Falling Shadows

Guardians of Reyth. Volume 1
By
Joan Lightning

The Lord of Light created the universe and filled it with light, but where we have light, we also find shadows.

First Printing: 2017

ISBN < 9781521125458 >

Published by P.J. Lightning
Bedfordshire, United Kingdom.

Contact- rykatu@hotmail.co.uk

Contents

Falling Shadows
Prologue

"After the conclusion of the cataclysmic War of Magic, the Lord of Light imprisoned His last enemy and made the remaining First Ones human. They joined with some of the survivors of the People and begat children. The Lord of Light gifted magic to those children and their descendants, so that they could find, serve, and protect, the other scattered survivors.

At that time, they were known as the Rykatean people (meaning 'Gifted people' in the language of the First Ones), because all had all seven Gifts of Power. Only later, after the Dark Time and the Rededication, did they take the name the Tyrean People (meaning 'People under oath'.)" Book of Light: History of the Protectorates – The Rebuilding.

Tam's birth

The worst day of my life began just like all of the good ones, Lonian thought numbly, *Just the same. How could it start just the same and end like this?*

Staring blankly at the warm wool-wrapped bundle in his arms, his mind roamed back to the start of the day when he had eaten firstmeal in the large communal meal-room of the Homestead. As always, he had found the bustle and noise of his extended family reassuringly embracing.

Kentarre Homestead was spread across the sides and top of a hill, with fields, pastures, and orchards, spreading down into the adjacent valley.

Hidden within the forest that covered the hill, and even within the hill itself, were the homes of the several closely-related families that formed this Homestead. Some were built of wood, some of stone, some of both. Some burrowed into the hill, some rose up around trees and utilised living branches within their structure. Some were small, for individual family groups; some were large, housing many families and their children. Tracks wound through the wood, the tree canopy, and through tunnels in the solid rock.

Lonian had grown up in the central Family House, which was a large half-timbered three-storey building, built against a rocky escarpment. The main structure and two wings lay on three sides of a central courtyard, with the cliff forming the fourth side. The cliff itself had been hollowed and carved by transmutation over centuries.

1

On its four floors it contained numerous bedrooms, workrooms, and storage areas. Some past transmuter had created an impressive system of crystal veins which ran through the fabric of the cliff, catching and channelling sunlight through to light the back rooms. Around it stood other, smaller, buildings, with orchards, gardens, fields, and barns close by.

Each family group had a set of rooms for private use, but the Homestead contained many busy communal areas, including kitchens, eating places, and guest-sleeping quarters.

In the meal-room, that morning, Lonian's parents had sat nearby, while his uncles, aunts, cousins, grandparents, great-uncles and great-aunts, had moved around, chatting, fetching food, and clearing plates, just as they had done every morning of his thirty four years of life.

After firstmeal, he took a horse and cart from the stables and drove his wife, Tamsin, and seven-year-old Tenji to the school in the outskirts of the city. The boy had slept badly the previous few nights, complaining of nightmares, and seemed unusually quiet, clinging to his mother's hand at every opportunity. Lonian did not worry; the memory of the bad dreams would soon vanish in the warm bright sunshine.

The thought that perhaps the boy's dreams might be a prophetic gleaning vision never entered his head - Tenji was very young and his single Gift was not strong. Later, his father would wish that he had paid more attention to his son's distress, but 'later' was too late.

He ruffled Tenji's hair before the boy reluctantly ran to join his friends in the field. When he had gone, Lonian kissed Tamsin.

"Please remember that you're more than eight months pregnant and should take plenty of rest."

His wife laughed affectionately.

"Oh, Lon, I'm pregnant, not ill. Don't worry so much! I know when to stop and rest and there are healers in the school."

Smiling ruefully, Lonian replied, "I know, but I always worry. I love you."

"And I love you. I'll be careful," she reassured him.

Tamsin climbed down from the cart and waved. The early morning sun made her long black curls shine around her smiling face before she turned and walked into the school. Her husband flicked the reins and the horse obediently set off towards the centre of

Tyreen. Lonian would be working today with a group of craftsmen building the new aisle for the Cathedral.

He loved nothing better than to see stone and wood combine into a functional and yet beautiful form, and the fact that his work was for the Cathedral made the task even more enjoyable for him. Under his strong hands, and guided by his transmutation Gift, the stone moved and flowed into scenes depicting the well-known stories from the Book of Light.

Years spent in the heat of the forge and under the sun, building homes and workshops, had burnt his dark skin almost black and made his body solid, with firm muscle that was strong without being bulky. His short-cropped hair was thick and black with just a few threads of grey beginning to show.

To be chosen for this work, when his Craftmastership was so recent, was a high honour, so he was supremely happy to have the opportunity to serve his God, the Lord of Light, in this manner.

Another honour had sprung from the first - the king of Tyreen had seen Lonian's work and had approved of it. The monarch had asked the Homesteader Craftmaster to mentor and tutor his eldest son, Prince Tarek, while the boy stayed at the nearby Kel Homestead, which was a kindred Homestead to Lonian's own Kentarre.

The date for this was just a week away and he was concerned about the proximity to Tamsin's due date, but his duty to Tyreen's king must come first. She would be well looked after by his family if he was away when her time came.

Lonian was a man who found pleasure in simple things and he was happy. He lived in a beautiful land and was doing work that he loved, for the God whom he loved. His skill had been recognised with a Mastership and his king had found pleasure in his mouldings, and, best of all, Tamsin was carrying their long-awaited second child who would soon enter the world.

Tenjian had been born within a year of their marriage but after that, for six long years, there had been no further sign of life from within Tamsin's womb. Homesteaders usually had large families, but year after year passed and Tenjian remained an only child.

Their son was not lonely, not when he had so many cousins to play with, but Lonian and Tamsin wanted more children. The lack of

3

further offspring had been the only worry in their otherwise contented existence.

Assured by the healers that nothing was wrong with either of them, they could only wait patiently. When the Lord of Light willed it, Tamsin would conceive again. Finally, one glorious day eight months ago, she had flung her arms around her husband and told him that she had a new life growing within her. He had been overjoyed! Life was good and Lonian was happy.

Today had begun just like the days that preceded it, but this day had now placed a new and devastating path before his feet. Time and happiness stopped as the sun began its journey towards the horizon. He heard someone call his name and looked around to find a grim faced Warrior who told him, oh so gently, that there had been an accident and that Tamsin had died but her baby was alive.

This morning, Lonian had been expecting to wait a few more weeks before he met his second son, but now he sat in his dusty work-clothes, on a comfortable chair, in an unfamiliar family room, in someone else's home, held the new-born infant in his arms, and tried numbly to find some way to make sense of what had happened.

He didn't see the wood-panelled room, which was well-lit, spacious, with thick carpet, soft chairs and well-made furniture. His eyes saw only two images: one was the child in his arms, and the other was Tamsin's face as they parted that morning.

He tried to feel the joy that the child's birth deserved because the baby could so easily have died with his mother. Tamsin's crushed body lay in an adjoining room, but her child was alive and strong, and his thick dark curly hair looked likely to be as full and beautiful as his mother's had been, and that was a cause for thankfulness.

The baby opened inquisitive grey eyes, like Lonian's own, and looked up at his father. Lonian forced himself to smile at his son, trying to project welcome and love at this tiny helpless infant who would never know his mother. The child knew nothing of tragedy, and his life and rearing were Lonian's responsibility and duty. He knew that he must put aside his grief for his son's sake.

But it was so hard.

"He is strong," Lady Aren said, "and I can find no sign of injury. Of course, I cannot use magic to be certain of that."

"No, of course," Lonian agreed automatically.

Everyone knew that babies were not strong enough to withstand healing magic. They would have risked a healing probe only if the child had been dying with no possibility of unaided survival.

"We are so sorry," Lord Jareth said awkwardly. "I cannot begin to express..." He faltered into silence.

Taking a deep breath, Lonian made himself look up into the sympathetic and guilty gaze of the older man. Lord Jareth was in his fifties though his neatly trimmed beard and moustache were deep black and unstreaked by grey. His lean build, smooth hands, and formal robes, all declared his status as a Sorcerer of high rank; his full title was Lord Rykatu Jareth.

Jareth was the only living Rykatu since the death of the previous senior Rykatu three years earlier. Until a new Rykatu was born, he and he alone possessed all seven of the Gifts of power. In all the world, only the Tyrean royal family and the Revered Father of the Congregation of Light held higher rank, and no-one possessed stronger magic powers than Lord Jareth.

The Rykatu must feel that he should have been able to save Tamsin, but some things were the Lord of Light's decision and men, even powerful Sorcerers, and even Rykatuii, had to accept that.

"There is no need for apology, my Lord. It was an accident and no-one was at fault. Accidents happen all the time. You have been very kind and I must thank you and Lady Aren for saving our child. Tamsin would be equally grateful."

If only she could.

Lonian was gratified to hear that his voice sounded completely normal, even when he used Tamsin's name. It would be most ungrateful of him to inflict his grief on Lord Jareth and his graceful wife, Lady Aren. They had tried to save Tamsin, but she had been beyond even a Rykatu's strength of healing. They could not save her, but they *had* been able to save the child that she carried. The child he now held.

He stood up abruptly. He had to leave this place before he lost control of himself. He needed to return home and then, and only then, could he give Tamsin the tears he owed her.

"My Lord, my Lady, I thank you again for your kindness. I must return home. I will return shortly for Tamsin when I have settled Tam with someone who can feed him."

5

They had chosen the name months before and he felt the rightness of it now that Tamsin was dead - her name lived on in her son.

"We can organise…" Lord Jareth began, but Lonian interrupted him, not noticing the powerful Sorcerer's blink of surprise.

"Thank you, my Lord, but I would prefer to bring her home myself."

"If you need anything, anything at all, please ask," Lady Aren said. "I do mean that."

"I know that you do, my Lady, and if there is anything, I will remember."

There would be no such need. His family would provide everything.

"You live in Kentarre Homestead, I believe?" she said.

Lonian nodded.

"Then I will order a carriage to take you home. No! Do not argue Craftmaster Lonian!" Aren held up a hand as he started to reject the offer. "You cannot hold reins and the child at the same time. You will hold your child and someone will drive you and that is an order!"

She was correct and Lonian reluctantly nodded acceptance of the carriage. He felt a slight tickle of magic use coming from her.

"It's ordered," she said. "They will be waiting for you when you are ready."

Lord Jareth abruptly frowned and then placed one fingertip carefully on little Tam's cheek.

"For a moment, I saw a Ponfour circlet on his brow," he murmured. "It is a Gleaning. A possible future, not a definite one, but he may bond one day."

"Light! I hope not!" Lonian muttered, and then remembered in whose presence he stood. Lady Aren's short hair, flowing movements, sword callused hands, and the sun-circlet on her brow, all reminded him that she was also Jareth's Ponfour, his bonded protector as well as his wife.

All those who became Sorcerers bonded with a Ponfour. Chosen from the best Warriors, the Ponfourii usually possessed fewer Gifts than their partners. Their training emphasised tactics and a wide range of physical skills that complimented the Sorcerers' magic orientated training.

Highly intelligent and experienced, the Ponfour was protector, advisor, confidante, and friend. When they bonded, the spell enhanced the Warrior's physical abilities, making him or her stronger and faster than they had been before. Ponfourii swore an oath of service to their partners and would die to protect them.

Jareth had fallen in love with his bond partner and they had married several years before.

Lonian grimaced at his thoughtless comment.

"Lady Aren, I apologise. I meant no offence to you. I have the greatest respect for the Ponfourii. Some of my family are bonded, but Ponfourii rarely have long lives."

Lonian looked down at his son.

"I will have no more children so I will hope and pray that this one will grow to be a farmer or craftsman, and marry and father many children, and live to see his great great grandchildren."

"Master Lonian. I understand completely. I took no offence." Lady Ponfour Aren smiled with gentle reassurance. "Now take your son home and I hope that he has the life that you wish for him."

"Thank you, my Lady," Lonian replied as he backed towards the door, bowing with his son held carefully against his chest. The need to leave was growing stronger. He had never before known such a strong urge to go home, but the home to which he wanted to return no longer existed.

Tamsin was dead.

Somehow he managed to keep his composure while he carried Tam through the halls of the Rykatu's large residence and out to the carriage. He could cry later, but right now his son needed him and that need was more important than Lonian's desire to grieve.

Jareth closed the door behind the bereaved man and listened to the footsteps fade away.

"Light! What a terrible thing!" Aren sighed. "That poor man!"

"Yes." Jareth nodded agreement, but his mind was still full of the images that he had seen when he touched the infant.

Ever sensitive to her Sorcerer/husband, Aren came close and laid a hand on his shoulder.

"Did you see more than a Ponfour Circlet?"

"Much more!" Jareth confirmed.

7

The images of his Gleaning were jumbled and many were blurred and vague. Of course they were – the child's life had only just begun and his path could take him almost anywhere – but there had been one sharp image.

"You must watch the family, Aren, and especially that boy. Also watch the royal family and if that boy shows any talent for battle, any interest at all in becoming a Soldier someday, I want him apprenticed in Tyre where he may encounter the royals as he trains."

Aren's eyebrows rose with curiosity.

"What did you see?" she asked.

Jareth pursed his lips thoughtfully as the images flowed once more through his mind.

"He may become exactly what his father hopes, but I saw one clear image of a likely future. I saw that boy, as a man in his twenties, with a Ponfour circlet around his brow, and beside him strode a slightly younger woman, while around the two of them flew a dragon and a grey heron with entwined wings."

Inhaling sharply with surprise, Aren asked, "Are you certain?"

"Very certain! The symbol of the Rykatuii entwined with the symbol of the main branch of the royal family. In one of his possible futures, that boy will be Ponfour to a royal-born Rykatu. Whether or not he fulfils that destiny, there will be a Rykatu born to the royal family and her birth cannot be more than five or six years away. No less than four, and no more than seven, or I am no judge of age, and born to the main royal line judging by the heron."

"That means Tarek!" Aren said with faint distaste.

Jareth smiled with understanding; Crown Prince Tarek was nearly fifteen years old and, like most boys of that age, could be irritating.

He nodded.

"Most likely, yes. With luck, he will have matured a little before he fathers a child."

"Did you know that Master Lonian is due to tutor him next week?" his wife asked.

"Is he? Can it be postponed? Or another Craftmaster found?"

"I am sure that it can or one could, but I think we should allow Lonian to decide that," she replied thoughtfully. "I do not think that he will appreciate further assistance."

"As you think best, my heart," Jareth replied.

The door that had so recently closed suddenly reopened and little Jathie's anxious face peered in.

"Meimei? Da? Are you cross? Did I do a bad?" the toddler asked plaintively.

Aren smiled reassuringly down at their only child as she picked him up and hugged him close. She met her husband's eyes and grimaced - at three years old, their son was just too young to understand either what he had seen or what he had done.

"No, Jathie, we're not cross," she told the boy, "We are just sad. It's not your fault. I'm sorry if you were upset."

"Why are you sad, Meimei?" her child asked, still looking a little uncertain.

Stroking his son's hair, Jareth spoke gently.

"Something sad happened today, Jathie - that's all. You don't need to worry about it. You haven't done a 'bad'. Actually, I am proud of you. Your Gift seems to be strong and that is good, but I want you to promise that you will only use it when your mother or I say that you may. Do you understand?"

"I pomise!" Jathie replied solemnly. "I pomise under Light."

Aren smiled. "Thank you, Jathie."

"I will teach you how to use it properly. I promise under the Light too," Jareth said with sincerity,

Light yes! The boy had to learn to control his power; there must be no more accidents.

26 years later......

Part 1: The Shadowbringer's proposal

"The imprisoned enemy's insanity grew ever stronger. He took the name 'Shadowbringer' and began to gather followers. With time, he learned how to grant them a portion of his own power. Their true name, we do not speak, because it is similar to his and he can hear it, but we call them Zindons." Book of Light: History of the Protectorates – The Rebuilding.

Dreams

Drawing his dark cloak protectively around himself, with a frown of concentration the pale man lowered the temperature in this tiny borrowed room to a more bearable level.

He was taking a risk, but both the Rykatu and her Ponfour were asleep and he was far enough away from them that the danger of them sensing his use of magic, and waking up, was minimal. Breathing deeply of the cooled air, he lay back, closed his eyes, and slid into sleep. This would be the most complex dreamhold that he had ever attempted; two minds were involved, one of whom was the most Gifted Sorceress in all of Tyreen.

Lord Xian was depending on him, so when he reached out with his dream, he did so cautiously – he must make no mistakes.

Rykatu Crystu was powerful, but his Lord had told him that she was also young and inexperienced, possessing absolute and arrogant confidence in her abilities which would effectively prevent her from ever suspecting that she was vulnerable. He was quite certain that she would never notice what he had done until too late.

The man found the minds, one already familiar to him from his last few days of work, and the other not suspecting the one great weakness that he was about to use against her. He had no doubt of his skill or of his inevitable success. His Lord would reward him richly for this and the anticipation whetted his skill.

His confidence in his own abilities was as arrogant and absolute and blinding as the Rykatu's but that thought did not occur to him.

Slowly, he touched the first mind, which was wide open and unprotected, and slid into the dream that filled it. With practiced ease, he controlled the dream and sent it in a new direction. He began to prepare the mind by triggering a memory…

<<< "Today we are going to start learning about the kingdoms we protect, which we call The Protectorates," Sorceress Laudia announced. "You've all heard of them, and probably heard some strange tales if you have Sorcerers in your families, so let's start by seeing what you already know, or think you know."

The group of children of mixed ages were sitting cross-legged around her in the sunny meadow near the school. She waved her arm and a map of the Protectorates appeared, floating above them.

"Any questions? Yes, Tam?" Five year old Tam's arm had shot up. He stood up and looked at the map, eyes wide, and tried to look at it all in one go.

"Is it true that school is different there? I mean..." He paused, trying to find the right words. "I heard that only some children go to school and they are all in classes all the same age and girls aren't allowed to fight and boys aren't allowed to cook." He stopped to breathe.

Laudia smiled at him, but he didn't see it - he was too engrossed looking at all the places he wanted to visit one day.

"Yes. Much of that is true," Laudia began, "although not all in the same kingdom. In Kest, only the children of important families go to school, the rest learn what they need to know by doing whatever work they must do. Like learning to farm by living and working on a farm, or being taught to spin and weave by your mother. They all learn to fight in special classes on Restdays but they don't call it school. In Eshiel, boys and girls both learn to fight, but only boys learn to use a sword. In Perrest, most children go to school and learn to read and write and learn about counting and history, but only the boys are taught to fight, and girls learn more about cooking and spinning and weaving. The Kingdom of Light has almost as many schools as we do, and nearly all children attend but few are taught to fight with a sword. And yes, in all of the Protectorates, they group children by age, instead of ability. They also expect attendance every day, even during harvest."

"But everyone is needed to harvest," one of the other boys said. "You have to get it in before the weather changes."

Laudia nodded. "Which is why we let you go and help, Firin, and you can catch up at your own pace when you get back. We know that gathering the harvest benefits us all and it's just as important as the things you learn here. However, in most of the Protectorates, they

12

like to keep ages together and they don't like going over the same lessons several times to help someone catch up, so children must attend every day no matter what else may need doing."

Tam put his hand up again. "Why?" he asked. "Why does everywhere do it differently?"

His teacher smiled again. "Because we are all different, Tam. It might be more orderly if everyone was the same, but it would also be boring. We are all different, so we do things differently. We, of course, have to teach magic as well as everything else and everyone learns that at his or her own pace. You can't rush it, so we don't. You will move through the classes when you need to, not as you pass an arbitrary age. That works best for magic, so we do it for everything.

That way made much more sense to Tam. He still wondered why some places didn't let girls fight – lots of girls were good fighters.

A noise from the road made everyone turn around to look as a rider galloped up to the big stone school building and stopped. The rider dismounted and ran inside the school. A few minutes later, Sorcerer Karig emerged and beckoned Laudia.

The children watched with great interest as she changed shape into an eagle and flew across. A few minutes later she returned and shifted back into her usual form. With a wave of her hand, the map vanished.

"We have a new princess," she told the class. "King Tarek and Queen Elish now have a baby girl and her name is Crystu. So everyone inside - class is ended for today and we are going to have some fun."

Tam sighed. He had been looking forward to learning more about the Protectorates. He wished that the baby had waited another hour.>>>

The connection to the Ponfour was secure so the pale man decide to move on to the Rykatu. Finding the shining cord, which was the metaphor that the Ponfour bond took in this man's dreams, he slipped into it. Holding his breath, he slid along the connection to the Rykatu's mind. As his Lord had predicted, the bond took him through her defences easily.

The Shadowbringer's devout follower was in Rykatu Crystu's dreaming mind now and began his work very carefully. Unlike the

Ponfour, she had the power to protect herself if she realised that someone was in her mind.

He would make her relive memories as well; the dreams should distract her while he created the doorway through which his Lord could come…

<<<Two year old Crystu staggered across to the door and frowned up at the handle.

"Doo igh!" she pronounced indistinctly around her thumb. Her Da was in the next room and she wanted to join him. She looked at the door itself and wished hard that it wasn't there. Suddenly it vanished just like the others had. Happily, she toddled through the space, unaware of the startled noises from the grownups beyond.

"Chrissie?" Her father stared from her to the missing door. "Did you do that?"

"I did warn you, my King," the tall lady said with a smile. "If Jareth is correct, your daughter is a Rykatu and you can expect her Gifts to start appearing much earlier than average. She's going to be a handful too - they always are."

Crystu didn't understand either the words or the look that the tall lady gave the grumpy beard, but he looked even grumpier than usual so she hid behind her Da's legs until Da picked her up.

"It's alright, Chrissie," Da said. "You can stay with me now you're here. Just please don't make holes in anything else, especially not the walls – they hold the roof up and we don't want it to fall down."

Looking up at her Da's face, Crystu grinned. "No holsh," she agreed, still speaking around her thumb. >>>

The pale man smiled in his sleep and slid even deeper into the dreams of the Rykatu and her Ponfour. He created a doorway in his mind and felt the glacial presence of his Lord's mind slide through the chain of connected dreamers, past his own dream, and into the opened minds.

Everything was proceeding as planned.

The Shadowbringer's offer.

Something is wrong here. Crystu thought, but the thought was so quiet inside her head that it seemed to be no more than a whisper. The bed in front of her eyes claimed her attention away from that faint sound and the whisper vanished from her thoughts.

"Can you save her, my Lady?"

The young Sorceress barely heard the anxious mother as she studied the dying child who lay unconscious on the bed.

Little more than a toddler, the child had been playing beside the road with her older sister when a noble's drunken son had deliberately driven his carriage at the two children. The older one had jumped clear, but the younger had had no chance to escape.

The boy's father, aghast at the actions of his wayward offspring, had done everything in his power to give the child a chance of life and to make apology. He had moved the family into this comfortable home and paid for the best of the local healers to attend, but his efforts and his genuine sorrow could change nothing.

All the attending healers had agreed that the child was dying and that all that was possible was to ease her pain until she left for the next realm. One of those local healers was present in the room at the moment. She was an elderly and experienced woman well regarded locally.

Crystu could feel that she possessed a small magical Gift, of which the woman probably was not even aware. The healer had managed to soothe the child into a deep sleep and had been treating the injuries with herbal poultices. Her experience and poultices, rather than her Gift, were the main reason that the child had survived this long.

Luckily, the woman's Gift was not strong, because she used it unconsciously and if it had not been so weak this child would already have died; the girl was simply too young for her body to survive the stresses of magical healing.

The only reason that Crystu was even considering making the attempt was that the child was dying anyway.

Crystu was here now, along with Tam, because of this healer. The woman had seen them in the street and recognised Tam for what he was - a Tyrean and a Ponfour.

With that unmistakeable sun-circlet tied around the brow of such a large muscular man, Tam did not need to shout that he was a

15

Guardian of Reyth and protector of a Sorceress. His face below the circlet confirmed it: his olive skin, which was even darker than Crystu's own deep brown, made his clear grey eyes seem almost to glow with the pure integrity and sincerity that also characterised his mind's aura.

Five years Crystu's senior, at twenty six years old, Tam was tall and handsome and possessed three of the most powerful Gifts - transmutation, illusion, and healing.

While only Crystu could sense Tam's aura through the magical bond that connected them, anyone with eyes should be able to recognise him as a Tyrean Ponfour, although Crystu had noticed that, out here in the Protectorates, few people seemed to use their eyes.

Most looked at Tam and saw a man-at-arms and if they considered his long braided hair unusual in a fighting man, no one would dare mention it, not when his broadsword, which he usually wore strapped across his back, was larger than most grown men could lift with two hands, and Tam carried it as easily as if it was made of straw.

The healer was unusually observant and she had recognised the two Tyreans riding through the market street in this tiny village of Tanjisford in the Kingdom of Borgan, and she had begged their help with the child. So here Crystu was, kneeling beside the bed, and trying to decide whether to attempt the near impossible.

Contrary to the ideas of many of the unGifted, healing was not a matter of waving hands and speaking incantations. It was powerful magic which placed a great deal of stress on the body of the person being healed, more stress than a young child could endure unless the Sorceress who was attempting to heal her was prepared to risk her own life.

Crystu would have to use her Gift extremely delicately and slowly, exercising total control over her power. Once she began, she knew that she would not stop until either the child died or the child was healed. She would be using her power continually, probably for several days without pause, and using it for so long meant that she would be risking burn out.

At best, Crystu would sleep for days after such a healing, at worst she could destroy her Seta and even die, but if she did not try, the child's death was certain.

The girl's skin was feverishly hot beneath Crystu's fingers, and livid bruises still discoloured her skin. She lay still and, to the eye, only the slight movement of her chest proved that she had not already crossed to the next realm. Crystu sent a gentle healing probe into the broken body and the crushed bones and torn flesh and infection confirmed that this little girl would certainly die within a day or two. Yet the infant's Seta was strong: she wanted to live and she was struggling with all her fading baby strength to live.

Sighing, Crystu glanced at Tam, who was squatting beside her. Tyreans were generally taller than was normal for the citizens of the Protectorates, and he was unable to stand up comfortably under this low ceiling. She could feel his emotions clearly across their bond; he was not at all happy that they were here. His compassion for the child was at war with his concern for his Sorceress. He knew what Crystu was considering and knew how dangerous it would be for her.

He also knew that, now that she had seen the child, his Sorceress would not walk away. Crystu yearned to be a mother of a large family one day, and she could not abandon a sick child to death without trying to save her.

She withdrew her healing probe.

"Your daughter is far too young for a safe healing. Do you understand that the attempt alone may kill her?" she asked the parents.

"We understand it, my Lady, but she's dying anyway. If your healing speeds her to the next realm she will at least be free from pain, and safe with the Lord of Light."

The child's mother spoke with the roughened voice of a woman who was holding back tears by sheer force of will and courage. So long as her child needed her to be strong then she could be strong.

The father held his wife's hand and nodded his agreement at her words.

"We put our trust in the Lord of Light. We prayed for a miracle and your presence is proof that our Lord has heard us. Whatever happens now we are grateful to you for coming here."

The Rykatu looked at the parents. They were poor folk, but honest, and both worked hard to provide for their family. This house would be luxurious to their eyes, but the luxury was clearly unimportant to them while their child was ill.

She smiled gently. "I will do my best."

17

"Thank you, my Lady! Oh, thank you!"

"Thank you!"

"Speak to her now. It may be your last chance," Crystu told them as she stood up carefully, mindful of the ceiling. She was not quite as tall as Tam, but her head was still in danger.

While the parents kissed their daughter and told her that they loved her dearly and that they wanted her to be well, Tam opened the leather bag and handed his Sorceress the robe that she had brought with her.

"I wish that I could take this risk instead of you, my Lady," he told her quietly.

"Your Gift is strong but you cannot use it finely enough for such a young child. She would die in minutes," she replied.

"I know it," Tam admitted, "but you are putting yourself at great risk. It will be hard to watch you and know that I cannot help."

"Yes," Crystu agreed, "but this is the child's only chance. You know as well as I that we are not here to avoid risk."

She understood Tam's unhappiness. The contradiction that lay in the heart of every Ponfour was the cause. Each one of them took an oath to protect and defend his or her Sorceress from all dangers. They swore to give their lives, if need be, to keep their bond-partner safe, but the nature of the Guardians' duty often meant that they went into danger together and fought together and died together. Ponfourii would be happiest if their Sorcerers never left the safety of Tyreen, but duty laid a path before their feet that all Sorcerers had to walk, and that path led out into risk.

Tam had sworn to die for his Sorceress, if necessary, and he would do so without hesitation or regret, but he knew that he could not protect her from her duty if her duty took her into danger.

The young Rykatu held the robe and looked at Tam. He nodded fractionally, understanding her unspoken request, and then he moved past her.

She did not look round while Tam ushered the parents and healer from the room, giving them instructions to bring water and food at regular intervals until told otherwise.

"This may take several days and once my Lady has begun she must not be interrupted for any reason."

"But what about...I mean if this takes days, she will need..." The woman's voice trailed off uncomfortably.

"I will take care of my Lady's physical needs," Tam replied firmly. "Apart from food and water, all Lady Crystu needs from you is your prayers for her strength; they are essential."

"Of course. We will pray."

The door clicked closed behind the family. Crystu expected them to hover uncertainly behind the door, but instead the footsteps moved away immediately as they went to fetch the water and food that were required.

She hoped that they would remember to pray as well; she would welcome any extra assistance from the Lord of Light!

Quickly, she peeled off her clothes and slipped on the robe, twisting her thick black wavy hair into a knot at the back of her neck to keep it out of her way.

Tam would see to her physical needs. He would hold food and drink to her mouth when she was hungry, and hold the pot for her when her bladder and bowels filled. His Sorceress must keep her hands on her patient to keep the magic flowing and would be unable even to loosen clothing when necessary which was why she had brought the robe and now wore nothing else beneath it.

A quiet knock at the door heralded the first of the water and food that Tam had requested. It would feed all three of them, but the child's need was the greatest. As Crystu healed her, she would place water and food into the child's stomach, and increase her digestion rate, to supply the required protein and energy for the body to heal.

Such a delicate task!

She was both eager to attempt what was almost impossible, and terrified by it at the same time.

"Lord of Light, guide your servants on this path. Help us to do your will and grant life to this child through your generous Gifts to your Priestess."

Tam's prayer spurred Crystu to begin.

Placing her hands on the feverish child, she sank her power into the broken body while her Ponfour crouched nearby and watched and waited patiently.

Something is wrong! What is it? The quiet thought returned with greater strength.

"No!" she said out loud suddenly, her voice echoing strangely in the bedroom. "That was days ago! I finished the healing and the child lived! This is a dream! A dream of a memory!"

19

Everything around her shimmered and began to dissolve. She remembered now that she had ministered to the child for two days, never moving from bedside. When she had finished, she had been so tired that Tam had carried her from the house in his arms, barely pausing to acknowledge the gratitude of the family. Such magic use would require days of sleep to recuperate her strength and her Seta. Was she in that sleep now?

She opened her eyes and saw Tam's familiar face smiling down at her. Light, but he looked so tired!

"Welcome back into wakefulness, my Lady."

"How long did I sleep?"

Even as she asked the question her time-sense told her the answer - three days.

"Three days," her Ponfour confirmed her body's knowledge, "but you have done yourself no harm, thank the Light!"

"And you've been awake the whole time? Tam! That's five days! You must be exhausted!"

He shrugged. "I can sleep when I am certain that you are fully recovered."

The young Sorceress nodded slowly. Something still felt wrong here, but what? Her mind felt muffled, as though she had cloth wrapped around her eyes and ears.

"The child?" she asked, trying to interpret what she was feeling.

"She is running and playing as though she was never injured."

Crystu sighed happily, then frowned and sat up and looked around.

This is still not right!

"No, this too is a memory! I'm still dreaming!" she exclaimed.

They had been staying in a guest house in Tanjisford but had left once Crystu was fully awake after the healing. They were travelling, as did all bonded Sorcerers throughout their lifetimes. They would travel for six months at a time, wandering through the kingdoms of the Congregation of Light hunting for servants of the Shadowbringer, or for any other creatures of shadow.

Tyreans were the Guardians of Reyth and they took their Guardianship seriously.

Crystu remembered now: they had journeyed to the next big town and had taken rooms in an inn.

20

She was asleep, and so was Tam - she could feel his mind's relaxation. She had encouraged his sleep magically, although he would probably scold her for it when he awoke. He had used his own healing power to speed her recovery and had been more tired than he would admit. He needed to sleep deeply but had refused to do so and risk leaving her unprotected, so she had waited until he was dozing and had placed a sleep spell on him.

If his Sorceress was threatened, the more powerful spell of the Ponfour bond would wake Tam to her defence, but other than that, he would sleep until she woke him.

He was asleep and so was she, and she was bored with dreaming memories. As a dreamwalker, she had the power to control her own dreams if she chose. She dismissed the memory dream and let her mind drift to find something else.

Colours and clouds swirled and then parted to reveal a tunnel that ran ahead of her for as far as she could see. The walls of the tunnel were grey-blue and translucent. Light flickered oddly in their depths and when Crystu touched the smooth damp surface it felt ice cold beneath her palm.

Not just ice cold - it was ice!

This was certainly no memory! She had never seen ice of such solidity and thickness that it could have a tunnel carved through it like this.

She looked up, but could not begin to guess how deep this ice might be.

For a moment, she considered dismissing the dream and trying again, but then shrugged; no dream could hurt a dreamwalker and this was an interesting beginning. She would see where it led.

Picking a direction at random she began to walk. With a thought she clothed herself in warm leathers and furs, adding a bow and well filled quiver as well.

There could be no real danger for a Rykatu in a dream, but she felt better with the weapon in her hand.

A strong sense of wrongness still nagged at her senses. Was her gleaning Gift trying to warn her about something? It did not feel like that, but she was uneasy; she kept seeing movement at the corner of her vision, yet saw nothing when she turned her head to try and see it clearly.

The tunnel grew darker.

And darker.

Soon Crystu was feeling her way along with one hand on the ice wall and she was beginning to feel irritated.

If this tunnel did not lead somewhere soon she was definitely going to dismiss this dream and try again!

"Ah, there you are, young one, please enter. We have been expecting you."

The strange voice emerged out of the darkness as though the shadows themselves had become sound. Each word seemed to slide around Crystu's head and then disappear into the ice.

Gripping her bow tightly, and reminding herself that she could leave at any time simply by waking herself, the young Rykatu stepped into and through a large black hole in the wall.

A change to the way that the air touched her face revealed that she had entered a large cavern. She could see nothing ahead but several points of light, like stars.

She moved towards them slowly, feeling her way one cautious step at a time.

Slowly, her eyes adjusted to the dark; she almost laughed when she realised what she was looking at. She had walked past the painting so many times in her life! It hung in the antechamber next to her father's throne room and she had always thought it the most unpleasant daub that she had ever seen.

Her dream had decided to recreate Tarreli's 'Shadowbringer in his Lair'.

There sat the Shadowbringer himself, with his body of shifting smoke and eyes of glowing molten iron that dripped hot tears to burn the floor.

He sat on his throne, made of skulls of course, and was surrounded by his minions, all of whom were smaller versions of him, although they squatted on the floor instead of reclining on thrones. The whole group was surrounded by smoke and moving shadows.

"Is this really how your people imagine me?"

He sounded amused and his minions cackled beside him.

"No!" Crystu replied boldly. "It is one person's vision which he decided to inflict on the rest of us by presenting his badly painted masterpiece to my father. I've never liked it. Whatever the Shadowbringer looks like, I doubt that he is quite so ... smoky!"

She waved her free hand to try to disperse the smoke that was wafting around her face. What was burning anyway? The ground was ice and ice would melt, not burn.

The figure before her chuckled and then, between one breath and the next, the dream changed.

As dreams do.

The ice-carved cavern was unchanged, but now a lush carpet lay beneath Crystu's feet, and she faced a group of the oddest looking men that she had ever seen.

Every person she had ever met in her life had dark skin. *These* men had skin that was as pale as milk, and their hair was white although they did not appear old. Their eyes were pink, except for one man whose brown eyes seemed to be pools of shadow in his bloodless face.

All wore plain black robes, and reclined on comfortable looking chairs, except for the man who sat where the Shadowbringer had been.

The throne had not altered - it was still made from bones, but the man sitting in it looked similar to the others except that he was taller, thin to the point of emaciation, and his face had an odd bone structure. Crystu was unsure, but she had the impression that he had no teeth in his mouth.

His clothing was indescribable. *Something* covered his body but her mind was unable to recognise it. Fur? Feathers? Leather? She had no idea what it might be.

Crystu stared at the peculiar people and wondered what her dreaming mind was trying to tell her. This did not feel like a gleaning and yet she could imagine no other reason for such a strange dream.

"I think that you do not believe that we are real!" The strange man said with a laugh. His voice still sounded as though it had been distilled from shadows.

"Please, try to leave the dream. We cannot proceed until you understand that I *am* the one you call Shadowbringer."

She shrugged, not liking this dream and seeing no reason to continue it; she would look for something more pleasant.

She dismissed the dream from her mind.

The room did not waver.

Suddenly worried, the young Sorceress tried again, but her efforts were in vain. Her dream remained unchanged and she fought

23

back the rising fear as she realised that someone else was controlling her dream.

This should be impossible! No one should be able to wrest Crystu's control from her! She was not only a dreamwalker, she was a Rykatu, possessing all seven Gifts, and her Gifts were stronger than everyone else's except the Senior Rykatu, Lord Jareth. Her dreams were guarded by her power and no one, not even Jareth, could enter her mind un-noticed, and yet somehow, not only had someone gained access, she had not noticed it until he told her.

And he claimed to be the Shadowbringer!

"How have you done this and why?" she demanded to know, trying to control the fear that was suddenly almost overwhelming. She was certain now that his claim was true.

Light! The Shadowbringer was controlling her dream! She was trapped within her own sleeping mind until he released her! Even Tam could not help her here. His three Gifts were strong, but he was no dreamwalker. Crystu was alone with the Shadowbringer and his minions.

She took a deep breath, feeling her dream lungs fill with dream air. The exercise was not real but it helped her to control her fear.

The Shadowbringer smiled. "Did you believe that your small power could keep me out? I am the creator of everything and you are scarcely more than a child."

"The Lord of Light is the creator of everything! *You* are just one of the First Ones, who is insane and suffering from delusions!" Crystu retorted. "You have used some trick to gain access to my mind and I demand to know how you did it."

"Demand?" The dream suddenly darkened as the Shadowbringer's anger affected his control. "You are full of fire, talking to a God as though to an equal!"

The dream stabilised and the light returned as suddenly as it had vanished.

"But I forgive you!" he declared magnanimously. "I know what you have been taught about me by the usurper, but it is untrue. He stole what I created and claims credit for it, but with your help I will take back what is mine."

He paused and then drank from a nearby container.

"I forgive you. You are a Rykatu and I have waited a long time for your birth. You asked why I have entered your dream and I will

24

tell you. I have chosen you to become my bride. You are young and strong and a Rykatu. Our children will be Gifted as your people are Gifted. Together we will create a new and Gifted race and, with them, I will escape my unjust imprisonment and regain my rightful place in this universe. In exchange for your service, you will become the most powerful woman on this world. Your Gifts will increase tenfold and all humanity will kneel to you. Your voice will be my voice until the day I am freed from this unjust imprisonment and on that day I will make you into a goddess."

Crystu stared at the enemy of all that was bright and good and felt a hysterical chuckle trying to force its way up her throat.

He was absurd!

He was insane!

"Become your bride?" she exclaimed scornfully. "Never! You are the great enemy, the Shadowbringer, the hater of life and Light, and I am a Priestess of the Congregation of Light and a Guardian of Reyth. I am sworn to defend these lands from you and to end your influence on this world. We are mortal enemies and I will never be your bride! If I was the only Guardian alive I would spit in your face rather than bear your children. They would be demons made of shadow!"

The room darkened again until only the creature's eyes were still visible - eyes of dark purple flame, full of fury!

"You defy me? You reject me? You owe me fealty and I will take it from you if you will not give it willingly!"

Flames surrounded Crystu and she staggered backwards to avoid the intense heat.

"You will regret your defiance! You will beg me to use your flesh in any way that I see fit! You will scream and plead for my forgiveness! You will come to me and throw yourself before me in surrender or I will plunge this land into darkness before this year ends! By the new year, your people will drown in blood, your Protectorates will become my slave pens, and the followers of Light will curse your name for bringing my wrath down upon them. I will destroy your people utterly and replace them with our children! Remember my words, Rykatu Crystu! You will watch as everyone that you care about dies screaming in agony to feed my people! Listen to my orders to my servants and tremble!"

25

He turned to the pale-skinned men sitting nearby and they fell to their knees.

"Go! Go out into the Lands of Light and cast my shadows where you walk. Find the innocent and the pure of heart and the brave and the strong and walk into their hearts and minds and make them my slaves. Sow despair and violence and heartache throughout all of the Protectorates until the followers of light understand that only in darkness is there strength and safety! The Guardians of Reyth will become a mockery, and a byword for uselessness, as the light fails across all of the lands that are ruled by the usurper. Go now and begin the work that I have given you!"

His pale-skinned servants jumped to their feet with broad grins and raced from the chamber in eerie silence. After watching them leave, the Shadowbringer turned back to Crystu.

"You have made your choice young one," he told her. "The time will come when you beg to be given a chance to remake it. For now, I release you back to your waking."

The dream turned to complete darkness.

"Lord of Light be thanked!" Crystu gasped as she clawed free of the enveloping bedcovers.

She sat up in the inn bed, sweat soaking her hair and covering her skin with a fine sheen of moisture. A sharp pain in her hands told her that her fingernails were cutting into her palms, so she forced herself to relax her hands and arms.

Slowly, her pounding heart slowed its pace and her breathing eased. She climbed unsteadily from her bed, walked over to the basin and poured water into it from the large jug beside it.

For once, she allowed herself to use a small amount of transmutation to warm the water, and then she began to wash the sweat from her face and body. As she washed, she sent her mind inwards, testing her Seta to be sure that it was untainted from this encounter with the ancient enemy.

How could this have occurred? How could even the Shadowbringer gain such entrance to her mind? It should be impossible!

One of the two most powerful Sorcerers in the world, she had trained from the age of five to hunt and kill shadow minions. She was supposed to find *them*, not the other way around!

The fact that they had *found* her was perhaps not so surprising, she admitted to herself. Healing that child had required use of powerful magic over a prolonged period, and if another magic user was in the vicinity he or she would be able to feel that use. Strong magic created an emanation that could be felt for several miles by someone sufficiently sensitive.

The more important question was how had the Shadowbringer managed to walk into her dream and hold her there against her will?

He possessed great power, but he was imprisoned and his Gifts were almost wholly confined within the walls of his jail. He could reach out his power only a short distance through its walls, which was why he relied on minions to spread his evil and do his bidding. Crystu did not know exactly where his prison lay, only that it was far from the Lands of Light and deeply buried. She was certain that the healing could not have weakened her so far as to allow him to reach her mind directly, and yet, clearly, the impossible had occurred.

Briefly she wondered if perhaps the whole thing had been an ordinary dream or a prophetic gleaning, but she dismissed both

27

thoughts. No ordinary dream could trap Crystu within itself, as this one had, and gleanings had a particular feel to them that this had lacked.

No, she could not deny the fact that, somehow, the Shadowbringer's mind had crossed the long miles, and strolled through her defences as though they were not there.

It should not be possible, but denying that it could happen was pointless. It *had* happened and perhaps the Elders could work out the 'how' later on. For now, Crystu must decide what she should do next.

Something still felt wrong to her senses, but Crystu was certain that she definitely was truly awake *this* time. What was it that was still setting her nerves on edge?

Where was Tam? He should have sensed her fear during the dream and woken up immediately despite the sleep spell which she had cast on him. He should be here now!

That was what was wrong – something was trying to block her sense of her Ponfour through the bond. Now that she was aware of that fact and fully awake, she easily threw off the influence that the Shadowbringer must have implanted in her mind during the dream.

Suddenly she felt Tam's presence again and he was close.

The door crashed open and Tam raced in barefoot, dressed only in a short tunic hastily tied, but with his short sword drawn and ready.

"What is wrong, my Lady? I felt your distress. Are you hurt?"

A puzzled and slightly embarrassed look appeared on his face as he saw that she was unharmed and was in the middle of washing herself.

Tam had been her Ponfour and friend for almost two years, and they had been travelling alone for nearly four months. He had seen her naked before today, but the difference between tending her as part of his duty, and bursting uninvited into her bedroom while she was washing, was considerable!

After casting a quick searching glance around the room to be certain that no immediate threat existed, he sheathed his sword deftly, closed the door, and turned his back to allow her a semblance of privacy as she dressed. She knew he would not leave until he knew the source of her distress.

She dressed quickly, trying to organise her thoughts and decide what to do. Tam would be extremely alarmed when he learned what had disturbed her sleep. She wondered whether it would be best to lie and tell him that it was just a bad dream and nothing more than that.

"No, Crystu! Don't even *think* about trying to lie to me!" Tam said suddenly without turning his head.

Crystu grimaced. Even after all these months, she still sometimes forgot just how much Tam could sense and interpret through the bond which they shared. She should not forget it because she could feel his emotions as easily as he felt hers, even if her interpretation of his feelings was not quite as accurate. Deceiving each other would require a great deal of concentration and effort.

"You must tell me the truth, Crystu," Tam continued. "How else am I to protect you? We're not in Tyreen, safely hidden behind the Great Shield. We're alone in a foreign realm, and must rely on each other."

Crystu finished dressing, walked across to Tam and placed her hand on his arm. He turned to face her and smiled. She lifted her head and smoothed back her hair, and then planted a kiss on his cheek.

"I wish that you would use my name more often, Tam, I like the way that you make it sound."

A smile flickered across his lips and he wagged his finger in front of her nose reprovingly.

"Don't think that you can distract me either!" he replied. "It won't work! I can feel that you're badly shaken by something. You *must* tell me what it is!"

Crystu sighed.

It had been worth trying. She felt reluctant to speak aloud what she had dreamed. She had an irrational feeling that if she said nothing, the dream would be just a dream, whereas talking about it would make it real. The dream had frightened her, she admitted to herself, and she did not like the feeling. Tam was correct: she must share the dream with him and then he would help her control her fear.

"You are my guide, my second pair of eyes, my protector, and most important of all, my best friend, and you're right as usual that I was thinking of lying to you. I didn't want to worry you," she admitted.

Tam smiled. "It is my job to be worried. I'm *already* worried! I can feel your fear and that worries me! Now sit down, start from the beginning, and tell me what has occurred."

"Yes, Tam!" Crystu nodded, restraining the impulse to smile at his tone of command.

She sank onto the edge of the bed wondering where to begin. Tam reached out to grab the corner of a chair and deftly turned it round so that he could sit in front of her.

"Tell me!" he repeated, projecting reassurance and support across the Ponfour Bond.

"I am not sure where to begin."

Crystu shuddered as the images of the dream rose in her mind and she felt once again the chill of that cavern of ice. She jumped as Tam wrapped a warm cloak around her; she had not realised that he had moved, so lost was she in her memory of the nightmare.

Smiling her thanks, she took a deep breath and began,

"A few moments ago, I awoke from a very disturbing nightmare, except that it was no ordinary nightmare. Tonight the Shadowbringer himself walked into my dreams and made an incredible proposal!"

Tam's eyes widened, and he inhaled sharply at her words, but he said nothing and nodded at her to continue, listening patiently as she spoke haltingly, trying to find the right words to describe what she had seen and felt.

When Crystu had finished relating all that she had dreamt, she looked at Tam, and he stared back at her in alarm.

"We must return to Tyreen quickly, my Lady; you are not safe here! I will not be easy until the Gate closes behind us and we are behind the Great Shield."

He rose and immediately began to pack the few things that Crystu had removed from her luggage when they had arrived in this inn the previous evening.

"May I at least eat first? And you should dress fully!" Crystu forced herself to laugh, trying to sound relaxed even though it was a futile pretence with someone who could feel her emotions almost as clearly as his own.

"We have time for food and I am hungry, as are you!" she continued.

30

Tam paused and then nodded. "I suppose that if he wants you to be his bride, he's unlikely to send someone to try to kill you. Very well, we will eat before we leave."

They entered the dining area and, filling plates with bread, cheese, and fruit, they sat and began to eat. This early in the day, they were alone in the room and Crystu was grateful for their solitude. She did not feel like trying to make pleasant firstmeal conversation with strangers right now.

She felt uncharacteristically nervous and Tam had strapped on his broadsword, keeping one hand near the hilt of his short knife while they ate. His eyes moved continually around the room and she could almost see his ears twitching as his keen Ponfour hearing strained to catch every sound in the vicinity.

Crystu could feel a greyness hovering over the room in which they sat. It affected the taste of the food in her mouth and cast a strange otherness onto the village scene that she could see through the window. Nothing seemed quite as it should and the long shadows cast by the rising sun seemed much blacker and deeper than usual.

Finishing their first-meal quickly, they paid the innkeeper. Then they gathered their bags, saddled their horses and left at a fast canter. Tam insisted that they wear armour in case they were attacked but Crystu had refused to wear her helmet until and unless danger threatened more directly.

They had been making their way back home at a gentle pace before they had stopped to heal the dying child, but Tyreen was still many days ride away even if they rode in a straight line across the fields. The mountains of home were not even visible as a blue haze along the southern horizon.

As they rode, the sense of doom that had been oppressing Crystu began to lift. The sun was shining brightly, the birds were singing, trees were beginning to bud, water flowed musically along shingled channels, and the early spring countryside seemed completely peaceful.

At midday, they stopped for a meal in a small inn in a tiny hamlet. The sun was still shining, children were playing in the stream, splashing and laughing at each other, old men sat in the sun and watched the visitors, and women chatted as they bought food from stalls set up on the green.

"You're feeling better now. I'm glad!" Tam remarked.

"In such a peaceful place as this, who could fail to relax?" Crystu smiled back at him.

At that moment, a quarrel broke out amongst the playing children. Their respective mothers stopped gossiping and rushed over to tear apart the squabbling children. They then began to accuse each other of failing to properly raise their offspring. The scene ended with children being marched away to their homes by scowling mothers, while the elderly onlookers cackled and offered advice on appropriate punishments.

Thick clouds drifted in front of the sun, and the corners of the suddenly emptied street acquired shadows as a chill wind whipped up previously unnoticed dust.

A faint tingling sensation prickled Crystu's skin and she knew that somewhere not far away someone was using magic but, strangely, she could not feel any clear sense of direction. To her surprise, Tam did not seem to notice it at all. His senses were not as sensitive as hers but he should be able to feel this, so why couldn't he?

Suspicion gripped Crystu and she immediately pushed it as far to the back of her mind as she could to prevent Tam sensing the shock that she was feeling.

Lord of Light! No! Surely not! Could it be? It would explain how the Shadowbringer had entered her mind! If she was correct then she dared say nothing to her Ponfour and he must not suspect what she was thinking. Somehow she must conceal her sudden realisation from him while she decided what to do.

Tam's life might depend on it!

"My Lady, you're shaking!"

Crystu gasped. Light! He had noticed already! She *must* fool him somehow! She forced her body to relax; her best chance was to try to hide the lie behind the truth of her fear.

"When the sun vanished," she began, "the images from my dream came back to me suddenly. How could he get into my mind like that? Was it the healing? Did I lower my defences without realising? Light, Tam, what about tonight? I can't go without sleep and yet I don't want another visit! I'm afraid, Tam! He walked in my dream and I could not eject him. Suppose he does it again?"

Even as she spoke, the truth of her words made her voice shake with renewed fear. She suspected now, how the Shadowbringer had

32

entered her dream and she did not know if she would be able to keep him out if he used the same method again tonight. The thought was terrifying! Good! Tam would feel her fear, and he should be satisfied with the obvious cause.

Light, she hoped that he would be satisfied!

Crystu knew that if she was correct in her suspicion then she needed help urgently. She knew what she had to do.

"Ponfour I must make of thee a request," she said, using the formal phrasing.

By long tradition the formal speech meant that a Sorcerer was invoking the Ponfour Oath of Service; no Ponfour would question an order given this way. Crystu had rarely given Tam formal orders since their bonding but this was one sure way to prevent him asking questions that she dared not answer.

"Name it, my Lady." Tam knelt. "I am yours to command, and you know that I will refuse you nothing!"

"We must go straightway to that church where we will prepare ourselves for what I must do. I will spend some time in prayer, and then, if no other guidance has been forthcoming, I must compose myself to dreamwalk. I will require you to safeguard my person while I am sleeping."

She spoke calmly, though her heart beat so strongly in her chest she could hardly hear her own words.

"My Lady! The danger! This is madness! You have not fully recovered all your strength after that healing! A dreamwalk from induced sleep requires considerably more energy than one from natural sleep. Can't this wait until tonight? We should not waste any time! We need to get you safely back to Tyreen as quickly as possible!"

Crystu had half-expected his protest and managed to smile calmly despite this evidence that her suspicion might be correct. Tam possessed a strong and absolute trust and faith in their God and he should have heartily approved of her intention to seek guidance from the Lord of Light, and, most important, he should *never* have argued with a request that had been spoken in the formal tongue.

"Why take such a risk?" he continued. "In whose dreams will you walk? Let me dissuade you from this action. We should keep moving!"

"I must first contact Jareth. I think that he needs t..."

33

Tam interrupted, again in a most uncharacteristic fashion. "Elder or Younger?" he asked with a strange intensity in his voice.

Jareth the Elder was the Senior Rykatu. His son, Jareth the younger (usually called Jathte by family and friends,) possessed six of the Gifts and had been travelling as a Sorcerer for five years. He and Crystu had been close friends at one time, although their respective duties meant that she had not seen him much of him since he had bonded his Ponfour and begun to travel.

"Senior Rykatu Jareth, of course," she replied. "This threat is too great for me. I need advice and Tyreen must be warned of the Shadowbringer's threat. I will need your support and protection in this, Tam," she added, waiting for his reply and wondering if he would continue his protest.

Her Ponfour was silent for a moment, and then he said, "I do not think you should do this, but as you are determined, I will stand guard at the door and keep you safe."

Crystu breathed a sigh of relief; she had feared a longer argument.

"Then we will begin immediately," she said, leading the way to the church.

The priest was overwhelmed to have Tyreans in his building. He happily agreed to close the church and allow them undisturbed use of it. Tam checked that all the doors and windows were locked securely and then he stationed himself outside the main door, sword in his hand. He was still unhappy with her decision but he had sworn to serve her and would protect her to his last breath.

Crystu knelt in prayer. Never before had she had such a desperate need for guidance. After several minutes of silent request, she rose to her feet and arranged seat-cushions and her sleeping furs to make a bed. Although a skilled dreamwalker could walk into another person's dream without themselves being in more than a light trance, Crystu was still tired from the healing and she knew that her call would be stronger if she slept fully. Jareth was almost certainly wide awake at this time of day, so she would have to attract his attention first.

Making herself comfortable on the bedding, she closed her eyes and slid with practised ease into sleep. As a dreamwalker, she could remain completely conscious even while her body was deeply asleep, and that conscious part of her mind guided her dreaming.

34

She pictured Lord Jareth walking on the far side of a noisy river, and began to shout and waved her arms in an attempt to catch his attention. This took patience because he would have to become aware of the attempted communication, and then he would need to find a secure place where he could safely go to sleep or at least, into a light trance, and join Crystu in her dream. Only then would it be possible to talk with him.

Suddenly the river disappeared, and then Jareth stood in front of her. A moment later, his Ponfour/wife Aren joined him. Unlike some Sorcerers Crystu knew, neither bothered to use the dream to make themselves appear younger. She saw them as they were in life.

They were both in their seventies. Aren's hair and Jareth's beard were streaked with grey but their sword arms and their powers remained strong, as was usual for Tyreans well into old age.

"What is it, Crystu?" the senior Rykatu asked. "I assume that you would not contact me like this unless the matter is urgent."

Quickly and concisely, Crystu related everything that had occurred.

"I couldn't understand at first how the Shadowbringer, or one of his minions, could have gained access to my mind. But, since I awoke from the dream I've become aware that something is wrong with Tam. I believe that he may be controlled."

There! She had said it! Light! The thought of it was terrible, but she was almost certain that it was true. While she had been asleep and recuperating from the healing, a shadow minion had entered Tam's mind and taken control of him. Tam was unaware of it and, except when the creature was actively controlling his actions, he would behave almost normally.

Almost.

These creatures, known as Zindons, served the self-styled Shadowbringer as the Tyreans served the Lord of Light. They were human in appearance and their lord gave them magical Gifts that were similar to those possessed by Tyreans.

"How sure of this are you?" Jareth asked urgently. "If you're right then you can't return to Tyreen. We cannot allow a controlled Ponfour into the Kingdom! It's a good thing that you did not decide to translocate back here."

"Examine the bond carefully, if you are correct there will be a noticeable cloudiness to his aura. We need to be certain!" Aren added.

Crystu closed her dream eyes and sent her senses out towards Tam's familiar mind aura. She could feel and taste the rich colours and flavours that were the way that her mind interpreted what she felt. His mind was still beautiful but in amongst the familiar rainbow swirls lay a new and unpleasant smokiness. It was a little like the smell of a firepit a day after it had been extinguished by rain.

She opened her eyes and looked at the figure of Lady Aren and nodded unhappily.

"There is smoke within his light," she confirmed.

Jareth muttered something that Crystu did not catch and Aren flicked a reproving glance at her husband before turning back to Crystu.

"Crystu, you know how dangerous this is, both for him and for you. The safest thing to do would be for you to kill him. He is well placed to injure you, or else he could place sleep on you and carry you to the Shadowbringer."

"I don't believe that is the purpose of this." Jareth shook his head.

"He's already had opportunities to do either of those," Crystu said at the same moment.

"It is far more likely that their plan is to get a controlled man into Tyreen - they have tried it before," Jareth replied. "They can't reach across the Great Shield to take control of someone, but where there is already a link to the mind..." He paused and then finished, "Your father will insist that you kill Tam."

"Is there no way to save him?" Crystu pleaded.

Aren and Jareth shared a glance and then Jareth nodded. "There is something that we can try, although it may not work."

"Please, whatever it is, I will risk anything!" Crystu exclaimed.

Jareth nodded again. "I think that we must." He smiled. "Whatever your father may think, I approve of your choice of Ponfour. We will save him if we can."

Aren added, "There is a good chance that we can free Tam's mind, just as long as the Zindon does not learn that you know of its presence. If it realises that it has been discovered it will destroy his personality and you know that we cannot heal that damage. You will

36

have to hide your knowledge from Tam and the Zindon for a few days. It will be difficult, but the Zindon's taint will make that a little easier because Tam will not be thinking so clearly as usual."

Relief flooded through Crystu. Aren would not say that there was a good chance of freeing Tam if it was not true.

"What must I do?" Crystu asked.

"You and Tam must come to the Cave of Cleansing at the gateway to Tyreen. We will meet you there with others in four days and then we will deal with this Zindon. Until then use no more magic unless you must, for you will need all your strength when we are ready to act," the elder Rykatu replied. He glanced at Aren who nodded and looked seriously at Crystu.

"Crystu, this is dangerous for you. We cannot leave you unprotected with a controlled Ponfour, so I am going to send Jathte to you, and also Seldar. If the Zindon decides to act before you reach Tyreen, if we are wrong about his intentions and he plans to try and abduct you..." Aren paused.

Crystu grimaced and nodded reluctantly.

"I understand. Their orders will be to kill Tam if that happens."

She met Aren's eyes firmly. "If it comes to that, I will kill him myself! I know that he would prefer to die by my hand than live as a servant of shadows, and it is my duty."

"Can you do it?" Aren asked gently. "It is not so easy to kill a friend, especially when you know that he is not acting of his own will."

Crystu swallowed with a mouth suddenly dry and shuddered at the thought but held the woman's eyes without wavering.

"I can do it if I must, but please," she could feel tears pricking her eyes and resolutely dismissed the sensation from her dream, "I do not want there to be a 'must'."

"We will do our best!" Jareth smiled grimly. "Now get back to your Ponfour and do whatever you must to make certain that he suspects nothing. Ride to the old tower in the Ursh valley. Jathte will meet you there."

Crystu nodded. She felt relieved now that the two elders were involved.

"Thank you, Lord Jareth, Lady Aren. You've given me some hope."

The two elders vanished from her mind and Crystu pulled herself back into wakefulness.

She took a deep breath. It was going to be difficult to fool Tam. She must hide lies behind truth and hope that he would not look beyond the obvious for another cause for her anxiety.

Striding to the door, she opened it to find Tam standing vigilantly on the other side. She smiled at him and allowed her relief to touch their bond. Every word must be the truth, and every emotion must be accounted for, if she was to fool someone who could feel everything she felt.

"Jareth and Aren are sending us some help," she said. "Jathte and another Sorcerer will join us and then we will return to Tyreen."

Tam frowned, and once again something flickered in the back of his aura that his Sorceress could not identify.

"Do they think that I'm unable to protect you without help?"

Crystu shook her head, trying to mask the disquiet she felt at his comment and to pretend that she had not noticed anything odd about it. The pious Homesteader would normally welcome any extra protection for her - a Sorcerer's safety was his or her Ponfour's first concern!

"Tam, if the Shadowbringer decides to attack us, he'll need a large group of minions to overcome even *one* Ponfour, but if we have *three* Ponfourii, that large group will need to be nine times larger," she reminded him, trying not to sound reproving.

Her Ponfour grimaced. "Of course you are correct! You will be far better protected by three Ponfourii and their Sorcerers than by me alone, and your safety is all that matters. I don't understand how I could forget that even for a second. The Ponfour Oath should make such forgetting impossible."

Crystu chuckled, thinking quickly; she had to distract him from this line of thought.

"The Ponfour Oath is powerful, but no Ponfour alive likes to admit that he may not be sufficient for his Sorcerer's protection. If you succumbed to a moment's wounded pride then it just proves that you're human," she told him. "There have been times when I've wondered if you have any imperfections at all. I think that I'm pleased to discover that your pride can overcome the oath, if only for a second. Perfection can be exhausting as a companion!"

38

A sudden swirl of surprise travelled through the bond at her words.

"For example," she went on before he could speak, "do you have to call me 'my Lady' every time you address me? Have I ever been offended when you have used my name? Of course not! You're my best friend, my closest companion, and friends use each other's names."

Tam grinned suddenly, and a trace of mischief shivered across the bond.

"Ah but, my Lady, if I used your name too often, the use would become commonplace," he said.

"But I like it when you call me by name!" she protested. His grin broadened but he did not reply. The feeling of mischief intensified.

"What? There's another reason, isn't there?" Crystu asked curiously. "What is it? Tell me! I order you!"

Her Ponfour laughed and shrugged.

"I know that you like me to use your name," he admitted, "which is why I use it so rarely because you're more likely to listen to me when I call you by your name."

Crystu gaped at him. "You... what?" she gasped. "You do it on *purpose!*"

He shrugged again. "Now that you know, I don't suppose that it will work so well."

"Count on it!" Crystu growled, not sure whether to laugh or be annoyed.

He'd been using her name as a way to make her more amenable to suggestions? That had never occurred to her. She opened her mouth, paused, and then began to laugh. Tam laughed too and they were still chuckling as they remounted.

At least she had distracted him from thinking about his uncharacteristic behaviour in placing his pride before her safety.

"Crystu!"

They had been travelling less than an hour when they heard the shout. They were riding along a track between fields, in an area of the land that had rolling hills that supported small coppices, interspersed with meadowland and cultivated fields.

39

Ahead, an old ruined tower had come into sight and, coming from it, two armoured riders were galloping towards Crystu and Tam.

Tam readied his short sword and positioned his horse in front of Crystu, while they waited to see who approached them with her name on their lips.

"Relax, Tam," Crystu said. "You'll need no sword with these two. I told you that they were coming."

She had recognised them immediately: they were Jathte, and his Ponfour, Trerisia. They came to a halt in front of Tam, who still gripped his sword.

Trerisia drew her own short sword and moved her horse forward. She was an impressive woman, even taller than Tam. Her unusual eye-catching, brilliantly-blonde hair was cropped in the usual Ponfour fashion to allow no grip for an enemy.

She did not appear to be heavily-muscled but that was deceptive; she had been first in all areas in her training class. She had been strongest, fastest, and most skilled in all forms of combat. Tam had similarly been first in his classes, but the two had never tested each other because Trerisia was a few years older than Tam and had finished training before him. Many longstanding wagers existed over who would win should ever they be matched against each other.

Now they regarded each other warily.

"If you wish a lesson in combat, I am more than happy to supply it." Trerisia's voice was low and musical.

Tam smiled at her. "I always enjoy a challenge and a good fight. It would be interesting to finally find out which of us is the better."

"Tam, I said relax! These are friends, not a threat." Crystu's voice was sharp. "The last thing we need is to be fighting each other."

"Agreed! Zia, lower your weapon!"

Jathte moved his horse between the two Ponfourii. "I understand that you fighters like to test yourselves, but please save your energies for our *real* enemy."

Lord Jareth's only son was twenty nine years old. His eyes were brown, but a little too unevenly placed on his head, and his ears projected more than was usual from his skull. His straight hair, also brown, tended to stick out at the back, although his beard was neatly trimmed. He was slightly shorter than Tam - about the same height as Crystu.

As he looked from one Ponfour to the other, the two of them slowly relaxed and lowered their weapons.

"Well, that's a relief!" Jathte smiled at Crystu as Trerisia and Tam sheathed their swords.

"Crystu, it is good to see you! I was so worried about you that I decided to not wait by the tower."

"I am glad to see you, Jath; the last few days have been...difficult," Crystu sighed, "and I fear the next few will be worse."

Jathte looked at Tam and smiled almost naturally. "It is good to see you again too, Tam, it has been a long time."

Tam nodded. "Yes, it has." He frowned. "I do not know what has got into me today. The Shadowbringer has threatened Crystu yet I allowed myself to be distracted by thoughts of a challenge. This is not like me at all."

Crystu suppressed a spurt of alarm; she had to distract him from such thoughts. "I didn't know that you know Jathte, Tam," she said quickly.

Tam looked at her and nodded. "He was my mentor during my first year as an Apprentice."

Jathte nodded as well. "We were good friends for a few years, but of course I was older and training to be a Sorcerer, and Tam was aiming to become a Ponfour one day. Our training took us along separate paths. It must be, what, fourteen or fifteen years since we last spoke together?"

"At least that," Tam agreed. "And despite my poor welcome, I am glad that you both are here to help protect Crystu."

He meant it. Crystu could feel his sincerity in the bond, but something odd still flickered in his aura. It was something to do with Jathte and it felt like a hint of shame and also sadness. It seemed uncharacteristic within Tam's aura and yet, strangely, it did not feel like something that the Zindon might have caused.

She pushed her curiosity aside. Whatever it was, it was unimportant compared to the Shadowbringer's threat.

As Jathte and Crystu resumed their journey, the two Ponfourii took up positions ahead and behind. Without speaking, Trerisia

41

assumed the frontal position, riding ahead by about twenty feet, carefully examining all the approaching side tracks and areas of concealment.

Tam, riding behind by a similar distance, also scanned the areas to the side and looked frequently over his shoulder to look for pursuit. Jathte rode by Crystu's side and began to talk of past times when they had both been students. He had been in his final study year when she began her second-level training.

Crystu remembered how embarrassed she had been her first day in the new level, when, to the annoyance of the instructors, Lord Andar had announced that he intended to observe the induction of a class that included the young Rykatu.

Lord Andar had been eighteen years old, pompous and arrogant, and believed that his familial relationship to the king and the young Rykatu Princess (he was her cousin), gave him rights which he had not earned. He was wrong, but the politeness of those around him meant that he had not yet learned that he was in error.

Jathte had begun his instruction that day.

"Oh, I remember it well!" Crystu laughed in response to her friend's reminder of the event. "He had come into the hall and was instructing me, in front of the whole class, to do my best and not dishonour our mutual family, and then... Oh, I could scarcely keep from laughing as his clothes changed from silk into cobwebs. He actually didn't notice for a full five minutes, until he scratched his nose and left his sleeve hanging from his beard. His clothes disintegrated as he ran from the room wearing nothing more than the colour in his cheeks - all four of them."

Jathte laughed with her. "I got a week's manual work in the Farm for that, but it was worth it. In addition, the Revered Father himself told me that it was the finest piece of transmutation he had seen in years. He also said they had no intention of telling the young twit who was responsible."

Crystu replied, "I also heard a rumour that Andar's carriage, which had been waiting outside, had turned into ice and melted in the heat, the horses breaking loose and bolting. No one would lend him clothing and so he had to walk home in just his bare skin."

"I didn't hear about that!" Jathte stared at her. "You don't mean to suggest that the Rev..." He trailed off in astonishment.

"Revered Father Teiron is a wise and good man," Crystu whispered, grinning. "He is also a skilled transmuter."

She continued at a more normal volume.

"Da told Andar it was his own fault, and that if he tried to pull rank on Sorcerers when he himself can barely manage even an illusion, then he was the world's biggest idiot and was lucky they had left him his skin in which to leave. It did him some good too: he came to see me a few months later and apologised for being an arrogant fool and I truly believe he was sincere."

Crystu was aware that Jathte was deliberately distracting her from the tensions of the last few days, and from what was likely to happen when they reached the gateway, but he did it so naturally that she couldn't take offence. Besides, it felt so good to laugh and he did tell the stories well.

They did not stop for food but ate on the hoof, from the stores of dried fruit, cheese, and bread, which they carried with them.

That evening found them in a sparsely inhabited area, hilly and rocky with little vegetation. They found a sheltered spot against a cliff with an overhang that gave some protection from the persistent rain, which had begun to fall mid-afternoon. Trerisia produced three rabbits and Tam, not to be outdone, had spotted edible tubers and a nest of large eggs.

Jathte dug a shallow hole, lined it with some large leaves, and placing the skinned rabbits and tubers in it, built a fire over the top. While the meat cooked, he pulled a small pan from his pack and scrambled the eggs to start their meal. By the time everything had been cooked and eaten, the sun was setting. They decided that Trerisia and Tam would stand watch for the first half of the night, and Jathte and Crystu would watch for the last half. Crystu looked at her bed and shivered. The thought of sleeping was frightening when the great enemy could walk into her mind, but she needed rest.

"Zia and I will watch your dreams, Crystu," Jathte told her quietly. "If there is the slightest sign that someone else is attempting to enter your mind we will wake you."

"Thank you!" Crystu replied gratefully.

43

When she awoke, the sun was shining and a pleasant smell of toasting bread filled the air. She looked towards the fire and saw Jathte stirring a pan of porridge with one hand, while the other held a long toasting fork with a chunk of bread from which the smell she had noticed emanated. Beyond him, she could see Tam and Trerisia also just waking.

"You were supposed to wake me to stand guard with you," she chided.

"I know I was," he replied," but I decided to let you sleep. Here, have some breakfast." Scooping some porridge into a bowl, he handed it to her along with a spoon and the toasted bread.

"Besides," he said quickly as she opened her mouth to continue her protest, "I wasn't alone for long."

He gestured towards the tethered horses, and Crystu realised that six horses now stood together.

Tam and Trerisia jumped to their feet as two armoured figures appeared from around a hill.

"Seldar and Trerin arrived here a short time ago, so I asked them to scout around," Jathte said with a slight smile.

He clearly enjoyed watching the consternation on the two Ponfourii faces as they realised that neither of them had been aware that others were in the vicinity.

Crystu looked at the two new arrivals for a moment, and then looked Jathte in the eye.

"Is your father planning to send *all* the biggest fighters to my aid?"

"I believe so," the taller of the two, a Ponfour circlet gleaming on his brow, replied, as he strode over and gave Trerisia a hug.

"Hello, Rinnie." Trerisia smiled. "So they finally let you loose on an unsuspecting world? I hope you haven't left anything vital behind this time. How much did you have to bribe this poor man to get him to agree to let *you* watch his back?"

Crystu looked curiously up at Trerisia's younger brother. She had never met Trerin before, but was immediately attracted to the mischievous glint in his eye. He had a merry face and an infectious grin, and his hair was as astonishingly golden as his sister's. He was also possibly the tallest man in all of Tyreen.

Trerisia was unusually tall even by Tyrean standards but Trerin's head topped his sister's by at least 4 inches. His Sorcerer was about the same age as her father, Crystu judged, and although considerably shorter than Trerin, was also much wider about the stomach.

Trerin grinned affectionately at his sister's expected gibes and Seldar laughed good-naturedly.

"It was quite the other way around: *I* bribed *him*!" the portly Sorcerer told Trerisia. "It was the only way I could persuade any Warrior to agree to take me on. But we complement each other well – Trerin forgets things and I bring too much!" He patted his over-ample stomach. "If the Shadowbringer's minions attack, Trerin will fight them and I will sit on them. The effect will be quite similar I assure you."

"Does Lord Jareth think me completely incapable of guarding Crystu?" Tam growled. Crystu could feel the uncharacteristic rage that surged within him as he stared at Trerin.

Jathte looked at him thoughtfully for a moment before replying.

"Tam, I can assure you that my father has no such thought, but you are one man, and the Shadowbringer's subjects are many. Surely you must agree that the more protectors she has the safer she will be and that her safety must be more important than your pride?"

The rage disappeared from Crystu's senses in an instant, and Tam opened his mouth as if to speak again then closed his eyes and took a deep breath. When his eyes reopened he was his usual calm self, though he looked puzzled, and Crystu could feel his self-annoyance for his loss of temper.

"Of course, you are right, and I know that Crystu is safer with many than with just me," he said. "I don't know what came over me. Please forgive my outburst. I should be pleased that others are present to take my place should I fall."

"I would prefer it if you *don't* fall, please ensure that you do not," Crystu said firmly, placing her hand on his arm.

Tam attempted a smile. "I will certainly make every effort to obey your order, my Lady."

His attempt at levity eased the awkward moment slightly, but a strained silence hung over the group while they ate breakfast, put on their armour, and set off again. Seldar joined Crystu and Jathte on the track, Tam resumed his position at the rear, Trerisia her position a little in front, while Trerin rode further ahead.

"We must hurry," said Crystu quietly, mindful of Tam's sharp hearing, "before it is too late."

"If it is not already," Jathte replied.

"There is still hope, I think," said Seldar, "but you're right: we have no time to waste!'

"I hope that you're right, Seldar, but I don't know how much longer I can sustain this pretence that I haven't noticed anything. You both know how hard it is to hide emotions from a Ponfour!"

"You can because you must," Jathte replied gently, placing a hand on her shoulder. "Tam's only chance is if we get him into the cave without the Zindon realising we are aware of the change in him."

His touch sent a burst of invigorating energy into her, and she smiled her thanks. "If ever I meet this Zindon in the flesh, I will teach him to regret this!" she promised grimly.

They travelled in silence for several hours.

As their path rose up into rocky hills, they began to encounter patches of mist, which was quite dense in some areas.

"Is anyone else hungry?" asked Seldar, as he reached round into a saddlebag, "I have some bis. . ." A great paw appeared from the rocks and sent him flying from his horse. Jathte ducked a second paw swipe, and smacked Crystu's horse sharply on the rump, making the animal, which had momentarily frozen with fright, break into a frenzied gallop for safety. They had been passing through one of the denser patches of mist when the attack began, but within seconds her horse had left the mist behind and was now running in clear sunlight.

Crystu managed to persuade him to stop and wheeled him round to return to her companions. As she galloped back, she tried to understand what she could see.

A patch of cloud hovered at head height above the others and parts of it had taken on a form something that looked similar to a dragon, albeit one made of mist. Despite its insubstantial appearance, it could apparently solidify its claws at will. Crystu had never heard of such a creature.

Tam and Trerisia were hacking at it with their swords, but their blades went straight through the creature's limbs without effect. She could see several Seldars, each of which vanished the moment one of the creature's attacks was directed towards him. Jathte was successfully blocking attacks with his airshield but, like the

46

Ponfourii, was unable to inflict any damage on the creature. He was wounded and tiring quickly. Trerin, who had been scouting the terrain ahead, came racing back over the hill to join the fight, but when he leapt to the attack he flew straight through the insubstantial creature without inflicting the slightest injury on it.

How could anyone fight mist?

Crystu laughed as the answer came to her; an absurdly simple application of transmutation should suffice. In fact, one of the first exercises practiced by children, as they began to understand their powers, should do the trick. The simplest form of transmutation was to change, not the element itself, but its form.

Gas to liquid to solid.

As long as it really was just mist. . .

She sent her consciousness ahead and plunged it into the creature. Yes, it was made purely of mist. A creature of mist? No, it was not a creature at all! She could feel the transmutation energy being used by someone else to transform parts of it from mist to solid and back again. The power being used to create and move the creature had a familiar feel.

Tam!

She could not allow any hint of recognition to colour her mind; the Zindon must not learn that she was aware of its presence.

At least she had one advantage: because the Zindon was working through another it would not be able to react as quickly as if it were wielding the magic directly with its own power. Marshalling her abilities Crystu struck and instantly transmuted the mist and air above the creature into water. Before the Zindon could react, the water fell through and into the mist and absorbed it. The combined water and mist dropped to the ground and flowed into the stream by the path.

It was over. The water in the stream was flowing too quickly to allow it to be easily used as the source for another attack.

Tam and Trerisia spun around thinking the disappearance of the creature was the presage to some other attack.

"It's over." Crystu's voice shook from reaction. "It's gone."

"Well done, Crystu!" Seldar's voice seemed to come from the air itself. "That was masterful!" and a rock transformed into the chubby Sorcerer.

47

"Indeed it was," said Jathte as he examined his reddened torn sleeve and the gashed arm beneath it. "I would never have thought of that. We owe you our lives. Yowtch! Oh, thank you, Zia."

Trerisia had walked up to him, grasped his arm firmly, and healed the cut.

"Just don't expect me to sew up the sleeve," she told him. "That's *your* job."

Tam had sunk to his knees panting with exertion. "Thank you," he looked at Jathte, "for sending Crystu to safety. However, my Lady," and he directed a stern glance at her, "next time someone sends you out of danger, please be so good as to *remain* there."

"I was in little danger I think, Tam," she replied, trying not to think about the fact that Tam *should* have followed her when her horse bolted. He was sworn to her safety and should have abandoned the others to stay close to her. "The creature seemed most intent on injuring Jathte and Seldar. It hardly seemed to be aware of me at all."

Her Ponfour closed his eyes and shook his head.

"Crystu, I hardly think we can count on that always being the case," he told her. Then he stood up and looked around at the completely clear day. "There is no trace of any mist now, but perhaps we should move on when we have rounded up Jathte and Seldar's horses."

He headed off in the direction the two horses had run. He didn't expect to have to go far as the horses of Sorcerers were well trained to run to a safe spot and then wait there.

Once again he was not behaving correctly, Crystu realised. After such an attack, no Ponfour would choose to leave his Sorcerer's side. Tam should have asked Trerin and Seldar to look for the missing mounts instead of going himself and leaving Crystu behind.

"I agree with Tam," said Seldar. "We shouldn't linger here even though I don't think that the mist will return today. In fact, I doubt that we've been walking through mist at all. I rather think that it was travelling with us and anyone even a few dozen feet from us would have been in clear sunshine."

"You're right," Crystu told him, forcing her worry about Tam to the furthest corner of her mind. "When my horse took me away I could see a fog only here above all of you. Everywhere else was clear. One thing puzzles me though: I could see many Seldars but none of them was real. That was an excellent illusion and it seemed to confuse the creature effectively."

"Ah!" said Seldar. "Well as you can probably guess, I am no expert with a blade nor am I particularly proficient in any system of hand-fighting. To protect myself while Trerin does the hard work I make an illusion that disguises me as whatever is most appropriate, while creating multiple images of me for the threat to waste its efforts on."

"It was impressive," complimented Jathte. "The images were extremely lifelike. I could not tell they weren't real until they vanished. Would you be willing to teach me the spell?"

"And me." Crystu nodded agreement.

"Oh, it's nothing at all, just a little trick," Seldar said modestly. "I'll be happy to show it to you."

"Perhaps not now though." Crystu had seen Tam returning with the horses.

Quietly, Jathte said to her, "You should talk to him about old times. It may help slow the process down. We still have three days to travel before we reach the cave."

Crystu looked at him sombrely and nodded.

The rest of the day's journey was uneventful, and in the evening they made a camp in a clearing surrounded by open woodland. Tam had killed a deer, which was soon roasting over a fire.

Crystu wandered over and stared into the flames. She breathed deeply of the delicious roasting smell as the deer cooked,

"That smell reminds me of the day I chose you for my Ponfour. Do you remember Tam?"

"How could I forget?" he asked. "I knew I was one of nearly fifty warriors who were being interviewed to be your Ponfour, and you had already seen most of them. I entered the room expecting a formal interview, seats, table, a row of faces asking carefully chosen questions, and perhaps some tests of strength or knowledge."

She laughed. "And instead you found yourself invited to eat roast deer and I threw red wine over you."

"I certainly did not expect that! Of course, had I known you had done it deliberately..." He smiled at the memory. "You seemed so embarrassed at your slip, I had no idea it was a test."

"Which you passed admirably. The previous person I threw wine on had become patronising and paternal and moved the wine bottle out of my reach! *You* dried yourself and the table, then asked if you could pour me another drink. You treated me just like a normal person who had had an accident, not like a silly child who couldn't be trusted with a glass. Then as we talked, you actually conversed with *me*. Not one of the others forgot for a moment that I am a Rykatu and the king's daughter, but you almost seemed unaware of my rank, and even called me by my name a few times. That was the moment I decided I wanted you for my Ponfour."

She smiled. "I knew then that we could become friends, I didn't want someone who would only ever see my station and who never forgot my rank."

"You decided then? Did you forget to tell anyone? I seem to recall it was at least three weeks before I received the invitation."

His words were teasing, and his eyes shone with the memory of the day he had received the formal invitation to become Crystu's Ponfour.

"Well, I still had several more to interview and more tests to think up. Besides, you might have refused the invitation; I needed to know if anyone else who would do."

"I could never refuse you anything, Crystu," he told her. "Receiving the invitation to become your Ponfour was the proudest day of my life. I hope we will be together for as many decades as Lord Jareth and Lady Aren."

"As do I, my friend, as do I."

They smiled at each other.

The moment ended when Trerin came over to ask if the roast was ready. Everyone gathered round the fire and enjoyed an excellent meal.

After discussion, they decided that they would stand watch, two by two, Trerin and Tam first, then Crystu and Trerisia, and finally Jathte and Seldar. Before Crystu went to sleep, she went over to Tam,

"You *are* going to wake me for my turn standing guard, Tam. I will do my share of this."

"As I said earlier: I can refuse you nothing my Lady, I will awaken you for your watch. Now go to sleep, Crystu."

"Thank you, I appreciate that."

Tam kept his word, and Crystu stood guard with Trerisia for the middle shift, and then woke Jathte and Seldar for their turn. When they were fully awake, she and Trerisia finally returned to their beds for the remaining part of the night.

Next morning Crystu woke slowly, listening to the sound of a mountain pipit's vibrant song. Her eyes flew open as she suddenly remembered that those plain sky-singing birds did not fly far from the Tyrean Mountains.

She sat up and looked out of the tent. To her amazement, she saw that the camp, which last night had been in a wood, was now in a meadow at the foot of the mountains that guarded the gateway to Tyreen.

The gateway, known as the Cave of Cleansing, was only a few hours travel from here. She looked across at Jathte and Seldar who were looking back at her and grinning at her surprise.

"How?" she asked.

"My father's doing," replied Jathte. "He walked in my dreams last night and told me he had gathered together all the strongest Sorcerers in the kingdom and that they intended to shorten our

51

journey. So here we are, almost at the gateway. Today we reach Tyreen."

The young Sorceress's eyes widened. "He moved all of us, and the horses and everything? With all the tents still up and people sleeping in them? I never felt a thing! If I tried that, the tents would all collapse and the horses would probably be on top of them!"

Jathte laughed. "Well, he has had a lot of time to hone his skills, Crystu, and he didn't do it alone."

Crystu looked around the campsite. The tents were still in their same places relative to each other that they had been when they pitched them in the forest and their pegs were firmly in the ground. She shook her head, wondering if she would ever be able to match Jareth's casual skill. He might have had help from other Elders, but he would have been the one coordinating and directing the merged minds.

"It's still impressive!" she told Jathte.

One by one, the other three woke to learn the astonishing news. They were all equally amazed that they had felt nothing when translocated such a distance.

Tam smiled with relief. "This is well done! We will soon have you safely home, my Lady," he said enthusiastically. Then he caught the look on Crystu's face and, through their bond, her sudden ambivalence, and misinterpreting both, continued, "After you have eaten, of course."

Crystu managed to smile back.

They ate quickly, each of them thinking ahead to their arrival at the Cave of Cleansing: the hidden gateway into Tyreen. As soon as everyone had finished eating, they set off, heading along the well-marked path into the foothills.

Crystu slowed to fall back and ride beside Tam.

"You look tired, Tam, did you sleep badly?" she asked.

"You shouldn't be back here with me," he replied. "You should be with Seldar and Jathte where you are safer."

She lifted her chin and replied with pretended haughtiness, "I think I demonstrated yesterday that I am fully able to defend myself at need."

"That is true," he smiled, "and I am glad of it. I almost feel sorry for any shadow minion who crosses paths with you. To answer your question – I slept deeply but had vivid dreams."

Crystu felt a stirring of alarm. "What kind of dreams?" she asked.

He looked into the distance toward Tyrean as he answered,

"I was back in my training days. Studying, practicing my gifts, attending lectures. Perhaps it was our talk yesterday because the Ponfour interview was one of the scenes I re-lived. It was all very vivid and detailed."

Crystu was relieved; surely dreams of his earlier life could only help reduce the Zindon's influence.

They rode in companionable silence for several minutes. Then Trerin rode over to join them.

"What do you want?" Tam growled. "Can't you see that you're interrupting?" He glared at the other Ponfour. Trerin did not react to the hostility and addressed Crystu without even a glance at Tam,

"Seldar sent me over here to take over the rear position from Tam," he told her. "He says that he will be happier if you ride with him and Jathte, and he thought that, after yesterday's attack, Tam would prefer to stay close to you."

"Perhaps he prefers my strong arm over yours," replied Tam.

Trerin paused before replying curtly, "Perhaps!"

Crystu saw the flash of anger in his eyes before he wheeled his horse to take up a position further back.

"You really are tired, my friend." She placed a hand on Tam's arm. "When we are back in Tyreen we can all get some much needed rest. Let's join Seldar as he asked. I think it was very thoughtful of him."

"I suppose so," he replied and allowed her to lead him over to where Jathte and Seldar were waiting.

"Besides," she whispered, "*I* would rather your strong arm was by me than that of anyone else."

As they rode, Crystu found herself chattering away about anything and everything that came into her mind. Tam seemed to be bemused by her babble and his irritable mood eased.

Soon they found themselves riding beside a river, and they knew that they were almost at their destination.

With the river to their left, Tam and Crystu rode around a rocky outcrop and found themselves looking at the cave.

"At last!" breathed Tam.

"Indeed!" Crystu agreed.

53

They cantered forward and entered the cave; the others were just a few seconds behind them.

Inside the large cave, they stopped and dismounted for the ritual wash. The waterfall issued from such a high point that its origin was not visible. Tumbling down the far wall, it collected in a small but deep plunge pool, before running out of the cave to form the river beside which they had been riding. A small rock projection within the waterfall caused a spray of water at waist height that was used for ritual cleansing.

Each, in turn, washed hands, feet, and face, then gathered beside the plunge pool.

"TAM!" Crystu had to shout to be heard over the noise of the waterfall. "WOULD YOU OPEN THE GATEWAY PLEASE?"

Her Ponfour nodded and walked closer to the waterfall, to the marked spot where he had to stand while he recited the short phrase which would open the gate into Tyreen.

Relying on the noise to mask his words, Jathte murmured to Crystu, "He doesn't know about the trap, does he?"

"We only tell dreamwalkers and Tam's not one, so, no - he doesn't know," she replied, watching Tam's mouth move.

"He will in a moment," Jathte said.

Crystu nodded. The phrase that opened the gate into Tyreen only worked if the Shadowbringer's true name was mispronounced the Tyrean way, but so far as Crystu knew, no controlled person would be able to say it that way. If Tam pronounced the word as a Zindon would, then the gate would open somewhere different. Crystu hoped that Tyrean belief (that Zindons, and those controlled by them, would never mispronounce their lord's name) was correct. They would soon find out.

After a moment, the water began to shimmer with rainbow colours, and the path stretched until it vanished behind the shimmer. Tam quickly led his horse along the path and crossed through the veil. The others followed hard on his heels.

The Cavern

As they passed through the curtain of light, they all felt a momentary disorientation. When the dizziness passed, instead of arriving in the small cave that opened out into the Treos valley, overlooking the city of Tyre, they found themselves in a huge cavern within which a group of some forty to fifty people stood waiting for them. Behind them, a similar sized group reclined in chairs, apparently sleeping. The walls of the cavern were completely smooth with no exits - the room was sealed.

Amongst the group waiting, Crystu could see many familiar faces. Lord Jareth was there, as was his Ponfour wife, Aren. Amongst the reclining group, she could see many who had been instructors during her training years - men and women she knew to be among the most powerful dreamwalkers and translocators in the Kingdom.

She gasped as she realised that her father, King Tarek, was also present. There was no time for more than a grim smile from him before her attention was drawn back to Tam by his puzzled voice echoing in the otherwise silent chamber.

"What is this? Where are we?"

Crystu looked over at Lord Jareth and her father. Did they expect *her* to explain to Tam?

Of course they did! She was his Sorceress and it was her duty. She realised that her bond to him and his to her would also make it easier for him to believe her. He would *feel* the truth when she spoke. When he understood, though, what would prevent the Zindon destroying his personality?

They must have some plan, she hoped, glancing towards the recumbent group. There had been no opportunity to tell her what it was, but they MUST have some plan. She could only follow their lead and hope and pray.

"The rest of you are not surprised to be here. What is happening? Crystu?"

Tam had started to walk towards her but stopped when Jathte, Trerisia, and Trerin all moved to place themselves between him and her, their hands on their sword hilts. Crystu could feel Tam's confusion so she forced herself to speak.

"I will explain, Tam." She took a deep breath and continued, "You're right, the rest of us expected this and we could not warn

55

you. However, I cannot explain to you if I cannot see you, so will all of you please step aside so that I can see my Ponfour?" Her tone was slightly sharp and, when they hesitated, grew sharper.

"Tam will not hurt me. It would take much longer than has passed to bring him to a point where that is possible, so step aside, NOW!"

The three looked at the king, who nodded, and they stepped to the side.

"Hurt you, my Lady?" Tam was incredulous. "Why, how, could anyone think I would ever threaten you?"

There was no gentle way to say it.

"Tam, you are controlled by a Zindon. That is why we have been brought here. You cannot be allowed into Tyrean until the Zindon is dealt with."

His eyes widened with shock as he took in her words.

"No, how can that be? You must be mistaken," he whispered but he could feel Crystu's belief in what she had said, and then memory replayed to him the words he had spoken to open the Gateway. He heard his own voice speak the Shadowbringer's true name and in that instant understood that he *was* controlled by a dreamwalking Zindon. The Zindon, realising his exposure, immediately struck at Tam's personality. Tam gasped, collapsing to the floor with his arms wrapped around his head, as his mind threw up barriers in a futile attempt to protect his mind from the creature.

"TAM! NO!"

Crystu raced to his side and thrust her mind into his, hoping against hope to find a way to defend him from the Zindon. What she found in his mind had her staring towards Lord Jareth, and the other Tyreans with him, in awe as she suddenly understood what their plan was.

Expecting an easy victory, the Zindon struck at the core of Tam's self and was repulsed. Astonished, he struck at Tam's Seta and was again repelled. Emerging from hidden recesses within Tam's mind, other minds became evident - minds that were as skilled in dreamwalking as the Zindon.

Joining together they poured from Tam's memories and struck at the Zindon. Finding himself unexpectedly threatened, he fled, leaving Tam undamaged mentally, but the creature took a small revenge as he left, searing Tam's skin as though he stood in a fire.

56

The minds followed the shadow minion; they could not allow him to reveal the secret of the cave trap. With them came other minds, and when they had established the creature's location, these other minds reached out and translocated him from his lair, depositing him bodily in the cavern.

For a moment all was still as the Zindon appeared in the centre of the cavern. He was swathed in an enveloping robe of featureless black, but the shape revealed by the draped fabric was that of a man. Perhaps he had once been a living man, but now a void lay where a living man would have his Seta. Whatever he might once have been, he was a servant of shadow and not truly alive as Crystu understood life.

She found herself suddenly furious and rose to her feet shaking with rage.

"You thought me so young and inexperienced that I would not notice the changes you were making in my Ponfour! A man closer to me than mother, father, brother, and you thought I WOULD NOT NOTICE? I will show you what it means to anger a Rykatu!"

Her power swelled within her, as she decided that translocation would be an appropriate punishment. Yes, she would translocate his feet first, then his limbs, in six-inch chunks to be sent to different parts of the cavern. Finally, she would transmute his head into solid rock and deposit it within the nearest volcano, to melt in the inferno.

The creature charged at her and she prepared to destroy him.

Crystu hadn't heard Tam get to his feet, and so was completely surprised when he pushed her to one side and, with a powerful swing of his sword, took off the creature's head.

"Killing the creatures is my job, my Lady. This Zindon was not worthy to die at your hands," he gasped as the sword dropped from his hand.

Barely able to stand from the pain of burnt flesh, the ravages of his ordeal clearly visible on his blistered face, Tam staggered and would have fallen had Trerin and Trerisia not stepped up to support him. Quickly Crystu refocused the power she had gathered and, reaching out, healed the burns that the Zindon had inflicted on his body.

As Crystu released the remnant of the power that she had gathered, she looked back at the Zindon's corpse.

"I expected more blood," she whispered as her knees buckled.

"Crystu!" Tam's voice sounded alarmed but distant.

"Tam, what is..."

She was unconscious before she could finish her sentence.

Tam had gasped as he felt the immense surge of power that flowed from Crystu as she healed him. Of course, he had known that Rykatuii were powerful but they rarely took the risk of utilising all their power in one spell. The danger of burnout, of death, was real and Crystu was still not fully recovered from healing the child.

Then, as she turned to look at the Zindon, his Sorceress collapsed and crumpled onto the ground and Tam could feel that she had badly depleted her Seta. He immediately tried to run to her side but found that Trerin and Trerisia's grips, which had supported him before he was healed, now restrained him and held him fast where he stood. He stared at Jathte who was the other side of Trerisia.

"I must go to her! She has overstrained her power!"

"I'm sorry," Jathte spoke sadly, "but we cannot take that risk. You have been in a Zindon's grip for at least five days we think. You are badly tainted from its control."

Tam turned to Trerin who held his left arm,

"Trerin, you understand, I MUST go to her." He spoke as one Ponfour to another.

"I do understand," Trerin agreed, "but so must you. Would you risk her with *me*, if it had been I who had been compromised?"

Tam knew they were right. Now that he knew that he had been controlled, he could feel the taint within himself. Until it had faded, no-one would trust him.

"I understand! You are right! You cannot risk it!"

Taking a deep breath and then exhaling slowly, he forced himself to relax his muscles and to accept the restraint.

"I cannot risk it either, until we are sure I am no longer a danger to her."

He watched as several people, including her father, gathered around Crystu's still form. After a few moments, her father picked her up and, surrounded by a large group of people, carried her out of a door that had appeared in the far wall. At a nod from Jathte, Trerisia let go of Tam's arm and followed them.

"I will find out how she is and bring you news," she promised Tam before she left.

Another group surrounded the corpse of the Zindon and Tam felt the tickle of magic use. When they moved away, the body had vanished.

They too left through the same door.

Only Tam, Jathte, Seldar and a small number of Ponfourii and other warriors remained in the cavern.

In silence, Tam allowed them to remove his armour and weapons, and then they escorted him through a different opening, leaving behind Seldar and Trerin in the otherwise empty cavern.

"He's a brave man," said Seldar.

Wrongly believing himself a coward, he appreciated courage in others. Especially those assigned to his protection.

He wondered if his young Ponfour appreciated just how much courage Tam's final words had shown. Seldar and Trerin had been paired for only a few months. Seldar's previous Ponfour had died saving a child from a flooded river and it had taken him many months to recover enough to bond with another. He had deliberately chosen someone who was as different as possible to his lost Arella. Trerin had a merry sense of humour and a love of practical jokes, which Seldar shared, but he was not given to deep considerations about life.

"Yes," agreed Trerin, who until that moment had never considered that there might be other forms of courage than that needed to fight an opponent who stood before you.

How would he react if someone told him that he, himself, was too great a danger to be allowed near his own sworn charge? That his heart, mind, and Seta, might be contaminated by the Shadowbringer?

Could he as quickly accept the possibility, or allow himself to be restrained while he was tested? Trerin did not know, and he hoped that he would never have to find out. If Tam failed the testing, if he was permanently tainted by the control, he faced restraint for his entire life.

59

Aftermath

Crystu woke slowly, her head pounding. She opened her eyes with difficulty because of the encrustations that were often the result of prolonged sleep. She saw above her head the canopy of her own bed, in her own room, in the palace.

Memory returned and with it the need to know if Tam was safe. That thought was followed by the hope that someone would be able to make clear some of the things that were still puzzling her about the last few days.

She climbed out of bed, feeling slightly unsteady on her feet. She found a bowl of steaming water on her table, ready for her, so she began to wash herself.

At one time, a maid would have helped the young princess to wash and dress, but once Crystu had begun to understand what it truly meant to be a Rykatu, she had decided to forego such assistance. She would have no maids when she began to travel, she had told her father on her ninth birthday, so she should get used to doing without them.

Her musing was interrupted by the sound of the door opening, and she turned to find out who would dare walk into her room without knocking. It was her father, of course, and he now stood in the doorway with growing embarrassment on his face as he regarded her undressed state. Crystu had a sudden flash of memory of the last time a man had walked in while she was washing.

"I'm s-sorry," her father stammered. "I thought you would still be asleep. I'll wait in the next room."

Crystu thought that Tam had handled the same situation with far greater aplomb, but she simply smiled and nodded at her father as he withdrew.

A short time later, fully dressed, she joined him in the adjacent room.

As she walked in, he hurried to her and all but crushed her in a bear hug.

"Chryssie, sweet daughter, I've missed you. The palace is so quiet without your voice."

"I missed you too, Da."

After a moment, he released her and, clearing his throat, strode over to the window and opened it. Crystu pretended not to notice that this was an excuse to keep her from seeing the tears streaming down

60

his face. By the time he had turned back, his face was dry again. One of his gifts was transmutation after all, and a king must keep his dignity, even with his daughter. He had fresh lines on his face, she realised, and his usually neatly clipped hair was sticking out by his ear. She could see a few grey hairs and was sure there had been none before she had left Tyreen earlier that year.

He must have worried continuously once he had learned what had happened. Crystu wondered how Jareth had persuaded him to agree to try to rescue Tam. Remembering how her father had reacted to her choice of Ponfour, and the many delays he had imposed before he had allowed them to start travelling, she was quite certain that his first suggestion would have been to kill Tam.

She could feel that she had been asleep for a long time, but her head still felt a little muzzy and she was unsure how long. She wondered why Tam felt so far away from her and why he felt so sad. What had happened while she slept?

"How's Tam?" she asked.

Her father frowned.

"That is still being assessed," was his cryptic reply. "I would prefer to hear how you are. You came close to burning yourself out by using far too much magic for too long. The Ponfour is supposed to risk his life for the Sorcerer, not the other way around, which you did when you healed him while you were still weak!"

Something in his tone chilled her. Had she really come that close, and did she just imagine it, or was he blaming Tam?

"How long did I sleep?"

He looked for a moment as if he wasn't sure whether to answer but finally replied,

"Five days."

Crystu stared at him aghast.

Five days! Such a long recovery meant he was right: she had indeed been close to burnout. No wonder her head was aching.

She sat down and carefully sent a tendril of her awareness into her own body and Seta. They were both intact, but she could feel that the energy conduits, along which her power was channelled, were narrower than usual. They also felt fragile, as if just one more burst of power would shatter them. It would be several weeks before she could safely perform any magic but the simplest spell.

Looking back at her father, she asked, "Da, are you blaming Tam?"

Her father looked at her and then away.

"Part of me is, yes. I warned you when you chose him, that he could be vulnerable to this kind of attack. A Ponfour with only three gifts, and none of them dreamwalking! A ridiculous weakness! He should never have put himself forward in the first place! The High Council has decided that never again will we accept anyone into the Ponfourii with fewer than four gifts, and one of those Gifts must be dreamwalking."

He took a deep breath, knowing she would not react well to his next sentence.

"Those few already bonded... well, we are still deciding about that."

Crystu felt a shock of fear run through her body.

"Decided? What can be decided? The bond is for life until death, and it can't be broken!" She stared at her father's unsmiling face, suddenly uncertain.

"Can it?"

"It is not widely known, but it can be broken. The spell is dangerous even if both Ponfour and Sorcerer have agreed and cooperate. If they do not, The Ponfour is likely to die and the Sorcerer will be weakened for many months at best, even if she was at full strength at the start."

The look he gave her was easily interpreted: he was wondering how long it would take for her to regain her full strength.

"I'm glad of it," said Crystu, "because were it not so dangerous, I fear that you would want me to agree to submit to the spell, and I tell you now, that I will *never* agree to this."

Her father smiled ruefully.

"Somehow I suspected that would be your answer. Still, you will be many weeks recovering your strength, and we will have other chances to talk about this."

He started to move towards the door.

"I will *not* change my mind, Da," she told him firmly.

"We'll see," he said without turning round.

"Da, wait, another moment of your time, please. Where is he? What has been done to him?"

62

The king turned in the doorway and looked at his daughter appraisingly.

"Can't you sense his location?" he asked.

Without hesitation, Crystu raised her arm and pointed in the direction where she could sense Tam's presence, somewhere distant. He felt tired, as though he had been working hard. She waited as her father judged how accurate she was, and then he nodded, and said,

"You're right, that's the direction. He's at the Farm. I should tell you that he has agreed to the bond being broken."

He saw the shock in her eyes quickly replaced by outrage.

"I think you had better talk to Lord Jareth," he told her. "He will explain everything."

King Tarek closed the door behind him as he left. He wondered, once again, how he of all people had managed to sire a Rykatu. No one else in his immediate family possessed more than four of the gifts, though his wife had five. Not for the first time, he wished his daughter had been no more than an average Tyrean instead of a Rykatu.

Explanations

Crystu stalked through the corridors of the palace seething with rage. Courtiers, soldiers, servants, all took one look at her face and quickly stepped out of her way. Her temper was well known, especially here in the palace.

"Agreed to break the bond indeed! Foolish stubborn man!" she muttered angrily.

Oh, she was sure it was true. Because his inability to dreamwalk had proved a weakness that had threatened Crystu, Tam could easily be persuaded into agreeing. He probably thought Crystu would see it exactly the same way.

Men!

She knew him extremely well!

Through the bond, she had sensed that he was constantly astonished that she had chosen him and that a part of him believed that he was unworthy of the honour. The recent events would certainly have added to that, as would the decision to bar non-Dreamwalkers from the Ponfourii in future.

The nerve of the council! Thinking that they could wrest her Ponfour from her against her will! Did they think her a child? Did they think that her decision to choose him had been based solely on his looks rather than on his skills? Maybe they thought that he could persuade her if they could not.

Before she set them right, she would speak to Lord Jareth and set *him* right if he tried to persuade her to choose a new Ponfour.

Leaving the inner palace by the main gate, she crossed the courtyard and entered the Hall of Councils. Jareth's study rooms and office were on the ground floor.

As she approached his office the door swung open before she could knock. Entering, she found Lord Jareth, the senior Rykatu, pouring a mug of her favourite spiced sweet drink, which he held out to her. Aren, his wife and Ponfour, sat nearby. On the table were placed plates and bowls containing fruit, bread and other breakfast foods which looked out of place in the wood panelled room with its overfull book shelves and work paraphernalia. A chair in the corner now held a pile of papers and folders which she guessed had been swept off the table to make room for the food.

Crystu looked at the prepared food and then at Jareth,

"You gleaned I would be here now?" she asked.

64

"Partly," he replied." I gleaned that you would be here sometime today, and I had asked for these things to be ready at need, and then I saw you cross the courtyard just now. I can see that you are furious and I can guess the reason for it, but before we discuss that, I think that there are some things that you must know. Eat, and I will tell you what I think you need to know, and then you can shout at me afterwards if you still want to. Agreed?"

He smiled at Crystu, and she reluctantly smiled back, then sat down and began to eat. Lord Jareth was a noble, honest, and trustworthy man and she knew that he would tell her the truth about everything.

"Firstly, to give you patience while you listen, let me assure you that neither I nor any of the senior Sorcerers here would consider breaking a Ponfour bond in anything but direst need, which this is not. I have told your father that."

"He said that the Council had agreed..."

"The Council agreed that four Gifts including dreamwalking should be the minimum for a Ponfour. Regardless of what your father may wish, Aren and I have made clear that there will be *no* attempt to break bonds that already exist."

"But Da said that Tam had agreed to it."

"Of course he has!" Aren shrugged. "At the moment he is certain that he is a weakness you don't need, and he is determined to persuade you of that when next you meet."

She smiled at Crystu.

"Some men are just too noble for their own good. I'm sure that you will be able to make him see sense. He may be sworn to your protection but you have certain advantages, even if you cannot use your *magical* Gifts at the moment."

Crystu stared at her for a moment wondering if she had imagined the slight emphasis on the word 'magical. Then she began to grin. Advantages indeed! Oh yes!

"I'm angry and I'm hurt, and I need only be honest about that." She threw an impish glance at Lord Jareth. "He'll never know what hit him."

"Hrrhh hm! If you two ladies have *quite* finished talking strategy?" Lord Jareth was grinning. "Then perhaps I can continue?"

"Please do."

"Thank you. Secondly, I will tell you that since you sent me that first warning, I have received many worrying reports, more than usual, from the Protectorates and have sent many Sorcerers out to assess and tackle any contamination. So far we have found nothing at all. Every rumour has been an error, mistaken identity, or exaggeration."

Crystu jerked in surprise, nearly dropping a piece of savoury pie.

"Which is exactly what I expected," Jareth continued, nodding at her reaction. "Tam has told us everything that he knows and I believe that this whole incident was a plot to manoeuvre a controlled Ponfour into the palace, probably for an assassination attempt. As best as I can tell, the sequence of events was this."

Jareth sipped at his drink for a moment to moisten his mouth before he spoke again.

"As you suspected, the accident that so badly injured the Borgani child was almost certainly deliberate. I believe that the Zindon arranged it, probably by controlling the young noble. He judged you to be a young and inexperienced girl who would be willing to risk a great deal to heal such an innocent."

The young Sorceress grimaced. "His judgement was obviously correct."

"Young and inexperienced, you may be, but *I* would have made the same choice," Jareth said firmly. "Our duty includes risking our lives to help innocents. Your only mistake was to perform the healing without taking any rest. That meant that you fell into such a deep sleep that Tam had to use his own powers to heal you, as well as go several days without sleep to guard you. This meant that he, in turn, required a deep restorative sleep, while you were still weakened, and that was the Zindon's opportunity to enter his mind."

"Of course!" Crystu interrupted. "He could not walk in my dreams, no matter how deeply asleep I was, but Tam..." she hesitated, not wanting to admit that her father had been correct.

"Was vulnerable," Jareth gently finished for her.

She stared at him, tears shimmering in her eyes. "And I did not notice for three whole days. I should have noticed sooner, I should have sensed the initial attack and defended him."

"Yes, you should," said Jareth, at the same moment that Aren said, "No, that is not your task - the Ponfour protects the Sorcerer."

Jareth and Aren looked at each other for a moment. It was clearly an old argument.

"You will find that Sorcerers and Ponfourii hold different opinions on this topic," Jareth informed Crystu.

"Very different," agreed his Ponfour and wife.

"Crystu, let me offer you this advice," Jareth leant forward. "Whatever mistakes you may have made, or may make in the future, by all means, regret them and learn from them, but do not dwell on them."

He held her eyes until she nodded her understanding.

"Now, where was I? Oh yes. Having taken control of Tam, the Zindon used his link to you to enter your dreams and to persuade you that there was an immediate, and severe, threat to the Congregation of Light and to Tyreen. I think he also somehow used that link to confuse your senses so that you would not realise that Tam was using magic while you rode."

"The things we saw while travelling?"

"Yes. They were illusions created using Tam's Gifts. All of it was intended to impel you back home to Tyreen as quickly as possible, and to keep your mind occupied so that you would not notice if Tam's behaviour was ever unusual."

Crystu smiled grimly. "He underestimated me."

Jareth nodded. "He did, but don't count on that in future encounters with the Shadowbringer's minions."

"If I hadn't realised when I did…" she paused, imagining the damage a Zindon controlled Ponfour could have wreaked before he was killed.

"It has happened once," Jareth told her. "A less observant Sorcerer, another Ponfour without the dreamwalking gift. Did you never wonder about your Grandfather's early death?"

Crystu stared at him in sudden shock, unable to speak at this unexpected revelation.

"We kept it quiet," Jareth continued. "Can you imagine the panic if people realised that a shadow minion once successfully penetrated Tyreen itself and assassinated the king?"

"Is that why my father objected to my choice of Tam? And why he now seeks to part me from him? "

"Yes." Jareth nodded. "Tarek came to the throne at the age of seventeen because a Zindon took control of a Ponfour, and murdered

67

his father, and you had chosen a Warrior with the same vulnerability."

"I see!"

Crystu realised that a great deal that had exasperated her about her father was explained by this new knowledge.

"And now Tam has been proved similarly vulnerable, my father fears for me."

She took a deep breath and looked up stubbornly.

"Then he must continue to fear, I chose my Ponfour and I stand by him!"

Jareth and Aren nodded in approval.

"And Aren and I are agreed that you chose a good one."

"Then why is he in the Farm? And why is he still being assessed? Surely five days is more than long enough for deep testing? I can no longer feel any trace of taint in his mind!"

The Farm was a sprawling estate, well warded with the most powerful and lethal transmutation spells. It was where the Tyreans held those shadow minions and other incorrigibles who had been taken alive in the long fight against the Shadowbringer. Part of it was also used as a place of punishment on the rare occasion that a Tyrean misbehaved.

"He is held in the Outer Farm while his status is still in doubt," Jareth sought to reassure her, "and he is treated with respect."

"But why is he held at all?" she asked again.

Aren answered her.

"Crystu, I was one of Tam's instructors. I have known him since the day that he was born. During the years of his training, he was tested many times and I know his mind and his aura well, but now there is something new about him that I do not recognise and cannot explain."

Jareth nodded agreement. "I have tested him several times in the past few days. I have found no traces or hints of taint, but neither can I find the cause of this change. Until I do, he must stay where he is."

"Could it not just be the normal change to be expected after surviving such an ordeal?" Crystu argued.

"Perhaps," Jareth admitted, "but until I am completely satisfied, he must remain imprisoned. Your father was most emphatic on that point."

"Then may l see him? Perhaps through the bond we share I may find what you cannot."

Aren smiled at her.

"I was hoping that you would say that."

Lord Jareth stood up and began to stack the now empty meal dishes as he spoke.

"Tam is undergoing further testing this morning but I will arrange for you to visit mid-afternoon when he works in the garden."

"You should rest till then; you need to regain your strength," Aren advised, as she too stood up.

"I won't tell you not to worry, Crystu," said Jareth as he escorted her to the door, "but do try to be patient at least for the next few hours. Come back after the mid-day meal, and I'll have my son escort you to the Farm"

Crystu knew that the next few hours would crawl so, as she was still tired, she decided to go back to bed until mealtime. The time would go past much faster if she slept.

69

Swinging the mattock over his head for added impetus, Tam struck the ground with it as hard as he could.

His task this afternoon was to dig over a field that had lain fallow for the several years. The soil was compacted, and the work was hard, but he welcomed it. He had found that he could become so immersed in the pure physical labour that he could forget everything else - at least for a short time.

Two trainee soldiers joined him in his labour. They had been sent to the Farm for a few days as punishment for some youthful misdemeanour involving the Revered Father's large dog and an illusory bitch (in season) overlaid onto a visiting bishop's travel bag. They seemed to be either in awe of Tam or afraid of him! Whichever it was, they left him to work alone for most of the time and he was grateful for that respite because he was in no mood for pleasant chatting.

Tam's morning had been spent, once again, in intense examination. The magical tests were intrusive and painful, but the results remained inconclusive. The Elders were still uncertain whether or not he had been permanently tainted. Tam was a little surprised that they had not warded him, but they had been content to accept his oath to refrain from magic use until he was freed.

One thing they *had* told him was that, except in a severe emergency, no Tyrean would ever again be allowed out of Tyreen unless he or she was a dreamwalker. Tam knew that he would never again travel in the Protectorates, and the knowledge was devastating. He had worked his whole life to become first a Warrior and then a Ponfour, and now he had lost everything that he valued.

He swung the mattock again and again and took out his frustration on the ground until the sweat was running freely down his back, and he silently rehearsed his arguments to persuade Crystu that their bond should be broken.

A Rykatu must travel. Tam would no longer be allowed to travel. Crystu must have a Ponfour to protect her when she travelled and Tam could not be that Ponfour. Therefore Crystu must bond with another, and that meant that their bond must first be dissolved. (He suppressed the pang of grief that thought caused.) Tam was sure he could persuade her. It might kill him, but that was a minor point. Better to die than live tainted anyway!

70

Tam knew that Crystu had awoken that morning from her long sleep - the sudden clarity of her mind across the bond had been unmistakeable. Tam could feel that she was recovering well and would regain her strength fully, and the knowledge that she would live had helped to sustain him throughout the tests of the morning. He had felt her sudden fury and guessed its cause, but he was sure she would see reason once he explained.

Almost sure.

He could sense that Crystu was moving now and he was soon aware that she was coming here. The closer she came, the less certain he was that she would accept his arguments but he had to make her understand.

When the mattock blade unexpectedly hit a buried rock, vibration raced painfully up both of his arms and brought him abruptly out of his reverie. The sound of voices caught his attention as the mid-afternoon shift of guards arrived. They exchanged the formal phrases with those they were relieving, and the earlier shift left.

The guards had apparently decided to give him the benefit of the doubt, at least so long as he didn't try to leave, and were even friendly within strict limits. One of the two came over.

"Lady Rykatu Crystu will be here shortly, Lord Tam. If you want to clean yourself for her visit, you may."

Tam nodded his thanks, quickly took his tools to the small storage shed. There was a large container of drinking water and he poured some into a bowl to wash his face and hands. He could do nothing about the sweat and soil marks on his clothes, but Crystu would not be offended by the stains of work.

He heard footsteps and came out of the shed to see his Sorceress striding across the field accompanied by Jathte and Trerisia. One look at Crystu's face told him, even without feeling her emotions through the bond, that she was in no mood to listen to reason.

Crystu walked up to him and looked into his eyes and then she slapped his face!

That slap hurt her – a Ponfour's skin and bones were as solid as rock – but Crystu ignored the pain as she glared at Tam.

"You agreed we should break our bond? After everything I went through to rescue you from the Zindon?"

71

Tam could feel the reality of her anger through their bond. Then he felt her mind touch his. Her eyes widened and her fury grew. She struck him again, harder.

"You actually believed you could talk me into this?

She stepped back and Tam felt her fury vanish in an instant, to be replaced by hurt. Tears filled her eyes and spilled down her cheeks.

"How could you? Do you know me so poorly? Is our bond that weak?" She span round and buried her face in her hands.

Her Ponfour opened his mouth but could not find any words. From the corners of his eyes, he could see the two guards trying hard to look as though they were intensely interested in something in the next field. The apprentice soldiers were staring unabashedly with their mouths open, and Jathte and Trerisia were grinning broadly at his discomfiture. Then he found himself unable to see anything but Crystu.

Every word that he had rehearsed, to persuade her that the bond should be broken, flew from his mind.

Crystu turned back to him and looked into his eyes. Her eyes were wide and filled with pain, and her cheeks were wet from her tears. Her lips trembled as she spoke.

"Tell me now, to my face, that you want to break our bond. That you no longer care about me."

Tam could stand it no longer; he could not bear to be the cause of her anguish.

"Of course I don't *want* that. I never *wanted* it," he whispered, barely able to speak from the tears closing his throat.

Crystu took a step towards him, a glimmer of hope colouring her emotions with vibrant gold.

"Then why did you agree to it, Tam? Why?"

Another tear slid down her cheek. As if in a dream Tam lurched forward and hugged her.

"They said it was the only way to keep you safe. They said I will never leave Tyreen again, and you cannot go alone…" he whispered into her hair.

His Sorceress pulled back slightly and looked at him. "Then you never truly wanted it? You just wanted to protect me as a Ponfour should?" she asked.

He nodded.

72

"I swore to protect you whatever the cost to myself."

"My brave Ponfour, to be prepared to pay such a price, but it is not necessary because if you cannot leave Tyreen, then neither will I."

"But a Rykatu must travel, my Lady."

"A Rykatu goes where she is needed, and I still believe the Shadowbringer threatens this land directly. I will stay here. Others can travel," Crystu replied firmly, and she pulled herself from his arms.

"So, that is settled," she said. "I command you never to speak of it again. Do you understand?"

Tam laughed suddenly as the strain of the last few hours suddenly vanished from his heart.

"You know I can refuse you nothing, my Lady."

"And don't you ever forget it," she told him, smiling.

He was certain that Crystu had quite deliberately manipulated him outrageously and yet her feelings and words had been totally genuine. How did she do that?

Only a few seconds had passed and yet now Tam was wondering how he could ever have thought that they should break their bond. The guards were still carefully looking at the next field and the apprentices were still gaping. The only things that had changed around him were the expressions on Jathte and Trerisia's faces. Trerisia was staring at Crystu with an expression of awe, and Jathte was looking at his Ponfour with the worried expression of a man who had suddenly realised that she was taking notes.

"Now!"

Crystu's voice jerked Tam's attention back to her. Her face was dry with no sign that she had recently been weeping. She placed her hands on either side of his head and sent her healing power flowing into him.

"Let's see if I can learn the cause and nature of this change in you that Lord Jareth spoke of."

She was silent for several moments as her power flowed through every pore in Tam's body, but then suddenly stepped back, eyes wide in astonishment. She began to laugh.

"Oh! Oh, but it's perfect!"

Tam stared at her, completely baffled, then he looked at Jathte and Trerisia, who were obviously equally bewildered.

"Lord Jareth must see this immediately. Come, Tam, we'll go to the palace!"

Grabbing his arm, his Sorceress started to pull him towards the track. Surprised, Tam took a step before rooting himself to the ground.

"Crystu, I can't just leave," he said, looking towards the guards who were hurriedly placing themselves between him and the track.

"But we must," she said looking at him and then at the guards. "Lord Jareth must see this immediately."

"We can't allow him to leave, my Lady, not without orders from the Council of Elders."

A sudden fury washed over her and she drew herself up. "I am the Princess Crystu, a Rykatu! I vouch for this man! He is my bonded Ponfour and he leaves with me!"

The man looked anguished and nervous but he repeated, "My Lady, we cannot allow it."

"Crystu," Jathte began, at the same moment that Tam spoke firmly and loudly.

"My Lady, this is unworthy of you. These men have their duty to perform, as do you. If they were to allow me to leave on your word, they would lose everything: position, rank, and, most important of all, honour."

The guards flashed him grateful looks before watching Crystu to see how she would respond.

Crystu stared at him for a moment and then her fury waned as suddenly as it had waxed.

"You are right, my Ponfour, as always."

She turned back to the guards.

"I apologise. My impatience to free my friend overcame my judgement. Perhaps, instead, a message could be sent to Lord Jareth requesting his presence as soon as he is able?"

"Are you sure you have found an answer that will satisfy the Council and allow Tam's freedom?" Jathte asked.

"Oh yes!" replied Crystu and she chuckled.

"Wait here with Tam, and I'll fetch my father if I have to drag him here by his beard," Jathte promised. He and Trerisia turned and ran back along the path towards the stables.

"Perhaps you would care to wait inside, my Lady?" suggested one of the guards. "The work shift is almost finished and, under the circumstances, we can end it early."

"That would be helpful," Crystu replied graciously. "Thank you."

As they walked towards the buildings, Tam had to ask, "My Lady... Crystu... are you sure you have found something that will explain the difference the council sensed within me? Something that is not a taint of shadows?"

She smiled back at him.

"Oh yes, very sure." She grinned.

Tam waited but she did not elaborate. He sighed.

"You're not going to tell me what it is, are you?"

Crystu threw him a dazzling smile.

"I don't believe so."

She laughed again, a tinkling merry sound, behind which Tam could sense mischief.

"You'll have to wait and find out with Lord Jareth. Consider it your punishment for the thing we are not going to talk about anymore."

Tam had a sudden uncomfortable feeling that, even though they were not going to talk about it, he would never be allowed to forget it.

The two of them were escorted to Tam's cell, which was spacious and comfortable. The door and windows were not barred but rather warded with mild transmutation spells, designed to discourage unauthorised exit.

Crystu sat on the chair and made herself wait patiently. She occasionally glanced at Tam and chuckled to herself, which he found disconcerting. Tam attempted to wait with equal patience, but this was difficult, partly because the only other seat was his bed. He felt uncomfortable perching on the edge of his bed while being laughed at by a beautiful young woman!

Another reason he found it hard to be patient was the growing feeling of hope. Tam had begun to believe that he would be interned in the Farm for the rest of his life, and the distress that he knew this would cause his father had been the hardest part of his incarceration.

The sudden unexpected possibility that this ordeal might soon come to an end, made each extra minute that passed until he knew, one way or the other, difficult to bear.

The door opened and in walked Lord Jareth with Aren. Jathte and Trerisia followed them.

"Well, Crystu, my son tells me that you believe you have found what the rest of the Council, including me, missed."

He sounded stern, but Crystu could see a reassuring twinkle in his eye, and Aren was smiling.

"I do, my Lord Jareth," she replied formally.

"The examinations conducted by the Council were no doubt thorough, but they assumed that the change in Tam was the result of his contact with the Zindon. That meant that the examinations were primarily looking for signs of taint in Tam's Seta, They found nothing because that initial assumption was incorrect."

Lord Jareth eyebrows rose. "Was it? Then what did cause the change?"

"I did," Crystu replied. "Link your healing power with mine and I'll show you!"

Both Sorcerers turned their attention on Tam and he felt the tingling as their magic penetrated his body.

"There, my Lord, do you see it?" Crystu asked.

"I do indeed!" replied Jareth. "You're right, Crystu, we...I... missed this because we assumed that the Zindon must have caused the change. I was wrong: this is not Zindon work. So, as I am now satisfied that Tam is no longer tainted in any way, he may return with us to my study where we can be more comfortable while you explain how and when this occurred. Tam, you are a fortunate man."

"My Lord," Tam replied, "at this moment, I am a very confused man! Would you be willing to tell me what it is you have found?"

The senior Rykatu glanced at Crystu, who said promptly, "You can wait a little while longer, Tam."

Then she relented slightly, and threading her arm through his, whispered, "Don't worry; it solves everything."

A short time later, after the official release procedures were completed, they travelled back to the Hall of Councils and were soon all sitting in Lord Jareth's study.

Tam held tightly to his patience as food and drink were brought and served but eventually could keep silent no longer.

"My Lord, please, I must know what it is that you and my Lady have discovered."

"I'd quite like to know too," said Aren mildly. "I think that he's been punished enough now, Crystu. It is time."

Crystu sighed.

"Oh all right, although I was enjoying myself. You're right, Lady Aren. Tam, the simple truth is that you have gained a fourth Gift. You now have the capability to learn to dreamwalk."

Jathte and Trerisia both stared with astonishment at Crystu when she made this pronouncement.

Tam gasped. What she had said made no sense!

"My Lady? How has this happened? I did not know it was even possible to develop a new Gift in adulthood."

"It's rare, but not unknown," Lord Jareth replied. "Usually it happens after the person has been healed of a serious widespread injury. We think that, sometimes, some trauma of birth can cause a Gift to remain unseen and unknown. If that person later sustains a serious injury that requires powerful healing, the original problem may be healed with the new. I have never heard of it happening in any other way."

Crystu nodded.

"In the cavern, I summoned all my power intending to destroy the Zindon. When Tam took care of that," she smiled at him, "I refocused that power and used it to heal his burns, external and internal. This must have healed some older injury, and released the dormant gift."

"The accident that killed your mother on the day of your birth could well have caused injury to you." Lady Aren sighed. "As you know, Tam, I was one of those who treated her and delivered you. We could see no sign of injury on you, but of course it is not safe to use powerful magic on a new-born child, so we could not probe to be sure."

Crystu's head snapped up at her words, and she gazed in surprise at Tam. She had known that Tam's mother was dead, but not that she had died the same day he was born.

She realised suddenly that an odd undercurrent was running through the room. Tam had glanced at Jathte, and then quickly looked away. Jathte seemed to be avoiding all eyes and was rubbing his nose. Lord Jareth and Lady Aren both seemed to feel awkward.

Crystu opened her mouth, but Tam, sensing her sudden curiosity, spoke first.

"Please leave it, Crystu," he said quietly. "It is no longer important."

She looked him in the eye for a long moment and then nodded her reluctant acceptance. There was no rush. They had years of partnership ahead and Crystu knew that she would get the story out of him eventually.

Jathte looked up, and for a moment he and Tam exchanged a look that Crystu could not interpret.

Lord Jareth took a long breath and then continued with the original conversation.

"It's not going to be easy, Tam. You have the capability to learn to walk in dreams, but learning to use it at your age will be difficult. *Very* difficult! You must not only learn to use it, you will have to train this gift to full mastery before you can both resume your travelling. I am certain that the king will demand nothing less. However, Crystu still needs time to fully regain her strength, and I believe that you, Tam, have sufficient motivation for the hard work that will be required."

"Indeed," agreed Tam.

The Sorcerer stood up. "I must inform the king of all this, so perhaps..."

Tam interrupted him. "Forgive me, but I still have one question."

Jareth sat back down. "Of course. What is it?"

"In the cavern, when the Zindon struck at my Seta..." Tam had to pause while he forced back the memory of that terrifying moment. He could feel Crystu sending him support through their link. He took a steadying breath and continued, "Many dreamwalkers appeared from within my own memories to attack it. How did that happen? How and when did they gain access to my mind, without the Zindon or me being aware?"

Jareth nodded.

"Do you remember the vivid dreams that you had the previous night, Tam?" he asked. "That is how and when. I walked in your dreams that night, triggering vivid memories of your past to hide my presence from the Zindon. I created a doorway through which a group of our most experienced dreamwalkers could enter your mind and hide within your memories. You have met all of them at one time or another, so they could hide their presence within your memories of themselves."

Tam thought about this for a moment.

"Wouldn't it have been easier and safer, to simply imprison me in the Farm or kill me?"

"Perhaps, but I decided it would be best to strike with over-whelming force to be sure that we could destroy the Zindon."

"I, for one, am grateful that you did," said Crystu fervently. "I would not have enjoyed training another Ponfour."

"Well, if that is everything?" Lord Jareth stood again. "I have just enough time before this evening's service to inform the king what has occurred. Otherwise, he will be shouting for the guard when you both walk into the Cathedral tonight. You will be there, I assume?"

"Yes, we will be there," Tam replied, at the same time that Crystu opened her mouth to prevaricate. While she was as faithful as any Tyrean, she was nevertheless only twenty-one and had had a stressful day.

She had hoped to spend the evening just relaxing in the palace gardens listening to the birds, and preferably not alone. Watching Lord Jareth and his Ponfour/wife had begun to give her some interesting ideas.

Tam looked at her with his solemn grey eyes, catching her reluctance and a hint of her speculations, and said to her reprovingly, "We both have a great deal for which to be grateful, and it would be rude to fail to give thanks to the Lord of Light for his assistance. Don't you agree, Crystu?"

"Of course, Tam, you're right." She sighed. "We do both owe him gratitude."

She smiled graciously at Lord Jareth, as he left the room to find her father and give him the news. She hoped that her father would be happier now with her choice of Ponfour. She might add a prayer about that during the service. Then she looked down at the clothes she had thrown on so quickly that morning and realised that they would not do.

"I must be properly dressed if we're attending service tonight," she exclaimed. "If you will excuse me, Lady Aren, Jathte, Trerisia. Tam, escort me please."

With that, she took Tam's arm and they left. The moon would be full tonight and bright enough for her walk in the gardens. She needed to find the right combination of clothing. Something dignified enough for the Cathedral, but relaxed enough for her walk, and elegant enough to remind Tam that she was also a woman as well as his Sorceress.

When their footsteps had faded down the passageway, Aren looked at Trerisia,

"That young man is in for an interesting time, I suspect," she remarked.

Trerisia laughed. "You may be right, Lady Aren. She is most accomplished in her arts."

Jathte was puzzled.

"Of course she is, she's a Rykatu. She has thoroughly practiced and perfected all her Gifts."

Unaccountably, his mother and Trerisia began to laugh. Jathte suddenly felt as if they were talking in another language, which just happened to sound like Tyrean.

As they walked towards the cathedral, Crystu paused and turned to face Tam.

"One thing still bothers me," she said. "Lord Jareth said that everything we saw on our journey, including my dream, was the Zindon using your power. But I think he's wrong! I believe that the dream was a true dreamwalk from or on behalf of the Shadowbringer, using our bond to circumvent my defences. I think that this was just the first strike - there will be another. His proposal and his threat were real."

"Then, my Lady, we will both have to work hard in the next few weeks. You to regain your strength and to add to it, and I to master this new Gift rapidly, so that we will be ready when that next strike comes."

Crystu nodded and sighed.

"Still, I hope for this one evening we can find something more relaxing to do? It seems like a long time since I last walked in the palace gardens."

She looked at Tam and smiled. "Perhaps, you would accompany me there, after the service?"

Tam smiled back at her.

"My Lady Crystu, you know I can refuse you nothing."

She took his arm and, smiling happily, went with him through the large cathedral doors, to attend the service where they would give thanks for their recent deliverance, and seek strength for whatever trials the future might bring.

Part 2: Learning to dream

"For the first four hundred years, all Rykatean People were blessed with the seven Gifts of Power, and their hearts became proud. They forgot their promise to use their Gifts to serve and protect the lives of the unGifted." Book of Light: History of the Protectorates – The Dark Time.

Controlling a Dream: A challenge

Lord Jareth began Tam's dreamwalking tuition the day after Tam's release from the Farm.

"Dreamwalking has two main skills which you must learn," he began.

"First, is the ability to walk into another's dreams and either watch, affect, or communicate. Second, is the ability to recognise when others are walking in your own dream, to be able to identify their nature, and to be able to defend yourself and eject them if they are enemies. You cannot even begin the second until you have mastered the first." He grimaced.

"The first step is the hardest part; you must learn how to slip at will into a lucid dream. You must be asleep and dreaming, yet aware that it is a dream. You must learn to be able to awaken at will and to choose where your dream will take you. Mastering this is essential because without this skill you will never be able to utilise your Gift. To help you do this, each night someone will enter your dreams and alter them until you become awake within the dream. We will do this several times a night, for as long as necessary, starting tonight."

Tam nodded his understanding, and the Senior Rykatu continued,

"Eventually, your mind will learn to create lucidity as the normal state. Only then can we proceed. In the meantime, you should review the basic visualisation techniques that you learned for illusion; the same skills are applicable to dreamwalking."

"Yes I know that you mastered illusion long ago," he said as Tam opened his month to make that same point, "but it never hurts to review the basics, and there is always room to improve the clarity of one's illusions."

Tam nodded. He knew that skills unpractised are quickly lost and no matter how skilled one is, there is always room for improvement. He would do as he was bid.

Jareth continued, "You should also try to tire yourself physically this afternoon. Then spend the evening in some relaxing pursuit. Have an early night and, once you are asleep, I will begin."

The elder Rykatu smiled suddenly.

"We're going to have to push you hard in this. Children often take many months to learn to control their dreams. I prefer not to have Crystu held inside Tyreen for that long."

"I will do whatever is necessary, my Lord. I, too, wish my Lady to be able to travel again as quickly as possible," Tam replied with determination. He wanted to be back out in the Protectorates again, not trapped within Tyreen!

Tam spent the rest of the morning sitting in a wooded garden, beside the river, practising the basic illusion visualizations as Jareth had instructed.

Although he had mastered these long ago, Tam recognized the wisdom of review. The danger of burnout through overuse of power caused one great problem: a skill unpractised quickly ceases to be a skill. Essential basics can be forgotten if not constantly drilled, but the Gifts could not *be* constantly drilled without high risk. Frequent review of the basic visualisation exercises was a way to minimise that problem because it used no magic but still helped keep the skill as a skill.

After he had eaten a midday meal, Tam went over to the Physical Combat training school for some exercise to try to tire himself physically as instructed.

The sprawling stone-built training school occupied a large area on the south-eastern edge of the city. It contained both open-air training courtyards, and indoor classrooms and gymnasiums. The central structure of the school stood four floors high, and the outer walls, doors, and windows were almost as ornately decorated as Tyre Cathedral's. The two buildings had been designed, over five hundred years earlier, by the same artist, who had used the training school to try out his ideas before designing the more important and even more impressive Cathedral. Everything he practiced on the school was taken to skilled perfection in the Cathedral. Tam, many of whose family had been master builders, had always loved both buildings. He knew that he would never be a craftmaster, but he had learned enough from his father to appreciate the pure skill and dedication that had made those buildings.

The flowing lines of the carved abstract designs on both structures pulled the eye upwards towards the sky. Those patterns were intricate with flowing lines that branched and subdivided and re-joined. Small patterns built larger ones and the whole almost looked as though it had grown up naturally from the ground, rather than been built by human hands, skill, and magic.

As Tam entered through the entrance into the main arrival courtyard in front of the central building, he looked up to appreciate the large archivolt above the doorway ahead. Around him, he could see many apprentices and trainees walking quickly from one building to another, many carrying bags containing various types of body padding. People of many different ages were all there to learn and train the physical combat arts. Some were training to be Sorcerers and some to be soldiers - they would be heading to compulsory classes and must be there on time. Others had completed their main training years before and were there to keep their skills sharp. Their practices were more informal: some attended the classes as they willed, and some followed their own personal training routines. This meant that any one class was likely to contain a wide range of ages.

Along with several others, Tam went in through the main entrance, then along several echoing halls until he arrived at the changing room for the class he would attend.

He changed into loose clothes and joined the class that was due to start in the adjacent room. The walls and floor of this room were lightly padded, and at one end were brackets and stands holding an array of weapons. Spears, swords, knives, and wooden staffs of varying sizes, were available to practice any form of combat. This was an internal room so had no windows, but the room was well lit by glowing stones set into the wooden ceiling.

The class was for those whose combat skills were already well practiced and consisted mainly of Soldiers, Warriors, and a few Ponfourii. A few older apprentices and younger Soldiers, whose abilities were of a lesser level, were allowed into the class so that they could practice against more skilful opponents and so improve their own abilities. A few people came in after Tam arrived, then suddenly the door slammed shut. Everyone in the room turned to look at the unexpected noise.

"Allyn!" The voice from behind the door sounded exasperated and then the door reopened and three Soldiers entered. The one in front, who looked far too young to be a Soldier, was seemingly being pushed in by the two behind who both wore expressions of mild exasperation. One, a young woman, removed her hand from the man's shoulder and rubbed her nose as though it was hurting. The instructor followed, close on their heels and the three quickly found places in the centre of the room, the younger one, who Tam assumed was Allyn, mouthing "I'm sorry," to the woman.

With the exception of the instructor, Warrior Laodir, who had been teaching for many years, Tam knew no one present. He suspected that most of them had probably identified *him*, judging by some of the looks coming his way, but no one had time to speak before the instructor saluted to the class and began a warm up session.

Within a few minutes, even the Ponfourii were perspiring freely. Instructed to choose a partner of similar size, Tam quickly found himself opposite another Ponfour during a punishing fitness circuit. One of each pair held a large pad while the other kicked or punched onto the pad at varying speeds - a short burst at full speed and strength followed by a period of less intense hitting, then full speed again.

Many were soon dripping sweat onto the ground around them. Those not sweating as much were told to work harder.

They stopped for a short rest and some water, before progressing to sparring. Tam noticed that, as was usual during the rest, the Soldiers and warriors had formed two groups by the windows, the apprentices were in the corner, and that the other Ponfourii had likewise formed a group at the other end of the room. He found he did not particularly want to face any questions from any of the others present, so deliberately did not join any of the groups as he sipped at his water bottle.

The break ended and three pairs stepped onto the floor, saluted each other and began to spar. The others watched - some shouting encouragement and suggestions. Another three pairs readied themselves for their turn. The sparring was full contact, with minimal protective equipment. For the most part, each group picked partners from amongst their friends, though Tam did see one brave apprentice ask a Warrior to partner him. He was easily defeated but did well enough considering the size difference between the two.

Two pairs of Ponfourii made up the next group. When Ponfourii sparred, they did not circle each other, or crouch, or raise fists to readiness. Instead after saluting they simply stared at each other, apparently totally relaxed. In an instant, they had clashed and one was on the floor, the other stepping back to allow him to rise. Then they resumed their stationary scrutiny of each other.

Tam knew that the relaxation was an illusion, (non-magical) and each one was, in fact, watching the other carefully, looking for the slightest hint of movement. That hint would be so slight that afterwards, the Ponfour would be unable to say what it had been; nevertheless, he would react to it so quickly that their movements appeared to be simultaneous.

His thoughts were interrupted by someone stepping in front of him. He looked up to see the young Soldier, Allyn, looking at him with a nervous yet determined expression on his face that made him look little more than a child.

"Lord Tam," he said in a rush, "would you consider partnering me for a bout?"

Caffy and Allyn had changed earlier for the class and then relaxed in the seating area in the courtyard, sipping cold drinks in the warm sunshine, while they waited for Arlton to join them.

"Are you certain?" Caffy said again, her clear blue eyes looking worried. "Absolutely certain? You know what will happen in the last thirty seconds."

Allyn nodded. "You know I have to do *something*!" he said plaintively. "Lord Urestine thinks I should go back home. He said I don't have any aptitude for fighting and I'd be a liability to any Septine. He thinks I'm not brave enough. He said I need to make a choice."

"It's not your courage he questioned!" Arlton said as he dropped into the seat beside Caffy. "He thinks you're hopeless, that's all, but he knows you're not a coward."

"That's not helping!" Caffy glared at him before turning back to Allyn, "How would challenging a Ponfour help, Allyn?"

The young man shook his head, trying to put into words what he could barely understand himself. "Lord Urestine thinks that I don't really want to be a Soldier or a Warrior or a Ponfour. He thinks I don't have the dedication. He thinks that's why I have so many accidents: because deep down I want to go home and paint pictures, but he is totally wrong!"

"Well, you do have a lot of accidents," Caffy pointed out, truthfully. She paused and then asked quietly, "Could he be right?"

"No!" Allyn denied it. "I don't want to go home and I don't want to be a painter. I like painting, yes, but it's not what I want to do. I want to be a Ponfour one day, but the Elders all think that I'm not serious about it. I have to show them that I am!"

"Most of our trainers think the same thing," Arlton said unsympathetically as he finished his drink. "Urestine just thinks it more."

"Arlton!" Caffy glared at him again, "He's just accident-prone. He'll find his equilibrium eventually!"

"*Just* accident prone?" Arlton shook his head, "Allyn, I like you, you're funny and good company, but when you point a bow and arrow, the most dangerous place to stand isn't in front of you, it's right beside you. I swear you can shoot them sideways! And how *did* you drive Urestine's carriage into the river?"

Allyn grimaced, remembering that incident. He'd been distracted by watching baby squirrels racing each other around a tree and had driven off the road.

"I missed the bridge," he muttered.

Caffy shook her head. "*How* do you miss a bridge that size?" she asked.

The young Soldier shook his head decisively. He knew what they were doing: they were trying to distract him in the hope that he would forget about it.

"No!" he said, "I'm doing it. Urestine said I have to make a choice and this is my choice. You know everyone who wants to be a Ponfour has to challenge one first!"

"And I also know that they discourage the practice by making the last thirty seconds of such a challenge, very-very painful!" Caffy pointed out.

Allyn shrugged, "That's so that we can prove that we can face inevitable defeat, and still fight, no matter the cost," he said, trying to sound as though the prospect wasn't scaring him almost witless. "Anyone, no matter how strong, may one day be defeated in battle.

Ponfourii swear to give their lives for their Sorcerers so if you want to be a Ponfour yourself one day, you have to show that you can face defeat and death if you have to. So I'll end up bruised and battered. It will heal eventually."

"Look!" Arlton gasped, unexpectedly, "Look over there,"

"What?" the other two looked around to see what Arlton was looking at.

A tall, broad-shouldered man with long hair, tied in a thick braid, was walking briskly across the yard, gazing appreciatively at the building ahead of him.

"Is that..." Caffy gasped.

"It's Lord Tam!" Allyn whispered with awe.

"I wonder which, if any, of the rumours are true," Arlton said.

"Probably none of them," Caffy replied, "and I don't suppose that we'll ever know."

Allyn's eyes followed the Rykatu's impressive Ponfour until he disappeared through the door, and then he sighed. "Maybe Urestine's right. I mean – I want to be a Ponfour but when I look at Lord Tam I can see why it's impossible."

"It's not impossible!" Caffy said angrily, "You're still growing. If you work hard, you can become like him. He was nineteen once as well."

Allyn laughed a trifle sourly. "Yes, and he was just as big then and didn't have a reputation for breaking anything and everything that comes within reach."

"Why don't you take it one step at a time?" Arlton suggested. "The Ponfour bond spell makes Ponfourii stronger and faster than they were before, and they were already all strong and fast because Ponfourii are chosen only from the best Warriors, and the Warriors are chosen from the best Soldiers. Concentrate on being the best at what you are and then you can aim for the next step, and then the next."

It was sensible advice, Allyn knew, but he felt that it was wrong. He knew what he wanted and he knew what he had to do. The feeling was almost strong enough to call it a gleaning.

He drained his cup. He wanted to be a Ponfour. He wanted to end the suggestions from so many people that he should give up and go home because he would never even be good enough to be a

89

Warrior. He knew only one way to show clearly that he had made his choice and would stand by it, and that was to challenge a Ponfour.

The Ponfour would be nice for part of the fight and would let him do his best, and then would spend the last thirty seconds teaching him what losing felt like.

It would be worth the pain!

"Are you certain?" Caffy asked again, meaning his intention to challenge a Ponfour and thus declare to the world that he was brave enough to be defeated in battle and that he intended to be a Ponfour himself one day.

Allyn stood up abruptly, "If I don't do it, they'll send me home sooner or later. If I do it, maybe they'll see that I really do want this. I'm going to do it."

Striding away from the table, he headed for the classroom, with his two friends close behind. When they reached it he opened the door, then slammed it shut so quickly that Caffy bumped into his back.

"Allyn!"

"Lord Tam's in there!" he whispered. "He's in the class. Lord of Light! I could challenge *him*!"

"Don't be an idiot!" Arlton said irritably. "You're not going to challenge anyone."

He reached past Allyn and reopened the door and together he and Caffy pushed their clumsy friend into the room.

The first half of the class passed in a blur. Afterwards, Allyn was unable to remember exactly which exercises he had done. He kicked, punched, and sweated, all the time wondering if he would dare to do it.

They stopped for a water break, and then the sparring began. Allyn watched, trying not to flick his eyes towards Lord Tam, who had kept apart from the others, and taking great care not to meet Caffy's eyes. He knew that she wanted to dissuade him. He knew that if any of the rumours were true, Lord Tam had had a difficult week and might not be in a mood to humour a Soldier, but Allyn was determined to try. What was the worst that could happen?

Well, Lord Tam might laugh at him and tell him to come back when he was older!

That would be humiliating, but Allyn told himself that he was used to being humiliated and it hadn't killed him yet so one more time wouldn't matter.

He found himself on his feet, pulling on padded gloves, and suddenly was standing in front of the Ponfour. Lord Tam looked up and suddenly Allyn found himself eye to eye with one of the highest ranked men in Tyreen. He took a deep breath.

"Lord Tam," he said in a rush, "would you consider partnering me for a bout?"

To Allyn's absolute embarrassment, his voice cracked on the last word, but Lord Tam seemed not to notice. The Ponfour looked at him consideringly for a moment, and Allyn wondered what he thought about what he saw. Caffy had told him only a few days ago that his latest growth spurt had left him looking like his arms and legs had been stretched. His muscles would catch up eventually, but at the moment he seemed to have bony joints everywhere. Allyn waited for the Rykatu's Ponfour to laugh and tell him to come back when he had finished growing, but instead, Lord Tam's face remained calm and courteous as he asked, "Are you challenging me?" and somehow managed to sound as if he did not think the idea ludicrous.

The young Soldier took a deep breath, heart pounding. This was his chance to back out and retain honour. He could pretend that no, he was just hoping for a chance to spar with someone stronger and learn a little, and did not intend a challenge this time.

He opened his mouth not knowing what he was going to say and heard his voice reply, "Yes, I am."

"You know what I will have to do for the last thirty seconds?" Tam asked.

Allyn nodded. "Yes, Lord Tam, I do." He was pleased that his voice sounded firm and resolute this time.

Lord Tam nodded and glanced at Instructor Laodir. Allyn held his breath as the Warrior looked at him and then nodded slowly to Lord Tam. Light! Laodir was saying yes! He was saying that Allyn was ready to challenge a Ponfour. Allyn felt elated; that approval in itself made him feel suddenly taller.

He didn't even hear Lord Tam say that he accepted the challenge and barely noticed that the other man had already put on his padded gloves, walked out into the centre of the room, and was now waiting for him.

A ripple of quiet laughter rolled over the spectators as Lord Tam quirked an eyebrow and remarked,

"It is customary for the challenger also to step onto the floor."

Allyn gasped and hurriedly moved to stand facing his opponent.

Light! What do I do now? he asked himself, as they saluted, fist to heart and then fingers flicked out in the gesture that mimicked the rays of the sun.

Should I try for speed? he wondered, but no, that would be pointless. Ponfourii were faster and stronger. Lord Tam would hold back his strength and his speed, but nothing Allyn could do would ever be fast enough to surprise him. So he wouldn't try.

Pretend it's Arlton, he told himself. *Just try the things that Arlton does to me, but do them back harder. I can't hurt Lord Tam so I don't need to worry about that. He can match me whatever I do, but so long as I don't do anything stupid, he'll be nice for two and a half minutes. I can't win; I just have to show that I can face what comes in the last thirty seconds.*

Raising his fists, he lowered his gaze to the centre of Lord Tam's chest, and relaxed. He flicked his left hand towards Tam's face following with a swift right punch also towards the head. As Tam parried the two high strikes, Allyn threw a round-kick mid-level and when Tam lifted a knee to block it Allyn threw himself forwards in an attempt to grapple with the big Ponfour. As he did it, he realised his mistake: he was off balance and sideways on.

Tam's left hand shot out to grab Allyn's left wrist. Allyn found himself spun around picked up from behind and dropped on the floor. He scrambled back to his feet, panting, and immediately had to jump to avoid a low sweep kick that would have sent him back to the ground.

Tam spun slightly too far, almost certainly deliberately, and Allyn quite literally threw himself bodily on the other man to use his own weight to knock him over. One part of his mind pointed out that compared to Tam his weight was miniscule and that Tam could easily pick him up with one hand, but the Ponfour allowed himself to be taken down to the floor with Allyn on top.

Allyn rained blows down on Lord Tam's face. Light! Even through the padded gloves a Ponfour's skin was like rock! Tam

92

threw some punches back upwards and Allyn wrapped his arms around one of Tam's, muttered a prayer, closed his eyes and threw himself sideways and round, trying to get his leg over Tam's head.

Yes!

He lifted his hips and then just as he thought that he would succeed in locking the elbow, Tam twisted, wriggled, and suddenly Allyn was turned and then rolled onto his side with Tam behind him, arms firmly wrapped around him. "Good try," Tam said in his ear and then let go.

The young Soldier got back to his feet. He was dripping sweat and already felt exhausted. Tam smiled and then moved and Allyn was now on the defensive, trying to block or avoid punch after punch and kick after kick while landing a few of his own.

As they span around each other, Allyn lost track of time. He had no time for thought, no time for anything except trying to find a way past the Ponfour's skilled hands and feet. A round kick hit Allyn's left side and instinctively his arm came up to catch the leg. Without thinking he stepped in, looping his right leg behind Tam's left as he lifted the caught leg and the Ponfour went down. Allyn jumped back just in time as Tam's foot kicked upwards at his face. Then Tam was back on his feet with a flip, smiling.

"Thirty seconds" Laodir announced and the smile vanished. Allyn suddenly understood that Lord Tam hated what he had to do next, but that wouldn't stop him.

A fist smashed into Allyn's face.

He staggered back, unable to concentrate as blows smashed into his ribs, legs, shoulders and chest. He should lift his arms and block, or *something,* but no matter where he put his hands, the fists and feet slipped by with ease.

"End," Laodir said.

The young Soldier fell forwards as the onslaught ended, but Lord Tam caught him and held him while he found his balance and caught his breath, and then the supporting hand let go so that he could stand unaided.

Allyn could feel blood running down his face and his lips felt strange. His ribs ached and he thought that his left thumb was probably dislocated. When had *that* happened? He could barely see through eyes already swelling closed, but could just make out the

93

Ponfour in front of him. Allyn took a deep breath, trying not to wince, and then saluted.

"Well done, Soldier. You fought well, with courage." Lord Tam told him.

Allyn grinned as best he could, saluted again and then returned to his friends, feeling two feet taller.

"I'm impressed!" Caffy told him, grinning proudly. Arlton nodded agreement.

"I really didn't think you would do it, but that was incredible. Good for you!"

Allyn could not stop grinning as he and his friends left the room when the lesson had ended. He knew that the aches and pains would be worse tomorrow when he had stiffened up, but he had no intention of asking for healing – the wounds were a badge of honour and he would wear them with pride.

"I am glad that you don't treat me that roughly when I spar with you."

Tam smiled at Crystu who was standing in the doorway from where she had watched the bout. He had felt her approach, of course, and had known that she was watching. Trerisia was with her and they had clearly just showered after their own workout. Both had wet hair and wore similar clothes of flowing silk in bright colours.

"My Lady, *you* are not planning to become a Ponfour so there is no need," Tam replied as he walked over to her.

"Is that the only reason?" She tilted her head down slightly to look up at him through her eyelashes.

Her Ponfour felt the power of that look but refused to play her game, even though he knew that she knew that he was deliberately refusing to be drawn in that direction. Trerisia was watching with interest.

"Of course not, my Lady; your father would skin me if I treated you that way. I cannot risk his displeasure, especially at the moment."

As he spoke he purposefully stepped closer, until she pulled a face and waved her hands at the powerful smell of sweat emanating from him.

"Oh! Go and wash! I'll wait in the courtyard."

"Yes, my Lady, my apologies, my Lady, I'll try not to sweat next time, my Lady," Tam said, bowing several times in the course of his sentence. He smiled as Crystu began to laugh at his nonsense.

"I'll be out in a short while, Crystu."

"Don't rush," she replied, "I'm sure I'll find something to look at while I wait." She eyed some of the well-built men walking past and allowed their link to convey her appreciation of the view.

"Crystu!"

Tam wasn't sure whether he felt amused or scandalised, or something else that he was not prepared to identify; not even to himself.

"Go and wash," she repeated, pushing him in the direction of the showers.

As he walked away he heard Trerisia speak but could not make out her words over the sound of a group of chattering children who came rushing past at that moment.

Tenjian

"Nicely done, my Lady!" Trerisia complemented her, as Tam walked away.

"Wasn't it?" Crystu grinned broadly. She had caught some of Tam's emotions at the end of that conversation, and she was fairly sure she had detected a hint of jealousy there.

Excellent!

The two of them walked slowly out into the main courtyard. In one corner of the square, a refreshment area offered fruit juices and savoury snacks for those training. Crystu took one of the spiced vegetable rolls that were her favourite, and both took glasses of a popular drink combined from several types of fruit juice.

They moved over to the far side of the square, where the ground dropped away to give a breath-taking view across the valley of Treos with the River Tyre flowing along its floor. On the far side of the valley, rising to blue-hazed rocky grandeur, lay the south-eastern part of the Tyrean mountain range. They were not as high as some of the mountains further west, but still impressive.

If she followed the path out of the square onto the hillside, and looked along the valley south-eastwards, Crystu knew she would be able to catch a distant glimpse of the Southern Desert. As a child, she had spent a large amount of time sitting on the grass, staring at that view, and imagining what it would be like when she could finally travel out into the Protectorates. The fact that no one travelled to the desert did not deter her from staring at it - it was still a part of the world beyond Tyreen, and was the only part that she would ever see until she was a Sorceress and began travelling.

"There are some free seats here, my Lady."

Trerisia gestured at the seating area positioned on the flat area of grass beside the courtyard. Crystu sighed, she had been trying for several hours to persuade Trerisia to call her Crystu, at least in private, but the woman refused. Crystu wasn't sure if it was because she was a princess, or because she was a Rykatu, but Trerisia apparently thought using her name would be inappropriate.

Crystu considered trying again to persuade her, but instead just smiled her thanks. She sat, enjoying the view of the mountains, and wondered briefly what it would be like to be someone unimportant with few Gifts, and to be able to follow some non-magical employment, only training soldierly skills for a few weeks each year. Rarely, if ever, required to face shadow minions, or worse, the over-formal respect of people with whom she would rather just be friends.

She could sense Tam approaching and she looked up as he appeared in a doorway and began to cross the courtyard toward her with his bag swung over one shoulder.

His hair was still damp from his shower and hung loosely down his back. Of course, being a Rykatu, a Sorceress, and a princess, did have some compensations, she thought as she watched him change direction to get a drink, before heading back toward her.

"TAM! TAM!" A voice shouted from an upper floor and an arm waved. "I'M COMING DOWN, DON'T GO ANYWHERE." The arm disappeared. Tam shook his head and walked the last few steps to where she and Trerisia were sitting.

"If we start running now, we may be out of sight before he gets here."

He sounded as though he was seriously considering it, and Crystu was a little surprised to feel, through the bond, a hint of genuine reluctance to remain until the man arrived.

"Tam," she said reprovingly, "that would be no way to treat your brother."

She looked over in time to see Tenjian emerge from the same doorway from which Tam had come a moment before. He waved and trotted over to join them.

Crystu had met Tenji only a few times, since she and his younger brother had bonded, and she studied him as he walked over. His facial features were similar to Tam's of course, though his hair was short and curlier, but she could see nothing else that would indicate their relationship to each other. Where Tam was muscular, with the broad chest and shoulders of a fighter, Tenjian was slim with the lean fitness of a runner. She remembered that he was a regular competitor in long distance endurance running and that he had won several races. Even now, in his early thirties, he regularly placed in the top ten.

He wore the simple uniform of the Soldier: loose sleeveless dark green belted tunic over brown trousers, with the added brown armband that proclaimed him an emergency reservist.

Crystu knew that the majority of Tyreans were not Sorcerers, Ponfourii, Warriors, or even Soldiers. In fact, on average, fewer than two thousand bonded Sorcerers were alive at any one time. They had a small permanent army of professional Soldiers and Warriors, but the majority of Tyreans, like Tenjian, were Reservists. They spent two months in every year in refresher training to keep their fighting skills reasonably fresh, but the rest of their lives were spent doing all the things needed to keep a nation alive. They ploughed, sowed, reaped, cooked, sewed, baked, spun, wove, fired, and smelted, to produce all the necessities that freed others to be active in the Protectorates. Should Tyreen ever need them to fight, they would do their duty as bravely as any Sorcerer or Ponfour, but in three thousand years, very few Reservists had ever left Tyreen.

Tenjian had neither the power nor the aptitude to be a professional fighter – he was, in fact, a jeweller, and a skilled one. He had only one Gift, that of gleaning, but his talent working with precious metals and jewels was almost a Gift in itself. Crystu knew that he was working towards his CraftMastership and she thought that it could not be long now before he gained it.

The young princess glanced at the particularly finely made Ponfour symbol on Tam's brow and then fingered the beautiful twisted brooch on her wrist. Tenji had made both and presented them as gifts on the day of their bonding.

When she and Tam had been travelling, they had carried many exquisite pieces of jewellery, crafted by Tam's brother, to exchange for appropriate coinage in the Protectorates.

As Tenji was here and wearing uniform, Crystu guessed that he must be within his two month refresher training period. As she came to that conclusion, he arrived at the table and bowed to her.

"Good afternoon, Lady Crystu, it is a pleasure to see you," he said politely, "and a good afternoon to you too, Lady Trerisia."

"Good afternoon, Tenjian, please join us." Crystu smiled up at him.

"Thank you, my Lady."

He sat down opposite her and looked up at Tam, who was still standing.

"Sit down, Tam, I want to hear all about it. There have been all sorts of rumours flying around. The silliest had you controlled by a Zindon and sent to the Farm until they were sure you weren't now a servant of shadows!"

Tenji started to laugh and then stopped as he realised that no one else was joining in. He stared at Tam whose face had gone blank, and then he looked round at Crystu. She had felt Tam's sudden shock at the insensitive reference and glared back at Tenjian.

"You don't say that that one was true?" Tenji sounded horrified.

He turned back to Tam, who nodded slowly.

"And here I joke about it at table! Tam, I'm sorry! I'm an idiot."

Crystu decided that his remorse was genuine, and to be fair, the rumour would seem unbelievable to anyone who knew Tam.

Tam sat down and poured himself some more juice.

"You couldn't know," he allowed and sipped at his glass.

The momentary awkward silence was broken when Jathte suddenly sank into the empty seat next to Trerisia. Even she jumped and he grinned at the unusual sight.

"I thought I'd find you here, Tam. My father asked me to remind you to get an early night tonight. Good afternoon Crystu, Trerisia, Hello Tenjian, are you here for your refresher?"

"Good afternoon, Lord Jareth. Yes, that's right."

As Tenji replied, Jathte ostentatiously looked around.

"For a moment I thought my father had appeared behind me. Please, Tenjian, I think you've known me long enough to call me Jathte."

Tenji looked uncertain for a moment but then nodded.

"I'd be honoured, thank you. I'll try to remember."

"How long do you have left to serve?" Jathte asked.

"It's my final day. Tomorrow I can get back to what I'm actually good at and leave the fighting to the musclebound types like Tam."

"I fight too!" murmured Trerisia, looking up into the sky.

"As do I." Crystu smiled sweetly.

Tam's brother looked at the two decidedly non-musclebound women and sighed.

"I'm misspeaking myself badly today," he said. "I apologise for any unintended offence, my Ladies. Please ascribe it to my being unused to such exalted, beautiful, and talented, company."

Crystu laughed. "Forgiven, as long as you don't mistake either of us for Tam again."

Tenji looked carefully between her and Tam.

"Very well, Lady Crystu, I think I have memorised the difference now. Ow!" Tam had stepped hard on his foot.

Crystu unsuccessfully tried to suppress a giggle and Tam decided to change the subject.

"Tenji, how is Narah? Isn't the baby due sometime soon?"

"Due?" Tenji laughed. "Tam, your niece is nearly three months old, and it's about time you met her. Why don't you come and visit now that you're back in Tyre? It's still your home after all! Narah would be delighted to see you, and it would put Da's mind at rest. He's been so worried by all these rumours and we didn't know for certain that you were back until I saw you just now! Come for dinner. Better yet stay the night! My Lady, surely you could manage without him for a few hours?"

Crystu looked at Tam. She could feel through the bond that the previous reluctance to see his brother had been replaced by a sudden longing to be in familiar surroundings.

The princess realised with shock that at this time yesterday they had only just been leaving the Farm. Had it really only been just one day? She had woken that morning feeling so refreshed and invigorated that the earlier horrors had seemed like something from years ago.

She had forgotten, if briefly, that Tam had had an unpleasant week. He was exhausted, and not just from the exercise that afternoon; he had faced the ultimate horror, been rescued, and then

99

had faced suspicion and deep, painful testing for a week while she lay unconscious.

He would never admit it, even to himself and especially not to her, but he needed some time to just relax.

"Tam, go home. That's an order. Don't come back either to the palace or here for at least a week."

Her Ponfour started to protest but Crystu shook her head at him decisively.

"I can find my own way back to the palace. Go. Meet your niece and see your father and *rest*."

"My Lady, thank you." Tam smiled at her and she could feel him already beginning to relax. He turned to his brother.

"How did you travel here, Tenji? Have you a horse in the stables?"

"Horse!" Tenji laughed at the idea as he stood up. "Brother, all this palace living has softened you. It's only six miles! I ran!" Threading his arms through the straps of his backbag he bowed again to Crystu.

"Thank you, Lady Crystu. Goodbye, Lady Trerisia, Jathte."

He was jogging backwards towards the path to the valley as he spoke his farewells and grinned at his brother.

"Come on, Tam! I'll race you!"

With that, he span round and raced off down the track.

"Tenji!" Tam looked down at his own large bag containing the various padded accoutrements required for a sparring class, sighed and, picking it up, made a hurried farewell to his friends before racing after his brother.

As soon as they were out of sight the others began to laugh.

"Well, what shall we do now?" Crystu asked.

Jathte and Trerisia looked at each other. "We have plans already. There's an exhibition of Larren's recent glass art in the Hall of Crafters. We're going to see it before joining my parents for dinner."

Something in Jathte's voice told Crystu that they didn't want extra company.

"In fact, we should be going now. Have a pleasant evening, Crystu," Jathte said as he and Trerisia stood up to leave.

Crystu watched them cross the courtyard to the gate and felt just a little abandoned. She took control of herself sternly; if Tam sensed it he would turn back immediately and she did want him to have some rest. If jogging six miles counted as rest!

She decided to wonder whether Jathte and Trerisia's trip to the exhibit was an indication that they were considering an even closer bond than they already had. Her speculations kept her amused while she returned to the palace.

Tam ran along the path, his bag bumping against his legs until he slowed to a jog. He could see no point in trying to catch up when Tenji had such a large head start.

He might have a speed advantage because he was a Ponfour, but Tam was also heavier than Tenji, hadn't done much distance running in some years, and was carrying an awkwardly large bag. Unless Tenji stopped and waited, Tam would not see him until he arrived home.

Nearly an hour later, Tam arrived at the sprawling Kentarre Homestead in which he had grown up. When he arrived at the Family House, he went to the front rooms that were the private domain of his immediate family. Tenji was sitting in the small kitchen, sipping at a glass, and trying to give the impression that he had been there for at least twenty minutes. The fresh rivulets of sweat still running down his face suggested it had been closer to five minutes but no longer than that.

There was a second glass of water waiting for Tam and, dropping his bag under the table, he picked up the glass and drained it. The water almost seemed to bypass his stomach to come straight out of his pores, and he realised that he now needed yet another shower and some fresher clothes.

"I won, as usual," Tenji said.

"You cheated, as usual," Tam replied. At that moment, their father entered and stopped in his tracks in astonishment.

"Tam! You're home. Thank the Light! I've been so worried!" Lonian enveloped his youngest son in a hug.

"With good reason, Da. The rumour about the Zindon was true."

Tam stiffened at his brother's words; he would have preferred to pick his own time to tell his father.

"It was?"

Lonian stepped back to be able to look at Tam's face and Tam nodded reluctantly. He knew his father wanted to ask questions but was relieved when all he said was, "Then I'm even more thankful to have you home safe, Tam. How long can you stay?"

"He's got a week, Da," Tenji said, "and orders to relax, so he can help you build Genaara's new workshop."

"Tam has a voice, Tenji, let him use it," Tenji's wife Narah commented as she came in carrying her baby.

"Hello, Tam, it's good to see you, here hold Sobri for a minute." Kissing Tam on his cheek, she deposited the child into his arms and then opened a cupboard and began to pull out plates.

"Your first evening home we should have a private meal so I'll go and fetch some supplies from the main kitchen." She smiled at him. "Don't drop her!" Narah vanished out the door, leaving Tam looking down at his sleeping niece.

"That's my Narah, always ready to draft another babysitter," laughed Tenji, as Tam sat down carefully, not wanting to wake the child.

"So is the other part of the rumour true?" his father asked. "That you are now a dreamwalker?"

Nodding as he looked up, Tam replied. "I still have to learn how to use it, but I do now have that Gift."

"How do you learn to dreamwalk as an adult?" Lonian asked curiously.

Tam shrugged.

"While I'm sleeping at first. I have to learn to recognise that I'm dreaming while I'm asleep. Lord Jareth said they would start walking in my dreams each night until I learned the skill."

"Then you'll be in no fit state to do much of anything for a while after today," Narah predicted as she swept back in carrying one bag of vegetables, and another with some cooked meat.

"So you can do your bit now and keep Sobri comfortable while I do this."

Five days later, Tam was more tired than he had known was possible. He was a Ponfour and could go for days without sleep if necessary, and yet he was so tired that he felt as if he was walking within a bubble that seemed to mute every sound. Only his will power kept his legs and arms moving during the day, and he was running short of that.

Part of the problem was the nightmares, particularly the recurring one where a Zindon laughed in scorn and fastened its teeth on his Seta and began to suck the light from it. In the dream, no saving minds rushed to his defence from within his memories. Instead, his life ebbed away into the jaws of the creature.

103

In another frequent dream, he found himself alone in the cavern without exit or light, trapped forever in the dark while the Zindon laughed and left him to his fate.

Each time he had either dream, he would wake, heart pounding, sweat soaking his sleep clothes, and with a need to light as many candles as he could find to banish the darkness.

The recurring attempts by Lord Jareth, Lady Aren, or other dreamwalkers, to rouse him to a lucid dream, also contributed to his exhaustion. Each night, seemingly within minutes of falling asleep, a dreamwalker would appear in his dreams, but each time he became aware of another's presence he awoke to full consciousness, rather than the conscious-but-still-asleep state that was intended.

Tam was waking many times each night, staying awake for long periods, and the time he *did* spend asleep was not restful. In addition to that, during some of his nightmares he sensed a shadowy presence just watching. He wasn't certain, but he had the uneasy feeling that this was the king. He wasn't sure which was worse, the nightmares themselves or the idea that the king, his Sorceress's father, was watching them.

During the day, knowing he was no fit company for anyone, he took his bow and arrow and hunted, but he caught less each day as he grew more exhausted.

In the evenings he sat in his family's private gathering room and stared into the flames in the hearth, speaking rarely. He could feel Crystu's sympathy and support through their bond and was grateful for it. Grateful too that she seemed to understand that he needed to find his own strength to work through this. He was aware that his father and brother were watching with concern, but, once begun, silence is a habit hard to break.

Finding the path

That night, Tam dreamt that he was hunting. He pushed his way through dense woodland undergrowth, bow in one hand, and searched for signs of life. The wood was grey and hazy, strange shadows lurched and twisted as trees moved in a wind that he was unable to feel.

He felt uneasy, peering through the gloom and behind him but could see nothing.

Ahead of him, he saw a moving flash of colour - a deer dashed behind a bush and he heard it moving away a short distance and then it seemed to stop. The gloom forgotten, he readied an arrow and crept after his prey. The creature moved away again, its passage betrayed by small movements of branches and occasional glimpses of a pale shape against the gloom. Tam could see a faint trail along which it seemed to be travelling. He followed trying to get a clear view for his shot, but it remained elusive. He followed the deer along the trail for what seemed to be hours but could get no closer. Again and again, the uneasy feeling of being observed had him peering over his shoulder into the surrounding forest, but he could see nothing but blackness extending back between the trees.

Suddenly he realised that he was expecting to see someone there - to see Lady Aren, or Lord Jareth, or another dreamwalker, attempting to awaken him to lucidity. The moment after he realised that, the truth awoke in him: he was asleep, dreaming, but aware that he dreamt.

Tam stopped and looked around him. The trail along which he had been walking shone with a faint shimmering glow, but around him the gloom of the forest seemed to thicken as if the air itself was turning into liquid.

Lord Jareth had said that a dreamer aware of the dream could change the dream, and that the techniques were similar to those used in illusion magic. Tam closed his dream eyes and pictured the forest as he had seen it that afternoon - bright, with the hot early summer sunshine streaming through the trees. He filled his mind with that image. Then he willed the image to expand outwards and merge into the dream.

He opened his eyes. The forest was bright and the sun shone through the trees exactly as it had in his image. A beam of light revealed the deer standing in a clearing. The deer shimmered and changed to reveal Narah smiling broadly. She nodded to him, mouthed "See you in the morning," and vanished.

"Very well done, Tam!" Lady Aren's voice came from behind him and he turned to see her walking along the trail he had followed. As she trod along it, it broadened into a clear path.

"And much faster than even I thought possible," she continued, "not only to achieve lucidity but to take control of the dream and alter it."

105

"I kept expecting to see you," he told her, "and then realised what I was doing."

Puzzled, he looked at the path that was now clear and wide. "What are you doing?" he asked.

"In a dream, a metaphor is more powerful than reality. This path represents the ability to be aware of your dream. No one could show you the path – you had to find it yourself – but once found, the path can be, and now has been, widened so that you will always be able to find it, no matter what shape it may take in future dreams. This was the most important, and difficult, part. The rest is a matter of training and repetition."

She smiled. "From now on, you will always be just aware enough in your dreams that you can choose to become fully aware at any time. No nightmares can ever again rouse you from sleep; if one begins you can simply become aware and change the dream as you wish. You will find your rest is as deep and re-invigorating as it ever was, perhaps more so."

Aren looked around at the forest, closed her eyes, and inhaled the rich smell of vegetation.

"Excellent, your attention to detail is impressive."

The senior Ponfour reopened her eyes and spoke briskly.

"Now, you should practice this over the next few days. As you begin to dream, you will see the path. It may not look as it does now - remember that this is a metaphor - but you will recognise it and be able to choose to walk on it. Take control of your dreams as you have done tonight; you should begin with places you know well and can picture clearly. Later you will learn more about metaphors as they apply to the dreamwalk. During the day you must consider the image that will help you to find the sleeping minds of others. Many find it helps to picture sleeping minds as stars shining in the night sky, each one glowing and distinct. Remain in your home for another week; you have had little rest for some time and it will take several nights to recover."

As Aren finished her instructions she began to fade and was gone.

Gazing around at the forest, Tam considered what he should do next. In the mountains nearby was a lake in which he had often swum. He closed his eyes and imagined it. When he opened them he laughed, and running down to the water's edge, dived in. His hunter's clothes vanished as he touched the water.

When he awoke the next day, he was tired but clear-headed. He now realised he had not been so awake for several days.

Looking outside at the early morning sunlight just beginning to filter through the trees, Tam realised that he was actually looking forward to the day. He would help his father and other family members with the building work. First though, he would go through to the communal area and start up the fire and begin to prepare the morning meal. It was about time he did his share of work!

Tam walked across the courtyard and into the large communal kitchen. Several others were in there already, as each person living in the Homestead took his or her turn at the chores.

Narah was one of those taking their turn and, as he entered the room, she ran over and threw her arms round him.

"Congratulations Tam, I'm so happy that you succeeded when I was on duty to see it. I'm so proud of you."

She let go and stepped back to look at him.

"You look much better now. For a while, I was afraid you were losing the ability to be conscious even while awake!"

"For a while I did," Tam admitted, "but I'm awake *and* conscious now, so what can I do to help with firstmeal?"

His brother's wife laughed.

"You can stir the porridge, Tam. No lumps, mind!"

She pushed him towards the large pot beginning to bubble thickly on the heating range.

"Quickly, before it starts to burn at the bottom!" she told him and slapped a large wooden spoon into his hand.

Yawning, Tam obediently began to stir. Lady Aren had been correct, he realised, it would take more than one good night's sleep to feel properly awake again, but at least now he felt more like himself.

In the back of his mind he could sense Crystu, still deeply asleep, and as he stirred the porridge he began to consider the stars. He didn't think that was a metaphor that would work for him, but he would consider it first - understanding it might help him find a better one.

"Uncle Tam! Da says we can pester you now if we want to."

Tam looked down to see his four year old nephews, Olin and Ovan, grinning back up at him.

Unforgivable! He had actually not noticed that they were missing!

He looked at Narah and realised that he had also totally forgotten that she was a skilled dreamwalker When not nursing a new child she would usually be teaching the older ones to use their gifts. He looked back at the boys whose faces were now looking uncertainly back at him.

"Did we do something wrong?"

Ovan's lower lip was starting to tremble; his uncle did not usually stare like that.

"No, no of course not!"

Dropping the ladle into the porridge pot, Tam knelt and pulled both boys to him in a fierce hug.

"I only just realised how unwell I've been, but I'm better now. You can pester me just as much as you want."

"That's a dangerous thing to tell them!" Narah told him. "Come on boys, go find yourselves bowls and Uncle Tam will serve your porridge."

She looked into the pan and grinned. "Just as soon as he's rescued the ladle that is."

Jumping to his feet, Tam was in time to see the end of the ladle disappear into the bubbling depths. He sighed.

"I'm sorry, Narah," he said, meaning more than losing the ladle.

"You've nothing to be sorry for," she told him, as she handed him a long handled spoon to use to find the lost one. "After you told us the first night, about how they planned to teach you to control your dreams, I sent a message to Lady Aren. I asked to be involved and she agreed. The next day, once they had told me exactly what they intended, I warned everyone in the house how it would probably affect you. Everyone understands." She paused to point to the washing bowl when he would have given her the porridge coated spoon newly rescued from the depths of the pot.

"We thought it best to keep the younger children away. They would have been confused and upset to be ignored by you."

Tam obediently washed the spoon, and then cleaned away the porridge that had dripped from it to the floor. The boys were still waiting for their breakfast, so he filled them a bowl each of porridge with sweetened fruit added.

"I haven't exactly been doing my fair share of the work," he pointed out to Narah as he placed the filled bowls in front of his hungry nephews.

"You went hunting," she replied.

"And caught little," he countered.

"Then you can make up for it now." An elderly woman came over. "We need more wood. I think you probably remember where the wood pile is, don't you?" She gave him a severe look.

Tam laughed; chopping wood had always been one of Aunt Tersha's favourite punishments.

As a child, he had honed his illusion Gift by creating incredibly detailed and life-like illusions of animals in places they should not be. Tersha had often been the victim of his pranks.

"I think I can find it, Aunt Tersha. Will a barrowload be enough?" He gave her a hug.

"Don't get porridge all over me!" she exclaimed before pushing him away. "Yes, a barrowload will be enough for now, thank you, Tam."

The mountain lake

When Tam returned with the barrow of chopped wood, the eating room beside the kitchen was filled with people. He deposited his load in the appropriate place, helped himself to some cooked meat and eggs, and crossed the room towards the table where his father, Tenji, and Narah, were sitting.

"...that princess has a devious and imaginative mind. I'd hate to get on her wrong side." Narah was saying as Tam approached.

"Crystu?" he exclaimed as he sat down. "Is there any reason you should?"

His brother's wife seemed flustered by his appearance and shook her head hurriedly. "No, no reason at all," she replied.

"Tam, you look much better," Tenji exclaimed. "Narah says that you managed to achieve a conscious dream last night, so you'll be able to get some rest at night now."

"That's right, I did. I finally succeeded. Lady Aren wants me to practice it for a few days," Tam replied and then grinned ruefully. "It will make a pleasant change to be properly awake again during the day."

109

"Ha!" his father said. "You seem more like yourself now, so perhaps you can help me today with the building? We saved some nice heavy jobs for you."

That set the pattern for the next few days. During the day, Tam helped his father building the new extension, and at night he practiced controlling his dreams, and in between, his nephews pestered him to their, and his, heart's content.

Again and again, Tam found himself returning to the mountain lake in his dream. It seemed to be important in some way, but he couldn't work out why or how. So, after a few days, he decided to go to the lake, in reality, to see if he could solve the puzzle.

Starting early, he crossed the valley and began to climb into the mountains. He walked beside the small river that flowed down from the lake until, after nearly two hours, he broke out of the forest and looked up at the mountain above him. The lake was not far from here.

He climbed up a short rocky rise down which the tumbling water roared and splashed, and there just ahead was the low dam that held back the lake.

The dam was built across a narrow gap between two spurs of rock. Built using transmutation, it was a smooth rock wall in which was set a sliding metal gate. The water in the lake flowed over the top of the gate, which could be raised or lowered to allow a greater or lesser flow of water. A wheel set in a pillar beside the dam was the control for this.

Tam climbed up over the rock spurs and then walked around the side of the lake toward the far end where two streams flowed into it from higher in the mountain, one flowing down gently from a higher slope, and the other crashing down over a sheer cliff nearby.

The lake below the waterfall was deep, and the water there could be dangerous; it frothed and bubbled as if boiling. The currents at that point were unpredictable because the water's churning constantly changed the shape of the underlying land.

Stripping quickly, he placed his clothes and bow on a large flat rock, weighted them down with a convenient rock to keep them from being blown away by the gusting mountain breeze. Then he waded into the lake.

110

The water was almost as cold as ice, but his body adjusted to it quickly. For a while he just swam leisurely, diving down to explore the bottom in the shallower areas, comparing the present reality to his memory of it in the past. Then he swam over to the side into which the two streams ran, and he floated, allowing the currents to pull him where they would.

Tam climbed out onto a large rock and dived back into the water. Then, as he had often done in childhood, he turned onto his back under the water and gazed up at the interface of water and air. He could see reflections from below him superimposed against the clouds visible above. The images rippled and changed, breaking apart and rejoining, slashed apart by bright ribbons of light as the surface of the lake moved.

A hint of an idea began to form of a metaphor for the dreamwalk. He surfaced, and trod water considering the image; it might work for him.

Swimming back to the edge of the lake, he climbed out. The warm sun quickly dried him as he lay on the grass, and he decided that tomorrow he would return to the palace and talk to Lord Jareth or Lady Aren about the next step in his training.

He dressed and returned home. On the way he caught a large deer, which he carried back on his shoulders, satisfied that the day had been productive in more ways than one.

Tam deposited the deer with those whose turn it was to prepare the meal. They would skin and clean it, and store the meat for another day's use. It was too late in the day to cook it for that evening's meal.

Enjoying the melodious birdsong, and the colourful sky as the sun sank towards the horizon, he walked slowly along the road to the workshops, where he found Tenji in his workroom finishing a particularly beautiful necklace. Narah was sitting nearby, sorting through recently polished gemstones to check if any needed further polishing before use. Sobri was sleeping in a cot to one side of the room, beside the shelves displaying finished jewellery ready for collection.

"That's beautiful," Tam said admiringly as he looked at the jewellery in his brother's hand. Tenji looked up briefly and grinned at the complement.

111

"It's a betrothal gift requested by someone in Tyre," he replied and looked back at his work. "It's almost finished, and just in time."

"I can take it up to Tyre tomorrow," Tam offered. "I'm planning to go back, I think it's time."

Narah burst into laughter.

"Oh! Lady Aren is good!" She grinned as both men looked at her in bewilderment.

"Tam, Lady Aren gave me a message to give to you as soon as you announced you were going back." She paused to breathe because she had spoken all on one breath. "She also predicted that it would be today."

She stopped, grinning.

"And the message is...?" Tam prompted.

"Tell him, that from the moment he says he's ready to come back, he is to wait seven more days. *Then* he'll be ready to return. Not before. She also said, that if you come back before then, she will personally… err…"

Stepping close, she whispered the rest in his ear.

Tam's eyes widened, and he swallowed.

"She said *that?*"

Narah nodded while Tenji looked on with curiosity.

Tam took a deep breath wondering if Aren would really do such a thing. He decided that if *anyone* would, that person was Lady Ponfour Aren, and she had the strength of power to manage it.

"Perhaps I should stay here a little longer then," he said, trying to sound dignified and knowing that he failed.

"Wise man!" Narah murmured.

Tenji looked from one to the other.

"What? What did she threaten?" he asked.

"Never you mind," Tam growled, at the same time that Narah said,

"None of your business, Tenji, I was instructed to give the message to Tam, not to you."

And with that Tenji had to be content.

112

Part 3: A widespread gleaning

"At the end of the Dark Time, the Lord of Light withdrew his Gifts from many of the Rykateans as punishment for their pride. He decreed that, from then on, only two people would possess all seven Gifts at any one time. Chastened, from that time they took the name 'Tyrean', and also the name 'Guardians of Reyth', so that they would never again forget that their first duty was to the unGifted of the Protectorates." Book of Light: History of the Protectorates – The Dark Time.

The vision

The next morning Tam went with his father to the extension they were building onto the forge and workshops. The new structure consisted of a low stone wall supporting a superstructure of wooden beams and bare wattle walls. The building was surrounded by a wooden scaffold to allow access to the roof where several people were carefully positioning tiles. A rope and pulley system had been set up on the side of the scaffold to lift large crates of tiles up to the workers on the roof.

Tam's first task was to carry the crates, from the road where they were stacked, to the building, attach each one securely to the pulley, and then hoist it up to the roof. After hauling enough crates up, he was asked to spend some time mixing the daub for the walls. Blending the clay with straw and horse dung was an unpleasant, smelly task, and he was glad when they stopped for the midday meal. He washed the clinging mess off his hands gratefully.

After eating, he began spreading the daub onto the inside walls. Suddenly, the air around him darkened. He looked out of the window, expecting to see that the sun had disappeared behind a cloud, but the sky was cloudless and the sun was bright.

For a second time, greyness seemed to fall over him, yet, for a second time, when he looked around all was still bright.

Tam suddenly understood: whatever it was, he was experiencing it through his bond with Crystu. He focussed on the link between himself and Crystu, attempting to understand what was happening to her. He could feel that she was starting to feel uncomfortable.

113

Whatever it was, was building in intensity, and she was becoming increasingly anxious.

"Tam! Tam! What is it?"

He roused to find himself leaning against the wall, with his father shaking his shoulder. Around them, activity on the building had ceased as people collected around two others who were apparently staring at something only they could see. He could think of only one explanation: a gleaning was affecting them and also Crystu. She was becoming increasingly distressed.

"I have to go," he told his startled father and, leaving everything, he sprinted along the road to the stables. "I need a horse, now!" he shouted.

A visitor about to depart, seeing the Ponfour symbol on his brow, dismounted rapidly.

"Use mine, Lord Ponfour, he's ready."

"Thanks," Tam muttered as he jumped onto the horse's back and urged him towards the road, using his sense of Crystu, through the Ponfour bond, to find his way towards her.

The gleaning was powerful and affecting several people at the same time. Tam wondered briefly how widespread it was but quickly put the question out of his mind.

Gleanings often came unbidden, and even if someone was rested and at his full strength, a powerful one could be draining and inconvenient, but Crystu had overused her power several times recently. Tam could feel that the onset of this vision was already making her uncomfortable.

More than two weeks might have passed since she last used her Gifts but she had come dangerously close to burnout, and the channels of power from her Seta would not yet have healed fully.

The gleaning would force her power to activate, and that could undo all the healing from her rest. As Tam urged the horse to go faster, he could feel that his Sorceress was beginning to feel pain as her power travelled along the still raw channels in her mind. What could he do?

He knew that healers could send Seta through a dreamwalking link, so was there a way Tam could send Crystu his own power to use instead of her own? Not by dreamwalking, that was certain - he was on a horse, did not yet know how to enter another's dreams, and neither he nor Crystu was asleep. It might be possible but Tam did not know the method.

Then it occurred to him that he already had a link to her mind, through the Ponfour bond, so perhaps he could use that in a similar way. Tam did not know if it was possible, and had never heard of it being tried, but he was determined that somehow he would find a way.

Visualisation was extremely important with all magic use. Many of the Gifts, such as transmutation, illusion, and shapeshifting, required a detailed mental image of the required end product. With dreamwalking, metaphors also were important, but again required visualisation.

These thoughts flashed through his head within a second. He could feel Crystu's pain growing as her power began to enflame channels only recently healed. He had to act, now!

The image came unbidden to his mind: the lake with its dam, the stream running down to the lower river. He concentrated on it. Metaphor! The lake was his power, the lower river was Crystu, and the stream was the bond between them.

He built the image in his mind, and then slowly lowered the dam wall to allow water to flow down the stream. He concentrated on the metaphor - the water was his power, and it was flowing towards Crystu.

His energy began to flow from him, along the bond, to Crystu.

The horse was tiring, and he let it slow to a more sustainable pace as he sent as much power as he could muster down the link towards Crystu. It was working, but would it be enough?

Crystu

The morning after Tam left Tyre to go home, Crystu rose early and made her way down to the kitchen in search of firstmeal. She hoped that none of her family would be up and around so early, particularly not her father. She was still angry at his suggestion that she should break her bond with Tam and choose a different Ponfour.

Even though Tam could now potentially learn to dreamwalk, Crystu knew her father still disapproved of her choice of Ponfour. She would have liked to talk the problem over with her mother, but at this time of day, her father and mother would undoubtedly be

115

together. Her two brothers had yet to bond so could not be expected to understand. So she decided to simply avoid all of them.

That left the question of what she should do to occupy herself for the next month while she recuperated from her near fatal over-use of magic.

In the kitchen, the servers were happy to find her some cereals and bread, which she took out into the gardens, out of sight of the house, to eat.

Crystu found court life boring and had done so even before she began to travel. She suspected that she would find the official duties even harder to stomach now after the freedom of travelling. In addition, those duties would mean being in the same room as her father, and, as she was still angry with him, she intended to avoid that for as long as possible.

She planned to spend at least an hour a day in exercise, but that still left many hours to fill. She considered visiting her former friends and acquaintances but dismissed the idea. Those who might be found around in Tyre were likely to be those whose Gifts were insufficient to qualify them as either Sorcerers or Soldiers, and whose attitudes made them unwilling to work in a craft or other area. Their experiences and conversation would be confined to gossip, and she had ceased to find that interesting *many* years ago.

Any who were Gifted enough to be Sorcerers or Soldiers, or dedicated enough to practice in another craft, were out travelling or training or working.

Whatever happened later, Crystu decided, the *first* thing she wanted was to talk to Lord Jareth or Lady Aren about how they would teach Tam to dreamwalk. She had a feeling that it would not be as easy as they had made it sound.

Several days later, Crystu was still bored and had taken to creeping out of the palace early each day and just wandering about the city. She knew her father was becoming irritated about that, but so far she had managed to avoid seeing him. That would probably get harder, she supposed, because a king usually gets what he wants in the end, but so do Rykatuii, and Crystu was every bit as stubborn as her father.

She had managed to have a long private chat with her mother, who had been completely supportive.

Queen Elish had told Crystu that she had told Tarek *exactly* what she thought of his insistence that Tam and Crystu sever their bond. She said that he had eventually agreed that he might have been wrong, but Crystu decided that she still wasn't prepared to forgive him for suggesting it in the first place.

As she wandered the city, she was constantly aware of Tam's rapidly increasing exhaustion. She had trouble stifling a twinge of guilt because she had made some suggestions to Jareth that would help to create the needed sleep deprivation.

Eventually, she would have to confess. No, not confess exactly, more like explain. Yes, she would have to explain to Tam about what she had done. She hoped that he would understand.

She was *almost* sure that he would.

On the fourth day, she had a surprise. She was exploring an area of the city she had not previously visited when she suddenly spotted a beautiful carving of an eagle, positioned in the display window of a craft house.

Frozen in the act of catching a rabbit, the bird looked almost as if it could burst into life at any moment. Even if the result of transmutation, it was an excellent piece of work, but when she looked closely Crystu realised that it was actually hand-carved.

The craftsman was inside, head bent to his latest work which was a lifelike carving of a gambolling lamb.

Crystu waited for his attention, not wanting to interrupt at what might be a crucial moment. When he finally looked up to speak to his visitor, she gasped in surprise - it was Andar, her distant cousin whose clothes Jathte had once turned to cobwebs. Andar had disappeared shortly after that event, but she had never imagined that he might have taken up a craft.

He was delighted to see her, and Crystu stayed with him all afternoon. The three of them (he was married now) reminisced and told stories and laughed.

She learned that after the cobweb incident, her cousin had found that people in the palace tended to snigger a great deal when he was about, so he had decided to leave and see if his hobby of carving could become something more satisfying. Apprenticing himself to a woodcarver, he had learned and then mastered his chosen craft. He had never returned to the palace and never intended to.

117

Crystu envied him his chance to just slip quietly away, which was something she would never be able to do.

Two days later, Calline (the queen's Ponfour), with the queen's knowledge (though not the king's) suggested that Crystu accompany her to a tavern on the outskirts of the city. It was a place largely frequented by professional Soldiers, and Warriors.

Many travelling Sorcerers and their Ponfourii also visited 'The Golden Moon' when in Tyre.

Crystu had known of its existence, but had never considered entering – her father would have a fit! Not that a Tyrean tavern was anything like a tavern in the Protectorates. It was cleaner for a start, and the patrons rarely became seriously drunk. Nevertheless, alcohol was present, and the atmosphere was convivial, and Crystu loved it!

Those who drank there were all widely experienced and had travelled in the Protectorates. They had experiences in common and were people with whom she could have a real conversation, without constantly having to avoid subjects and questions which others might find disturbing. Like why a Zindon had not bled much when it was beheaded and then chopped in two.

She started spending her mornings rebuilding her strength and fitness, and her afternoons at The Moon.

Lady Aren told her when Tam succeeded in controlling his dreams, and Crystu could sense his rapid improvement as he regained alertness. She knew that her own recovery was also proceeding well.

So long as she continued to abstain from magic use she would be back to full strength within a few more weeks.

Waking one morning, feeling alert and full of energy, she jumped out of bed and dressed quickly. She found her mother, with Calline, waiting for her in the eating room.

"Crystu," her mother said briskly, "it's time you started doing your share of the family duties. We've been patient as you were recuperating, but you're clearly well enough now to take your turn. It will only take an hour or so."

Crystu nodded reluctantly. Her mother was correct: it was indeed time she started doing her share of 'The Duty'.

"Of course, Mother," she replied. "What do you need me to do?"

"There's an anointing service in the Cathedral this morning, a new group of youngsters entering into the Service of the Lord of Light. A member of the family should be present and it's your turn."

She smiled as Crystu nodded acquiescence.

"Thank you, sweetheart, your father and I both appreciate it."

Crystu dressed in the formal red silk robes required for the occasion and, looking wistfully up at the clear blue sky, stepped into the Cathedral and allowed herself to be ushered into the Royal Seat. The service was mercifully brief, although she enjoyed the singing and found the sacred readings inspiring. The Revered Father was away in another city, but the priest who stood in for him in his absence read well and had a warm rich voice.

When the service was finished, Crystu slipped out a side door, rushed home and changed. She had decided that she wanted to climb into the mountains and enjoy the rest of this beautiful day.

Leaving a brief note for her mother, she took some travel food from the kitchen and then headed into the countryside. She intended to go as far as she could until she felt hungry, and then find somewhere with a spectacular view while she ate. She decided to take her bow because even the Palace could use fresh hunted meat occasionally and she did not want to lose her skill.

Following a familiar track, Crystu started up through the woods. As she approached a clearing, the sky suddenly darkened and she looked up. She expected to see that the sun was behind a cloud, and was surprised to see it shining brightly, in a warm blue sky, with no clouds anywhere nearby. She frowned in puzzlement and looked back at the path. Again, it seemed as though a shadow had fallen over the wood but, again, when she looked up, the sky was cloudless.

Feeling unexpectedly nervous, she stopped and looked around her, trying to find the source of her anxiety. The wood seen from the corners of her eyes gained deeper shadows, and she heard a sound, like wind in the treetops, yet when she looked around, the leaves were not moving; the air was still.

Her breath became faster, and her heart started to beat more quickly. Greyness seemed to surround her, and suddenly she understood - it was a gleaning and it felt powerful!

A gleaning would activate her Gift without her control, and it would use as much of her power as necessary to show her the images that it carried.

Rested and at full strength, she would be in no danger, but her mind channels were not yet fully healed. A flow of power would undo the healing of the last few weeks and, if great enough, would cause the burnout she had so narrowly avoided less than three weeks earlier. If she were still in Tyre, she could ask for healers to strengthen and support her mind channels, but she was alone on the mountainside, too far away from help, and not yet strong enough to translocate.

Crystu turned and began running along the path. It was a futile effort; she could already feel the power beginning to flow from her Seta

Images began to take shape in front of her eyes despite her efforts to reject them. The still tender channels resisted the flow and pain started spreading through her head and down into her body. Fear gripped her as she began to realise that this gleaning would be extremely strong and would require much power to run its course.

Power which she did not currently have!

Her pain grew in intensity, and blood flew unnoticed from the side of her mouth where she had bitten her lip, unable to feel the little pain against the greater. She tripped and fell, coming to rest with her back against a large tree trunk. Suddenly the pain eased and then vanished.

Crystu sobbed with relief at the wonderful nonfeeling, yet the gleaning continued to build. She realised to her astonishment that the gleaning was now drawing its power, not from her Seta, but from energy that was pouring out of her bond with Tam.

His power? How was this possible?

She had never heard of such a thing, yet he was doing it. Somehow Tam was using the bond between them to send her the Seta that would power the gleaning - she would survive it after all. As the gleaning became so powerful that its images took over her senses, she had time for one more thought: Tam was pouring all his energy into the link between them. She would survive but would he?

Eventually, the gleaning began to ease slightly and Crystu became aware of her surroundings again. Her eyes could still see only the images of the gleaning and she could not move, but she could feel that she was being carried. An arm was under her knees and another behind her back, while a slight swaying motion told her that they were on a horse. She knew it was Tam; he had come for her. His power was still flowing down the link between them, but she could feel that it was starting to falter - he was tiring.

Somewhere nearby and getting closer, she could hear voices and sounds of activity like people coping with some sort of emergency. Perhaps this gleaning was widespread.

"Look, it's Tam; he has found Crystu." A voice she didn't recognise.

"Someone fetch Aren and the queen."

"She's coming."

"Here's the queen."

"We need healers quickly!"

Crystu felt the jar as Tam slid off the horse still holding her. He seemed to sit down on the spot as though unable to walk.

"Tam, where was she?"

"What's he doing? Why doesn't he speak?"

Hands tried to remove her from his arms, but they could not release her from his grip.

Then her mother's voice sounding relieved and worried at the same time.

"Crystu, can you hear me?"

The young Sorceress tried to respond but could not open her mouth or even nod. She felt her mother's fingers on her face and then her mother's mind was sliding into hers. She felt her mother's healing probe investigating the channels in her mind, then it slid towards the bond.

"This is extraordinary!"

"Elish, is she alright? What's happening?" That was her father, joining the group gathered around them.

"She's not injured, the channels are stressed but not ripped. She has not burnt out. The gleaning isn't drawing on her power at all - it's using Tam's!" Crystu could hear the awe in her mother's voice.

"Tam's power?"

That was Lady Aren, clearly just arrived. Then Crystu felt Aren's mind joining her mother's to probe into her mind. She would have

121

moaned in frustration, but could not make a sound. How long would it take them to realise that Tam needed help?

"I see it, Elish. You're right: the gleaning is using Tam's Seta through their bond. That's the only reason Crystu's alive! She is not recovered enough to have survived such a powerful gleaning otherwise!"

"No, It's not Crystu who needs buffering," Lady Aren told the healers trying to gather around Crystu. "Tam. It is his Seta being used; concentrate on him!"

Crystu felt her mother and Aren's minds leave hers, and a moment later felt the renewed strength in the energy flowing across the bond. The healers, with her mother and Aren, were using their Gifts to support and strengthen Tam, as he poured his power into her. A hand grasped hers and she realised that her father was squatting beside her.

The gleaning weakened suddenly and then dissipated completely. As soon as it had released her, Crystu could see and talk again. Around the courtyard, she could see clustered groups of people gathered around others who had obviously also been caught up by the gleaning.

"How long?" she gasped. "How long did it last?"

"About forty minutes," her father told her. "Almost everyone with the gleaning Gift was affected to greater or lesser degree."

"Forty minutes?"

She tried to move but Tam still held her fast, though the power flow from him had abated. He seemed oblivious to all around him, while her mother, Aren and several other healers worked to bring his mind back to awareness.

Suddenly he blinked and drew a deep breath. Through their bond, Crystu felt his fear for her melt into relief.

"Crystu? Are you well? Did it work?"

He released his grip on her and, letting go of her father's hand, Crystu twisted around on Tam's lap, threw her arms around his neck, and kissed him.

This did not have quite the intended effect, because her unexpected movement unbalanced him and he fell backwards onto the floor, knocking sideways the healer who had been behind him.

Hands were proffered in assistance and, eventually, everyone was back on their feet including Tam, who seemed extremely tired but otherwise unharmed by his expenditure of power.

"Tam! You were amazing! How did you do it?"

"I would like to know the answer to that myself," said Lady Aren,

"As would I," said the king, and Crystu's mother nodded agreement.

"But not now," Aren continued. "Tam is exhausted, and there are still many others to tend to, before we begin to make sense both of this occurrence and of the gleaning itself. I have never known such a widespread and powerful gleaning. Clearly, the Lord of Light is anxious that we are warned of some forthcoming event."

"Indeed," King Tarek agreed. "It will take several days to gather together and begin to make sense of all the images. Crystu should return to the Palace, and I believe Tam was recuperating at his home. I will order a carriage to take him back."

Crystu felt Tam's sudden stubborn resistance to that suggestion and was not surprised when he spoke.

"My King, grateful though I am for the offer of a carriage ride home, I must respectfully decline. I will not leave my Lady Crystu again."

King Tarek looked astounded and not at all pleased at this defiance. Crystu wondered sourly what Tam would have to do to gain her father's approval if just saving her life was not enough.

Lady Aren pursed her lips, glanced at Tarek but spoke to Tam.

"Tam, I believe I made it quite clear that I expected you to take several days more rest. Under the circumstances, I will overlook your disobedient return to Tyre, but you still need that rest, especially after your astonishing feat this morning. You are hardly awake now and will in all likelihood sleep for at least a day. You must return home."

Her Ponfour remained stubborn, although Crystu was intrigued at the sudden hint of deeper colour that appeared in his cheeks, and ...was that embarrassment she could feel in their link?

"Lady Aren, I am aware that I have disobeyed your instructions. You may carry out your threat at your earliest convenience, but I will stay with my Lady Crystu."

123

Crystu realised that this debate could continue for some time unless she stopped it herself.

"The solution is simple!" she announced. "I will go with Tam to his Homestead, and stay there. That easily solves both his need for rest, and mine."

There was sudden silence as those around her absorbed her remark and began to react.

"Tam, not a word, that's an order."

She silenced her Ponfour's objection before he could do more than draw breath.

"Da, I will be very *very* stubborn about this!"

Staring her father defiantly in the eye, she held her breath, wondering what he would say, but then her mother spoke firmly.

"Well, I think that's an excellent idea, I'll have some clothes packed for you immediately."

Elish smiled at Crystu before turning to her husband. "Don't you agree, dear?"

She phrased it as a polite question, but the look in her eye left the king in no doubt that he had better agree with his wife.

"Of course, that will be acceptable," he replied with dignity. "I'll leave you to arrange it all, Elish, while I go and see if Jareth is able to begin interpreting the gleaning."

With that, he turned and left, trying to suppress the smile that might reveal too much of his inner thoughts.

Guest of the family

A short while later, Crystu and Tam were in a carriage heading towards his Homestead. Crystu had packed only her travel clothes, and Tam had taken the opportunity to locate his armour. He found that it was sorely in need of attention, so it and his sword were also placed in the carriage. The horse he had borrowed was resting in the palace stables and would be returned to its owner the next day.

For the first few minutes after they set off, Crystu closed her eyes and allowed the images from the gleaning to pass through her mind: the larger moon obscuring the sun with a flash of brilliance at the edge before the light vanished, a heaving darkness, red and green flames, dust, a spider's web, a screaming cat, a circlet on the ground, and other things less clear. She sighed, perhaps her dreams that night would allow her to begin to make sense of it all.

124

Opening her eyes, she found Tam regarding her solemnly,

"Crystu, when we reach the Homestead, do you wish to be a visitor or a guest?"

She stared at him blankly for a second before she understood his question. Of course! Homestead tradition gave different meanings to those two words.

If she stayed in the Homestead as a visitor, she would have a room in the Visiting Quarters, have a reserved seat at table, and be served first with the best that was available. She would not be expected to do any chores and would be addressed as her rank dictated.

If she stayed as a guest, she would be treated as a member of the extended family. There would be no titles and no reserved seating. She would sleep in a family guest room, and she would eat what the family ate. She would also be expected to do her fair share of the work.

This would be her first visit to a Homestead, and she found the prospect of being part of a large extended family exciting, but being invited as a guest was both an honour and a big responsibility.

"Before you answer," Tam continued, "you should take into consideration the fact that like most Homesteads, we keep animals and birds and we also farm."

Crystu understood: he was warning her that the chores might include cleaning stables, or worse.

She looked at him and smiled at the slight hint of challenge in his eyes. Through the link, she could tell that he expected her to rise to it.

"I would be honoured to be a guest in your home, Tam," she told him, and was rewarded by a slow smile.

They sat in companionable silence for the rest of the journey.

The carriage stopped outside Tam's home and they got out. Lonian emerged from the house at a run.

"Tam, you're back, is the Rykatu safe?" and then he stopped and bowed as he saw who was standing beside his son.

"My Lady, I hope that you are well?"

"Da, we have a guest." Tam stressed the last word. His father looked at him in surprise, and then looked at Crystu again, giving her an evaluating look with familiar grey eyes.

"Guest, is she?" he said at last.

125

The young Rykatu nodded, holding her breath. As Tam's father, he could revoke the guest invitation, which would be extremely embarrassing, both for her and for Tam.

She had met Lonian only once, at the Bonding Ceremony, and that had been a formal occasion with no opportunity for in-depth conversation. He had opposed his son's application to become her Ponfour, and she did not know how he felt about her now that she and Tam had been bonded for almost two years.

Lonian smiled suddenly.

"Then guest it is! Be welcome in our home and Homestead, Crystu."

"Thank you, Master Lonian," Crystu replied, trying to mask her relief. "I've never stayed in a Homestead before. Please tell me if I do or say anything I should not."

Tam's father nodded.

"For your first time we'll make allowances, but we will also correct. You'll soon learn our ways, Crystu. The first thing to remember is that there are no rank titles between family. Here, I am Lonian and you are Crystu."

Crystu smiled at him. "Thank you, Lonian. I think I will like that."

While they were speaking, Tam and the carriage driver had offloaded her bag and Tam's armour and sword. Crystu thought Lonian looked surprised that she had just the one bag with her. She threw it over her shoulders and waited while Tam hefted the bag of armour, which was an awkward shape and clanked noisily.

Picking up the sword with some effort, Lonian headed briskly for the door. Crystu waited for Tam, who was now close to falling asleep on his feet and was struggling to control the bag of armour which kept slipping off his shoulder with each step.

When he realised that they were not keeping up with him, Lonian spun around, looking closely at his son for the first time since they arrived.

"Whatever's the matter with you, Tam? You look half asleep."

"He *is* half asleep," Crystu explained. "During the gleaning, he found a way to pour his Seta down the bond for me to use. I would probably have burnt out if he had not, but he has exhausted himself."

"Tenji!" Lonian roared into the house. "I need you!"

126

Then he propped the sword against the wall, just inside the door, and came back to take the bag of armour off Tam.

"You'd better get straight to bed, Tam, don't worry about Crystu, we'll take care of her."

Tenjian appeared through the door, but before he could speak Lonian pushed the large, heavy bag at him, with a muttered, "Here hold this."

Then, supporting Tam, who was now struggling just to walk, he indicated that Crystu should precede them into the house.

"Tenji, show our guest to the family room, and then bring Tam's bag."

A few minutes later Crystu was alone in the family's private room. She wandered around the room, peering at books, pictures, and ornaments, then the door opened and Lonian and Tenji entered. Lonian sank into a chair while Tenji poured everyone a drink.

"Well, sit down, and tell me precisely what Tam did, that saved your life and left him in such a state," Lonian ordered.

Then he smiled reassuringly. "Don't worry, I'm not blaming you, that gleaning was widespread. Almost everyone with the Gift was affected."

"Except me," Tenji grinned. "My gift is too short-term focussed and I didn't have so much as a shimmer in my eyes."

Lonian continued, "Tam said that you were in danger, and then he dashed off shouting for a horse. It must have taken him at least half an hour to reach you in Tyre, by which time the thing was almost over. So what happened?"

"I had gone for a walk in the hills," Crystu replied. "I walked in this direction so I think he may have found me slightly sooner than if I had stayed in the city. He can sense my position, as I can his." Lonian nodded and Crystu continued, "You know that I nearly burnt out recently and am still convalescing. The gleaning triggered my power, but my mind has not healed enough. The pain was intense and getting worse, when suddenly," she took a breath, wondering how to put everything into words, "suddenly his power came pouring down the bond, into me. The gleaning fed on that instead of my own."

Lonian frowned thoughtfully. "I have never heard that such a thing was possible except through direct contact or a dreamwalk."

127

"Nor I," agreed Crystu. "I have no idea how he did it, but he found a way. I would have died if he had not. When my senses began to return, he was carrying me down to the training school. The healers there were able to bolster his Seta enough that he survived"

"Otherwise, he would have died when his Seta was depleted," the Homesteader stated flatly.

Crystu nodded.

"I opposed him applying to be your Ponfour, do you know that?" Lonian looked her in the eye.

Crystu swallowed to moisten her suddenly dry throat.

"I know it," she replied, "and I think I know why."

"Oh? So tell me why?" Lonian challenged her.

She looked down for a moment, then lifted her eyes to meet his gaze squarely.

"Because it is rare for a Rykatu to go through his or her entire life with the same Ponfour. Some have three or more during their lifetime."

"And why is that?"

"Because they are killed protecting us."

She looked at Tenji, who was listening quietly, and then back at Lonian.

"I looked at the records myself when I first began to realise just how dangerous it is to be a Ponfour," she said.

Tam's father nodded.

"It's not so bad for those warding lower ranked Sorcerers; they may go their entire lives and deal with nothing worse than the odd plague. But whenever they find something truly evil..." He paused.

The Sorceress nodded and finished his sentence. "They call a Rykatu to deal with it."

"Exactly," Lonian agreed.

Tenji said quietly, "Tam looked at the records too, Da, he knew what he was choosing."

"Yes, he did," Lonian agreed. "Which is why I was wrong to oppose him. I had hoped that he would become a craftsman like me, and like Tenji, but he had and has the right to choose his own path and he chose well."

Crystu's eyes widened at the unexpected statement. Lonian saw it and grinned.

"Thought I was going to say I think he made the wrong choice, didn't you?"

She nodded.

"We all have to return to the Light eventually, one way or another. If he dies defending you, his death will mean something. You will make it mean something, won't you?"

She nodded again, firmly, unable to speak for the lump in her throat.

Lonian smiled at her and repeated his earlier words. "Be welcome in our home and Homestead, Crystu, as a member of our family."

Her first morning in the Homestead, Crystu awoke excited and eager for the new experience. In her entire life, the only people to ever treat her as just a person called Crystu, instead of a Princess or Rykatu, were her parents, brothers, a few close friends, and Tam.

Everyone else looked at her and saw only her rank. Few others ever addressed her by her name, but today they would. Of course, everyone here would know who she was, but they would follow their custom: as a guest she was a family member and must be treated the same as any other.

She dressed quickly, in the plain brown leather trousers and sleeveless top that she had brought with her, and walked through to the family kitchen.

The sun had only just risen when she opened the shuttered window and looked out, but she could see that people were already busy at work out in the fields. Tam was sound asleep and from what she could feel of his sleeping aura, would remain so for another hour or two at least. She was surprised and relieved that he was recovering so quickly but his Seta although still depleted was rapidly rebuilding itself.

Crystu looked at the small cooking range. It was a standard type and she quickly started a fire large enough to heat a pan of water. She smiled wryly as she realised that she was more used to cooking over a campfire while travelling than to using a proper oven. At home in the palace, she was not expected to help cook, but she had been schooled in most methods of cooking. While the water heated, she rummaged through cupboards until she found the spices, leaves, and dried fruits she wanted for her favourite morning drink. When the water boiled, she added the ingredients and moved the pan further from the heat to simmer. She didn't know if the rest of the family would like it, but Tam had, the first time she made it for him, so she made enough for all in the hope that they too would enjoy the mild stimulant.

While the drink steeped, she opened the outer door and stepped outside. The birds were all singing loudly to greet the sun. The air still held onto its night-time chill, although the stillness and the cloudless blue sky suggested the possibility of one of those hot summer-like days that can occur in the middle of spring. Crystu inhaled deeply of the crisp air, savouring the rich smells of an open wood in spring.

"Well, good morning, Crystu. Eager to be put to work? That drink smells wonderful."

She turned to see Narah leaning out of the open kitchen window with a friendly smile on her face.

"I hope you like the drink; it's my favourite, and yes I'm ready. When do we start?"

Narah laughed at her enthusiasm, as Crystu stepped back inside and checked the drink - it was ready. She poured both of them a mug.

"That's delicious," Narah said after a moment. They sat quietly as they drank. The two women had chatted the previous night and Crystu knew that they could become good friends.

Today she would be helping Narah and the others on the rota to prepare and serve breakfast to the whole family. Crystu knew that her inexperience in such things meant that she would probably be chopping, stirring, and washing, but she didn't mind. They finished their drinks and Narah placed little Sobri into a carrier. Then the two of them walked across the yard, to the main kitchen, leaving the rest of the drink to keep warm for Lonian and Tenji.

When Tam woke, the light pouring through his window made it obvious that the sun had been up for several hours. He stretched and swung his legs off the bed. Sending his awareness deep into his inner being, he examined his Seta and the channels of power. He found no damage, thank the Light – his Seta was still low but would fully replenish with a few more good nights' sleep.

Next, he focused his attention on the Ponfour bond; the emotions he could sense were clear - Crystu was extremely happy. Tam allowed her location to tug at his mind and guessed from the direction and strength that she was in the main kitchen.

Good!

After he had washed and dressed he walked through to find out what it was that was giving her such satisfaction.

He was astonished to find her elbow deep in washing water, happily washing the morning's dishes, and surrounded by a group of young women, some of whom were drying as she washed. They were all chatting as if they had known each other for years. She looked over her shoulder at him and smiled and her entire face seemed to light up with it. Tam thought that he had never seen her so relaxed.

"Tam! You're awake earlier than I expected. I saved you some food. Go and sit down and I'll bring it to you."

The last sentence had more than a hint of royal command to the tone, but remembering that she was staying as a guest, he suppressed the urge to respond with a 'Yes my Lady', and just nodded and did as he was told. The room was empty at this late time of morning.

Crystu followed a moment later with bread, cheese and fruit, and a large mug of the spiced drink she liked.

"Eat it all, Tam," she said as she put it in front of him. As soon as he saw the food he realised just how hungry he was. He hadn't taken more than two bites, however, when Ovan raced in shouting,

"Uncle Tam! Aunt Crystu! There's a Lord and Lady come to see you, I showed them to the visitors' room."

"Did you ask their names?" Tam asked, at the same moment that Crystu, staring at the boy in surprise, exclaimed,

"Aunt?"

"It's Lord Rykatu Jareth and Lady Ponfour Aren!" Ovan replied, sounding as if he could hardly believe what he said.

Tam sighed and, gazing regretfully at his meal, stood up.

"Children address all women, who are not in their immediate family, as either Aunt or Grandmother. It's the custom," he told Crystu, who suddenly realised he had not had time to eat his meal.

"You're famished, Tam, you should finish your breakfast. Jareth and Aren will understand."

"My L.." Tam stopped and corrected himself. "Crystu. I am *not* going to send a message to Lord Jareth, the head of the Tyrean Army, to tell him that he should wait while I have my firstmeal. It would be," he paused, searching for the right word, "inappropriate."

"Don't be silly, he can hardly demote you," she pointed out, "you're *my* Ponfour,"

"We are both under his command," Tam reminded her, "and we shouldn't keep him waiting."

"I suppose you're right," she admitted resignedly. "I'll let Narah know that we may be occupied for some time."

Tam took the opportunity to take another bite washed down with some drink and then, when Crystu returned from the kitchen, they left to answer the summons.

132

He followed Crystu into the visitors' room and, as she sat down, took his official position standing just behind her chair. She had taken a seat facing Lord Jareth and looked around as she made herself comfortable. Tam wondered what she thought of the room. It was on the ground floor, in the halls and rooms built within the cliff. It had large windows, which gave a wide view of the fields beyond the edge of the wood. The walls were plastered and painted with floral designs and the wooden floor had been sanded to a smooth finish. The chairs were designed for comfort and the low tables held scented flowers. Against two walls were bookshelves and a low cupboard containing books of many different kinds, and children's toys and games. Everything in the room was intended to make a visitor feel welcome and relaxed. Lord Jareth, however, managed to look as formal as if he was sitting in his own office. Lady Aren was standing a little behind Jareth's chair, showing clearly that she was there in her role as Ponfour, not wife, and that their visit was official.

"Good morning, Lady Crystu, Lord Tam." Lord Jareth began.

Tam started slightly at being addressed in that fashion by Lord Jareth. Lord Jareth smiled slightly seeing his surprise, but it was Lady Aren who explained.

"Lord Tam, I was reminded yesterday that as Crystu's Ponfour you now have rank equal to my own and that it is about time we all started to remember that. I was told that it is wrong to continue to address you as if you were still one of my students."

"It would be inappropriate?" Crystu asked sweetly, deliberately choosing Tam's own word from their earlier conversation.

He had to struggle to not glare at her.

"Exactly," Lord Jareth confirmed. "I have been as remiss in this as Aren. Largely, I suspect, because Lord Tam has never made any attempt to claim the title which is his due."

"M-My Lord," Tam stammered, "I am not used to such..." he paused, trying to find the right words to explain his discomfort, when Crystu interrupted.

"Then it's time that you were, Tam. Oh, I mean Lord Tam." she turned back to Lord Jareth. "I assume that this is an official visit, my Lord?" He nodded. "Then we should all use the correct forms of address."

She smiled sweetly at Tam.

133

He stared back at her for a moment and then managed to say, "Yes, my Lady."

"Good! Now that we have settled that, we should get to the purpose of this visit." Jareth spoke briskly. "Lady Crystu, I need you to tell me the details of yesterday's gleaning as you personally experienced it, and then Lord Tam, I will want you to explain exactly how you did what you did."

Tam could feel Crystu's concentration as she sought to clarify the images from the gleaning.

"The larger moon blotted out the sun, and then a grey mass rose into the sky and obscured the eclipse." she began. "It grew thicker, and I could feel a gritty texture in my mouth. It was followed by many blurred images of hooded figures, seen dimly against the darkness. Fighting figures. A Ponfour circlet lying on the ground. A large cat screamed in a farmyard, and a spider span a web across giant trees. A huge rising dark mass towered ever higher. Finally, a mountain lake in sunlight with a river rushing downhill from its lowest point, and many streams feeding into it at the upward end. The last image felt like it was intended to give guidance in some way, but I do not understand it"

Tam stared at his Sorceress in surprise, as she described the lake, thinking of the image he had used as a focus when he sent her his energy. Lady Aren saw his movement,

"Does that last image mean something to you, my Lord?"

"It does, my Lady," he replied.

Lord Jareth and Crystu looked at him enquiringly.

"Lord Tam," Jareth began, "everyone who experienced the gleaning saw similar images. Several of us felt that the lake was intended as some form of instruction. If it has meaning for you, please explain it."

"It is similar to the image I used to allow me to transfer power to my Lady, yesterday," Tam began. "I could feel her pain as the gleaning started to draw on her Seta, and knew I had to do something. I know that there is a way to send healing energy through a dreamwalk link, but I do not know how that is done. It occurred to me that Lady Crystu and I already have a link and that perhaps it could be used in a similar manner. There is a lake in the mountains above here that has been a favourite spot for me since childhood. It has a dam at one end with a controlled water outlet. The water feeds

134

into a stream that flows down towards the river. The image of that lake came to my mind suddenly and it seemed that it was a perfect metaphor that might allow me to send Seta to my Lady. So I concentrated on the thought that the water in the lake was my Seta, the lower river was my Lady, and the stream between them was the bond between us. When I opened the dam, the water flowed rapidly downhill, and my power went with it. It is slightly different from that described by my Lady, in that only two streams feed into it from uphill."

Jareth nodded. "I see, and I think I begin to understand. Let me consider this for a moment."

He sat back, brows furrowed in deep thought. The others waited patiently. After several minutes he sat up suddenly.

"Yes, I think that may be the answer!" he announced.

"Lord Tam, using magic for forty minutes or so could not in itself have caused your fatigue. We all have used magic for longer periods without problem and the spell does not seem to be complex. I think that the only reason you were in danger yesterday was because you sent your power down the link in an uncontrolled fashion and so nearly exhausted it. If the gleaning had lasted much longer, you would, at best, still be deeply asleep at this moment. I mean no criticism by that; it was an impressive achievement. However, as a spell, it is of little use unless it can be controlled, so I want you to practice it until you can send controlled amounts of Seta at need through the bond. When you can do that, I will require you to instruct other Ponfourii in this spell. At the same time, you *must* start dreamwalking. I know you have learned to control your dreams so you must now begin to enter others. The closer a person is to you in physical distance the easier it is to find them and enter their dreams. Begin tonight."

Tam nodded. Jareth leaned forward.

"Dreamwalking is a complex and tiring spell for a beginner. It does get easier with practice, but training both of these techniques at the same time will be draining for you. You must be sure to practice no more than two out of three days. Each third day you should do no magic of any kind."

Crystu spoke up.

135

"I will make sure of that, Lord Jareth. He's still a little depleted from yesterday and I don't want him to burnout." She smiled sideways at Tam.

Lord Jareth looked at Lady Aren.

"We must also make sure that all who can heal and dreamwalk learn how to use the *dreamwalk* to transfer their Seta to another. All healers can learn it, but the need has been rare enough that few do. That must change!"

Suddenly, Tam understood what Lord Jareth was thinking,

"You think we could combine the two spells?" he asked. "Have several people use the dreamwalk to send safe, controlled, amounts of energy to a Ponfour who relays it to his or her Sorcerer?"

He saw Crystu's questioning look.

"The multiple streams feeding the lake, in your vision my Lady. Energy coming from others to keep the lake safely full," he explained.

"That was exactly my thought, Lord Tam. That way, the Ponfour would be in no danger of burnout," Lord Jareth said. "If the process needed to be prolonged, we could rotate the healers. No one would be endangered, including the Sorcerer receiving the energy. If we can perfect this combined spell in time it could be a useful tool against the servants of the Shadowbringer."

"In time?" Tam queried.

Crystu answered that.

"The rest of the vision, Tam, can only have one interpretation: the Shadowbringer is moving. Even as we speak he has begun his plan, whatever it is. Remember, in my original vision, he prophesied that the land would be in total darkness by the new year. We may still only be in mid spring, but he has begun to move."

Lord Jareth nodded.

"Exactly! I was wrong to think that your dream was just something to make you race back to Tyreen and distract you from what had happened to Tam. He *is* planning a major attack on the Congregation of Light. Not only yesterday's gleaning, but the rediscovery of a lost spell, confirms that your original dream was a true message from the Shadowbringer."

At Crystu's puzzled look, Jareth shrugged. "There is no need to conceal the truth from you two. Tam's spell is not really new and neither was it truly lost. 'Hidden' would be a better term."

"Hidden?" Crystu queried.

Jareth nodded. "You know that there are spells which are forbidden."

"Everyone knows that!" Crystu interrupted. "Spells from the dark time which verge on dark magic, but what Tam did for me did not use dark magic!"

"No, it did not!" Aren agreed.

"I did not intend to imply that it did, and if I can finish my sentence you will understand." Jareth lifted an eyebrow repressively at Crystu who nodded acceptance of the mild rebuke.

"Please continue, my Lord," she said apologetically.

"Thank you. As I was saying, you know that there are forbidden spells, but there are others which are so dangerous they are actively kept hidden from us by the First Ones themselves. The elders know of their existence in theory, but not the details of their practice. The fact that one of those spells has suddenly been rediscovered, apparently spontaneously, suggests that the First Ones believe that we will need it."

"Dangerous?" Tam repeated at the same time that Crystu said, "There are others?"

Jareth nodded. "Yes, Tam, as you discovered, the transfer of Seta from one person to another can risk the life of the donor. The records say that all of the hidden spells are dangerous to those using them. And, yes, Crystu, there are others, but unless the First Ones decide that we need those too, I will not discuss them at this time."

His tone made clear that he had finished with that subject.

"The important thing now is that this spell has re-emerged. This tells me that we are going to need it to combat whatever the Shadowbringer has planned. Unfortunately, we do not know where he has begun his new strike, but I received some other guidance from the gleaning and I know that we must begin to assemble the largest army that Tyreen has ever mustered."

He leaned back in his chair.

"I believe that we must begin this immediately or we will not be in time. We will need almost everyone who is able to lift a weapon. This means that I will need both of you back in Tyre as instructors as soon as the healers are satisfied that you are back to strength, Lady Crystu, but until then I think it would be best if you stay here away

137

from the temptation to begin using your gifts before you should. If that is alright with your family, Lord Tam?"

"Of course. My Lady is welcome to stay as long as she needs," Tam replied.

Crystu laughed. "I expect they can find me more washing to do." Tam smiled slightly.

"If that is your preferred occupation, my Lady, I'm sure Narah will arrange it, but you may become tired of it after a few days."

Crystu laughed again.

"Well, then I'll clean the animal pens," she declared, "or sweep the yard, or," she paused at a sudden thought, "I'd like to see your lake. Would you take me there one day? We could hunt on the way back."

Her sudden enthusiasm made her eyes sparkle as she looked up at him over her shoulder, and Tam could feel it reverberating infectiously across their bond. He found himself smiling fondly at her, momentarily forgetting that they were not alone in the room. Then memory returned, and he schooled his expression back to a correct appearance of attentive respect and answered,

"Of course, my Lady. Whenever you wish."

The sound of Lady Aren suddenly developing a cough suggested that his temporary lapse had not gone unnoticed.

"If the two of you have finished planning your rest-day?"

Lord Jareth's severe tone was belied by a twinkle in his eye. Then he relaxed and smiled at them.

"Enjoy the next few weeks as much as you can. Once back in Tyre, there will be little time for either of you to relax, and if we are correct, there are dangerous times ahead."

He glanced at Aren. "I think that covers everything unless you can think of anything I've forgotten?"

"Tenjian?" she replied.

"Of course! Thank you for reminding me."

"I think Jathte would be very upset if we forgot," she replied cryptically.

Moving from her previous position behind Jareth's chair, she sat down in the chair to his left.

"Now that the official part is over, perhaps we can prevail on Tam to invite us to stay for the mid-day meal? That will give us a chance to talk to Tenjian."

She looked at Tam. "Well?"

"By all means, Lady Aren, you may both eat with us."

To his surprise, she frowned, and Tam sensed Crystu's sudden amused anticipation.

"I said the official part is over, Tam," Lady Aren said, suddenly smiling broadly. "You can stop calling me Lady. My name is Aren, and my husband's is Jareth. Sit down and try using them."

Tam's eyes widened, and Crystu began to laugh helplessly, her delight and amusement at his discomfort were all too clear.

At that moment Tam's stomach chose to remind him and everyone else in the room how hungry he was, which sent Crystu into a fresh paroxysm of laughter. The absurdity of the situation was too much, and shaking his head ruefully, he sat down beside Crystu. A little while ago, two of the most important people in Tyreen had insisted on calling him Lord, and now they were insisting that he should dispense with their own titles. The whole notion was difficult.

"My La..." he stopped himself and began again. "Aren, I'm a Homesteader from a craft family."

Jareth interrupted him.

"Not any more, Tam. As the queen reminded me last night," he nodded at Crystu's start of surprise, "in terms of rank, the king is first, followed by his immediate family," he nodded again to Crystu, "followed by the Revered Father, and then by the two Rykatuii, and then by their Ponfourii. Everyone else in Tyreen is below."

"You'll get used to it. I did," Aren added.

Tam looked at her in surprise and she nodded.

"Yes, I too was once a 'Homesteader from a craft family', Tam. The rank and formality are the price we had to pay when we chose to become Ponfourii to Rykatuii," she said, smiling fondly at her husband. She looked back at Tam.

"You must have known it when you chose," she pointed out.

"I did, but it wasn't the most important consideration at the time," he admitted.

"If it had been, I wouldn't have had you," Crystu said, smiling up at him. His stomach chose that moment to rumble again. Her smile broadened into a grin, and she turned to Jareth.

"Jareth, Tam had only just awoken when you arrived, and he had slept almost a full day. He's had nothing to eat, and it's almost midday now."

139

"Of course," Jareth said. "In that case Tam, you have a decision to make - shall we all be formal or informal for the meal?"

Tam smiled, relieved. "Thankfully, my Lord, custom is clear on that matter - visitors receive formal address."

Aren laughed and, speaking to Jareth, said, "Oh, he clearly needs more practice!"

Jareth nodded.

"I agree." Unexpectedly, he grinned mischievously, as he looked back at Tam. "In that case, Aren and I, as visitors invited to eat here, would like you and Crystu to join us at our table."

Crystu began to laugh again.

The smile dropped off Tam's face as he realised that Jareth clearly knew Homestead customs perfectly. Tam would have to be treated as a visitor by his family, including being addressed as Lord, while at the same time he would have to try to remember to be informal with Jareth and Aren.

Even his father and brother would be required to use the title if they spoke to him, and he was gloomily certain that his brother would find the situation every bit as amusing as Jareth, Aren, and Crystu, clearly did.

It was going to be a *long* mid-day meal.

As Tam had feared, the meal was long and embarrassing. He had felt the eyes on him as he took his seat in the visitors' area, although he did not manage to actually catch anyone staring.

The worst moment had been when Jareth had called Tenji over to ask about an item he was crafting. Tam's brother had raced away to fetch the item then, on his return, after handing it to Lady Aren, had punctiliously asked whether Lord Jareth, Lady Aren, Lady Crystu, and Lord Tam would care for more drink.

He proceeded to pour drinks for all of them with great attention to ceremony, with just a quiver of his mouth to indicate his internal laughter. Tam could not even glare at him without committing a severe breach of custom, so was forced to resort to dignity instead.

Crystu was laughing internally. Her emotion seemed to dance up and down the bond, but no trace of it existed on her face or in her voice as she conversed. Tam wished he had the same skill.

After Jareth and Aren had left, Tam went back to the eating room. He felt a strong urge to do something, anything, to prove to his family and to himself that he had not suddenly become an aristocrat, regardless of any titles others might insist on inflicting upon him. He filled a trolley with used crockery, pushed it into the kitchen and looked for a free washing sink. Finding one, he filled it with hot water and began to wash the dishes. He ignored the slight ripple of laughter that spread around the room, though his ears felt hot.

He reminded himself that it is not really possible to die of embarrassment. Aunt Tersha watched for a moment and then intercepted the next plate before he could put it on the drainer.

"Tam, work it off on the woodpile, please - it's better able to take the strain."

She picked up the mug that he had placed to dry a moment before and held it up to show him the large crack that had appeared down its side, caused by the force with which he had placed it.

"You're too strong to wash up in this mood, and I don't want to have to repair all the crockery in one afternoon." As she spoke, the side of the mug blurred and moved as she repaired the ceramic with magic.

His aunt was right: the large amount of frustration that had built up during the meal would be better released on the wood than the crockery.

"Sorry, Aunt Tersha, I'll do that."

"You're a good boy, Tam, even if you are a lord now." She grinned at him and pushed him out the door.

He decided that they needed a *large* amount of wood!

Tam placed the log on one end upon the flat rock and swung the axe one-handed in a large circle that impacted exactly in the centre of the log. Its two halves flew in opposite directions. He placed one half on the rock and soon had quarters. Over the next two hours, he systematically worked his way through the entire woodpile until it was all chopped into usable pieces.

As he worked he felt the tensions and frustrations of the day melt until all that was left was just enjoyment and satisfaction in the job he was doing. He didn't even realise that Crystu was watching until he turned round to check that he had chopped all the logs, and saw her leaning against the house wall. She held a tray with a jug of juice and two beakers.

She laughed. "I think that's the first time I ever made you jump. You were concentrating so hard on the work that I didn't dare interrupt in case you swung the axe into your leg. Here." She put the tray on the ground and handed him a beaker which she then filled from the jug.

"I thought you could use a drink, it's a hot day for that sort of work."

"Thanks," he replied and drained the mug, only now noticing the tickling feeling as the sweat ran down his face and torso. Crystu poured more juice for him.

"I also came to apologise, Tam," she said.

"For what?" he asked, surprised.

"For laughing at you when we were with Jareth and Aren. I should not have. I don't fully understand your reluctance to use the title, and yet," she paused, trying to find the words for her thoughts, "the thing I am enjoying most about being here as your guest, is the way everyone treats me as just one of the family. For me, it is a rare and treasured treat, but for you, it is normal. I can understand that you don't want to lose that."

He looked down at the axe at his feet and then back at her.

"You are correct: that is what I fear - that one day I will wake and there will only be Lord Tam, with no trace left of the Homesteader."

"I don't think that is very likely to happen to you," she replied, "but if it does, I promise to send you out to chop wood until you remember who you are."

Tam smiled at her.

"I appreciate that, my L.. I mean, Crystu. I will hold you to your word."

"Still, I *am* sorry I laughed. Although," she looked impishly up at him through her lashes, "your face when Jareth invited us to eat with him, was very *very* funny." She grinned, and Tam felt his lips begin to twitch,

"I suppose it was," he admitted. Then they were both laughing together, which Tam reflected was much more enjoyable than just being laughed at.

They took the tray back into the kitchen, still laughing.

"Do you really want to see my lake, Crystu?" he asked as they put crockery away in the cupboard.

142

"Oh yes, please!" She nodded eagerly.

"Then we'll go on Restday," he told her. "Guests are never on rota on a Restday, and if I'm on it, I'll swap with Tenji; he owes me after this afternoon."

They left the kitchen, both completely oblivious to the knowing glance exchanged by Narah and Tersha.

"There's something I must tell you."

Tam opened his eyes and turned his head to look at Crystu. She was sitting on the grass beside him and looked uncharacteristically nervous. They were beside the mountain lake, enjoying the warm sunshine on what both knew was likely to be the last Restday they would be able to take fully for themselves.

Crystu's strength was almost back to normal levels, and she would soon be proclaimed fit enough to resume magic use.

It was odd, he mused, that although they could heal people who had come as close to burnout as she had, they had learned that such healing actually slowed the return to full strength - it was far better to let the recovery proceed naturally.

Once she was able to use her Gifts again, they would return to Tyre and become involved in the gradual build-up of the Tyrean army.

Although no word had yet been received suggesting where the Shadowbringer was at work, all Tyreen knew that it was only a matter of time before they would have to fight to defend the Path of Light.

On their journey up to the lake, Tam had sensed that Crystu had something on her mind and that it involved him. He knew she was trying to find the right time for it and had clearly decided that time was now.

"What is it, Crystu?" he asked.

Expanding his sense of her emotions, he sat up as he realised that she was feeling apprehensive and guilty about something.

Guilty?

Whatever could she be feeling guilty about?

She looked down for a moment, took a deep breath and then looked back at him. He raised his eyebrows in an encouraging fashion.

"The first day after that you went home, I spoke with Jareth at some length about how they would teach you to control your dreams enough to allow you to learn to dreamwalk."

She stopped to take a deep breath before continuing.

"He told me that he had looked at the records and been able to find only three previous cases, in eight hundred years, where someone had gained the ability to dreamwalk in adulthood."

She looked him in the eye. "Tam, two of those three were never able to achieve a lucid dream. The third did so, but only years later, after a time when she had suffered extreme sleep deprivation. He told me that they intended to try to replicate a similar state in you in hope that it would enable you to achieve the controlled dream state. So I..." She stopped again and looked down again.

Beginning to suspect what it was she was going to say, Tm waited.

"Go on," he prompted when she remained quiet.

His Sorceress looked up again.

"Well, Ponfourii can easily go for days without sleep, so I suggested that in addition to just deliberately waking you each time someone appeared in your dreams, that if they *also* induced nightmares then the time that you *did* spend asleep would be far less restful."

Tam stared at her, remembering some of the truly terrifying dreams that had sent him lurching from his sleep, heart racing and sweat flowing freely.

When he didn't speak, she continued in a quiet scared voice,

"I also made suggestions about what you would find most disturbing, so that the dreams would be as effective as possible."

He looked at her and shook his head as the full meaning of her words sank in.

"You...composed those dreams? The sealed cavern, the Zindon, all of it?"

Crystu nodded.

"And the shadowy watcher?" he continued.

"I thought you would think it was the Zindon," she explained.

"Ha! Worse than that!" He began to chuckle. "I thought it was your father!"

The revelation was shocking, but he could see the necessity, and it had worked - he could now enter another's dreams. He chuckled again.

"I now see what Narah meant: I too hope I never make you angry enough to do that again. You know me too well, Crystu."

"You're not angry? No, you're not!" she exclaimed.

"Of course not, Crystu," he replied. "You did what was necessary. I understand."

"Oh! I'm so glad," and she threw her arms around him.

145

He hugged her back and then, because some things just have to be done, in one flowing movement he rose, picked her up, and taking two steps to the edge of the lake, threw her in as far as he could.

Her squeal as she hit the cold mountain water was immensely satisfying!

The King's decree

Tam and Crystu stood on a balcony of the Royal Palace and watched the activity in the valley below. The meadows that usually contained nothing more than cattle now held tents and people. The army of Tyreen was beginning to gather. Many of the tents were empty as yet, but others held equipment and stores of food. Around Tyreen, everything an army could require to feed, clothe and equip its soldiers was being readied for translocation.

In addition, people were arriving in Tyre. They had trained all their lives for this and each person knew where he or she had to go to join the correct group. The groups had pre-allocated areas in the valley, and as sufficient of their members arrived, they began to assemble the tents that would be their sleeping, eating and training quarters until the time to march arrived.

The junior Rykatu and her Ponfour had been back in Tyre for several weeks and had been extremely busy since their return.

For the first week, Tam had spent several hours a day teaching his power transferral technique to other Ponfourii. He soon discovered that Sorcerers and Ponfourii alike could learn to successfully transfer Seta to their bond partner, but *only* those whose bond had the extra depth to it. Once he realised that, Lord Jareth quickly arranged for those known to have the deeper bond to be called to Tyre for the training.

The hours spent teaching those who, like himself, had a much stronger bond than the usual, quickly showed Tam that his theory, about what that bond meant, was correct. Nearly all of those he was teaching had married their bond partners, or were engaged, or were clearly likely to marry. Even Trerisia and Jathte were now wearing betrothal gifts, one of which was the item that Tenji had shown Jareth and Aren when they visited the Homestead.

Put simply, if a Sorcerer bonded someone who was also his or her ideal life partner, the bond was stronger and would deepen further with time.

Tam could understand why this was not common knowledge because there might be some who would be deterred from bonding if it were more widely known. Also, it was a private thing and he knew that he would not want to discuss, with *anyone*, the exact nature of his relationship with his Sorcerer.

147

He wondered if the king knew about it. That might explain his continued hostility towards Tam, even though he now was acquiring some mastery of his dreamwalk Gift. The thought brought him back to the present, and the angry Rykatu beside him on the balcony. Just half an hour ago, the king had announced that unless Tam could pass two tests he would not allow Crystu to leave Tyreen when the army marched.

Tam must invade the king's dreams and resist expulsion from them, and he must defend his own dreams against an intrusion by Lord Jareth.

Even Lord Jareth had seemed surprised by this announcement. Fully half of the ordinary soldiers were not dreamwalkers and they would need powerful wards in place to protect them outside Tyreen - wards which would also protect Tam should he still require it.

In addition, the junior Rykatu traditionally travelled with the less powerful Tyreans and fought with them at the front of the battle.

Unhappy about the thought of Crystu fighting in a major battle, Tam wished fervently that she could stay safely far from it, but he would never try to stop her performing her duty. He would of course fight beside her and protect her to the best of his ability.

Crystu was furious with her father at his decision and had made her anger extremely audible. She had then stormed out of the room, leaving Tam to deal with an awkward moment. Crystu could stamp from her father's presence, Tam could not.

Fortunately, the queen had come to his aid by suggesting he should go after Crystu and calm her down. He gratefully left the room and tracked Crystu using the bond, until he found her on this balcony overlooking the growing encampment in the valley.

"It's not fair!" she snarled. "Many in the army can't dreamwalk, and of those who can, few could pass these tests."

"They are not assigned to your protection, my Lady," Tam pointed out, "I am."

He could feel her stubbornly refusing to admit that the distinction was valid, so he continued,

"There is still time before we will march, and l gain understanding, skill, and strength, each time I practice. Lord Jareth says I will soon be ready to learn how to eject someone from a dream, or resist ejection from another's, but I *must* first learn to identify correctly whose mind I am entering. As you know I still sometimes get that wrong."

His reminder was deliberate and succeeded in his intention. Crystu smiled at the memory despite herself.

"Yes. It was lucky it was my mother you mistook for me and not my father. She at least was amused when you changed her dream."

"Perhaps, but she still ejected me so hard I had genuine bruises when I awoke."

Crystu laughed.

"I've often wondered how she does that. I asked once, but she refused to say."

Looking out across the valley again, she sighed.

"I think what really angers me about my father's demands is that he seems to think I'm still the child I was before we bonded. I have grown, but he will not see it."

"Crystu," Tam felt the informal address more applicable to what he was about to say, "telling the king that he is a stupid, senile, half-wit, with the Gifting of a waterbird, was *probably* not the best way to persuade him that you have become an adult."

She laughed and shook her head.

"Perhaps not, but it is true."

Leaning on the balustrade she gazed at the distant horizon where it was visible between and beyond the mountains.

"I wish we were still travelling, Tam, just the two of us, getting ready to sleep under the stars."

She straightened suddenly and the bond reverberated with her sudden decision.

"Get our travel things, Tam, and follow me, I will not stay another night here in the palace. I will find us something to eat out there in the mountains."

As she spoke, her body seemed to both stretch and shrink, her clothes melting and reforming, until a large golden eagle stood upon the balustrade. The bird leapt into the air and flew southwards. Tam grimaced as she disappeared into the distance,

"I hate it when she does that!" he muttered.

A chuckle behind him made him spin around, to find Queen Elish and her Ponfour Calline wearing similar expressions of amusement.

149

"You could always try spanking her," suggested Crystu's mother. "It never worked for me, but you have some advantages. You also have my permission to try it..."

Her smile broadened at his shocked expression; surely she could not *really* be suggesting...?

"I intended to have a word with Crystu," the queen said, "but it can wait. Well? Didn't she just give you a task? Off you go."

"Yes, my Queen," Tam replied and hurried to his room to pack a bag for Crystu and himself. Spank her indeed! Although he had to admit he was sorely tempted to try it!

It was difficult to guard someone when she could fly off into the sky and he could not. She might not be in any danger from shadow creatures here in Tyreen, but even a Rykatu can have an accident.

She was right, though: it would be pleasant to spend some time away from other people. Tam was conscious that he had recently been the cause of rather too much amusement! That, he decided, had to stop!

Part 4: Invasion

"For over three thousand years has Lord Xian languished in his prison beneath the ice. Deceived and betrayed by Taris, his former servant, he was overcome and laid low by the usurper, his powers reduced and contained. We have dedicated our lives to ending his long suffering and now the time is nearly upon us. The next few months will be exhilarating! I am honoured to command His armies and looking forward to victory. This plan will destroy the Tyreans and leave their lands open and unprotected.

We will seize the so-called Protectorates of Tyreen, Lord Xian's intended will kneel at his feet, and their children will have the power to free him when they are grown. We vow to live and die in his cause. Soon I will sit on the throne of the Kingdom of Light and, one day, Lord Xian himself will enter Tyreen and make it his." Xiantona Cherex's journal.

The Port city of Bein, the Kingdom of Light

Darshen Coe, known as Dash to family, friends, and customers alike, swore as he wiped the dust off another table.

Catching sight of his wife's expression at his impiety, he hurriedly muttered an apology to the Lord of Light. Though surely a man could be forgiven the occasional oath when faced with such never-ending shadowborne dust!

If only the wind would change. He licked his finger and pointed it hopefully at the sky, trying to persuade himself that the long black dust cloud looked thinner, but the wind had not changed. The long cloud carried by that wind still stretched from beyond the distant horizon, over the ocean, and gathered itself into a blanket high above the city and slowly fell to coat the land beneath.

The origin of the cloud was, Dash knew, a volcano hidden beyond the rim of the sea. It often spewed its dust into the air, for weeks at a time, but usually the cloud remained on the horizon instead of coating the tops of honest men's tables.

"Darkness cover all! Will it never stop?" he muttered crossly.

"Dash!" Dara protested. "Don't use language like that! You may call it down on us!"

"Call it down? Call it down? It's already coming down all over my food-yard!"

He was the owner, manager and head bartender of The Sailors' Well. His establishment was located beside the High Road into the city, about halfway between the city boundary and the main docks. This meant that everyone travelling by land, to and from Bein,

151

walked or rode past his inn and, as the High Road was a long one, many would stop for refreshment. As a result, Dash was more than moderately wealthy, and generally enjoyed his life.

The port city of Bein had grown up on either side of the River Bee at the point where it emptied into a large northwest looking bay, known as Bein Bay.

At the far side of the bay, where its waters met the sea, high rocky headlands projected from either side, to form a large, partially enclosed, naturally sheltered, harbour.

Very deep, and with docks lining both sides of it, the bay had ample room for moorage for even the largest of ships. On the southwestern side of the bay, a series of regular rocky shelves stepped upwards to join the western mountain range. The oldest parts of the city were situated on these shelves and the major road from the docks to city centre ran close to the foot of the lowest of them. On the northeast side of the harbour, the hills above the docks were smoother in shape and not as high. Anyone moored on that side had a much greater distance to travel to reach the traders' area in the city centre so it was a less popular place to dock. Between the southwestern mountains and the north-eastern hills lay the Bein Plain with the river flowing in the centre. The plain between the mountains and the river was completely filled by the city and its fields, meadows, and orchards. Five bridges crossed the river: one at the docks, one at the south-eastern extremity of the city, with the rest in between. The southern plain was rich, fertile, farmland and meadowland.

The Sailors Well had its main building beside the High Road, but the property stretched backwards and upwards onto the next shelf. It was part bar, part restaurant, and part hostel.

Dash was in his early fifties, a genial, good-natured man who was both respected and liked in his community. He and Dara had worked hard for over thirty years to make the well a thriving concern, and they continued to do so. Both enjoyed the work for the wide range of interesting people they had the opportunity to meet.

From Dash's position, on the upper terrace, he could see across the roofs of the intervening buildings, to the north-eastern docks and the sea beyond. Three unusually large ships were in the process of mooring out at the furthest dock. They were too far away for him to be able to see any detail of design, but they seemed to dwarf the dockside storage buildings that he knew to be of large size.

"That's odd," he remarked.

"What's odd?" his wife asked. Dash pointed at the ships.

"See those ships at the furthest dock?" he asked.

Dara looked where he was pointing.

"What about them, apart from their size," she asked curiously.

"They've moored at the furthest dock," Dash replied, "but there are many empty berths closer to the city. Whatever they're shipping will have to be carried an unnecessary extra distance."

"You're right: that is odd," his wife agreed, "but I expect they have their reasons, and I also expect you'll get a chance to ask Enneth about them when he comes in this evening."

Enneth the Harbourmaster was a regular customer of long-standing, and a close friend of Dash.

"Now," Dara continued, "if you've quite finished doing Etra's job for her, you should be making sure the kitchen is ready to start serving the evening meals. It's almost time to open."

They went inside, the three ships temporarily forgotten.

"Ah, Enneth, the usual?" Dash welcomed his friend into the private barroom reserved for close personal friends.

"Actually, no! I think I'll have a Sunfire, and have one yourself on me."

Dash's eyebrows rose.

"Did someone die and leave you a fortune?" he asked, as he unlocked the cabinet and removed two small bottles containing a rich amber coloured liquid. He waited until Enneth had placed two large gold coins on the bar, before opening either bottle.

"Better than that!" the Harbourmaster replied. "Eccentric visitors!"

He saw Dash's blank look and explained, "Three ships arrived today."

"I saw them," Dash interrupted. "They docked right at the far end. I thought it seemed odd."

"The oddness doesn't stop there," Enneth stated, shaking his head in remembered bemusement.

"How so?" Dash asked.

Enneth glanced around the room to be sure it was still empty. Then he pulled out his purse and shook it. It chinked in a most satisfying way.

153

"They said that they wanted to rent the entire northeast docks, to be berthed there in complete privacy. They were prepared to pay whatever I asked."

"Did they have good money?" asked Dash, who had known customers occasionally try to pay with unusable outlandish currency.

"Not at first. They had strange coins I'd never seen before," Enneth said, "but then they produced some tradable goods that Bantriss was happy to buy from them, and they used his money to pay the docking fees. There was plenty left over too!"

"Bantriss bought their goods? So, they had jewellery and such like?"

"That's right, some of the finest work I've ever seen. As good as Tyrean, though some odd designs – they like pictures of eclipses for some reason. They had precious stones too."

"Is that why they're here then? To trade?" Dash asked.

"Apparently not," Enneth replied. "The two, who came onto land to pay the fee, said that this accursed wind was preventing them from sailing home, so they had been forced to land to wait it out."

"Why do they want to rent that entire side of the bay? Did they say?" Dash asked.

"Well, that was another strange thing! They said," he leaned forward to whisper, "their God does not permit them to mix with others."

Dash did not understand.

"Their God?" he repeated blankly. "How many do they think there are? There is only one that I ever heard of."

"Precisely!" Enneth nodded. "Like I said - strange."

He took a gulp of his drink, and Dash shuddered at the disrespectful use of the fine expensive drink and sipped his own, savouring the warm flavour.

"There's more," Enneth continued.

"More? What could be stranger than that?"

"The two who came ashore..." Enneth paused for effect.

"Well?" said Dash impatiently.

"They were wearing so many clothes, all I could see was their eyes."

"What?" Dash exclaimed. "In this heat?"

The weather for the past few days had been stiflingly hot.

154

"Yes! In this heat! So I asked them, 'Aren't you hot?' and they said that their country is so far to the north, that the sun never rises much above the horizon, so they're not used to the strength of it here. So they wear the clothes to keep the sun off their skin to stay cool." Enneth spread his hand wide. "Have you ever heard of such a thing?"

"Not I!" Dash replied. "Did they say what their country is called? Maybe Father Arnath will know of it."

"I did wonder if they were Kandarii - the stories say that's a strange place, but, no, they said they come from a place called Shannet. They called themselves the Shantoo. At least, that's what it sounded like."

Enneth took another swallow of his drink,

"I've never heard of it or them, but I don't know the name of every region in the Protectorates. You may be right that Father Arnath will know of them, but of course, he's on his annual Sabbatical and you know how long those last. We can't ask him till he returns."

"Well, hopefully, the wind will have changed by then, taking this shadowbred dust, and the Shantoo, with it."

"I'll drink to that," Enneth raised his glass and took another gulp. "I still haven't told you the oddest thing about them though," he said wiping his mouth.

"Something even odder?" Dash leaned forward. "What could be odder than everything else?"

"I said I could only see their eyes?" Enneth waited until Dash nodded, then he continued. "Well, I've seen brown eyes, blue eyes, green eyes and grey eyes before, but never until today have I seen pink eyes."

"Pink eyes?" Dash was intrigued. "Pink eyes! You're right my friend: they are clearly the oddest visitors Bein has ever had."

"They are indeed." Enneth drained his glass. "Now I have to arrange for the boundary of the rented area to be marked out. They wanted the north-eastern docks and the land that overlooks them with effect from sunrise tomorrow. They said that the area will be protected, but we have to be sure no-one even tries to cross the boundary."

"Protected? How?"

"They didn't say." He got up and started for the door. "I'll see you tomorrow, Dash. Light bide with you."

155

"And you too," Dash replied automatically, his mind on the strange things he had been told.

He wondered how long it would be before Father Arnath returned; he had already been gone longer than usual.

Father Arnath had been the Bishop of Bein Cathedral for over 10 years, and one of Dash's closest friends for only slightly less time. He had a theory about the priest's regular and lengthy absences, but would never dream of invading his privacy so far as to actually ask if his idea was correct. Besides, he and Arnath both enjoyed playing a game, where Dash would drop subtle hints about Arnath's origin, which Arnath would pretend not to have heard, feigning deafness and changing the subject. Dash was almost certain that the old man was Tyrean and far older than he admitted to being, despite being fit and surprisingly strong.

"You're the Zindon!"

"That's not fair! I'm always the Zindon! I want to be a Sorcerer this time!"

"You can't be a Sorcerer! You swear when you're losing! Sorcerers never swear. That's why you're the Zindon: because you speak like one."

"Darkover! I do NOT swear,"

"You just did then!"

Simet Coe-Jersa looked away from his squabbling friends and gazed over at the hills.

Today was a restday and he and his friends had ridden out to the north-east hills to play their currently favourite game of Sorcerers and Zindons. This game was best played away from grown-up eyes because, while not actually banned, it tended to incur a certain amount of disapproval from adult quarters. Many held that it was bad luck for someone to pretend to be a Zindon - suppose you attracted the attention of a real one?

The boy didn't believe in Zindons, or in Sorcerers for that matter, but the game was fun to play, although the rules were restrictive. Unless you won the part of the Rykatu, you had to declare your powers at the start and couldn't use any other pretend Gifts for the rest of the game.

He looked back at his still squabbling friends and sighed. He was bored because it always took so long for the arguments to end. Everyone wanted to be a Rykatu and no-one wanted to be a Zindon. By the time they finished arguing about it, they would have barely enough time left to play it.

His eyes strayed back to the hills. Just out of sight was the painted line, with its warning signs, that marked the boundary of the land rented by the Shantoo. A little way past that line was the rocky cliff that overlooked the north-east docks. It was the day after the Shantoo had arrived, and Simet was burning with curiosity. He had been listening just outside the door of his adoptive father's barroom last night, as Enneth told Dash all about the newcomers. People with pink eyes, who swathed themselves with clothes to keep the sun off their skin? Simet could not imagine such a thing! His own skin was as exposed to the sun as he could manage without outraging decency.

At thirteen years of age, he naturally thought that curiosity was its own justification for rule breaking. With a quick glance at his friends, he decided that he had time to run over to the cliff and take a peek. He would be back before they had made up their minds. Personally, he didn't care which role he played, so long as the game eventually took place. None of his friends noticed him creep away, so intent were they on their disagreement. Simet dashed over the hills, following a familiar track to a place where an ancient rock slide made it possible to scramble a fair way down the cliff toward the docks. When he reached the collapsed part, he started to climb down. Eventually, he found a ledge that gave a good view of one of the enormous ships. No-one was on deck that he could see, but he stared at what was visible with avid curiosity.

Even if he had looked upwards, it was unlikely that Simet would have seen the large winged shape above him. Had he spotted it, he would have immediately have recognised a creature of legend. The perimeter was indeed guarded - by derstrals.

Derstrals were believed, incorrectly, to be extinct. About as large as a medium-sized dog, they were winged lizard-like creatures with an effective camouflage: rapidly changing pigment cells enabled a derstral to almost perfectly replicate the land, sea or sky on either side. From below, against a clear blue sky, the derstral was effectively invisible. Intelligent and easily trained, and possessing inch long razor sharp claws, the creatures were ideal guard animals.

The creature dived at the intruder, its razor claws tearing long bloody streaks down his back as it dragged him off the cliff. Too shocked to even scream, Simet fell towards the ocean and the rocks hidden below its surface.

His friends, having finished their argument, looked around for him but assumed that he had become bored and wandered off. He had left his horse behind so would come back.

Two hours later, with still no sign of him, his friends were getting angry thinking he was deliberately choosing to hide. Tish, his best friend and next oldest of the group, told the others to ride home; he would stay and wait for a while longer.

Tish waited until the sun was almost on the horizon before reluctantly riding back, leading Simet's horse. He was scared; he knew that Simet might play a joke and hide, but not for that length of time.

158

Dash was becoming seriously annoyed with Simet, it was the same every Restday: off he'd go with his friends, promising to be home before evening service. This was too much though! He'd never been this late before, and Dash had decided it was time to become a little stricter until the boy began to take his promises more seriously. He heard the hooves clatter in the yard and rushed out.

"Simet, you're late again!" he started, then stopped as he recognised Tish, with Simet's horse, but no Simet. The look in Tish's eyes made Dash hesitate, and fear suddenly gripped him.

"What is it, boy? Where's Simet?"

Tish slid off his horse and looked up at him, a tear sliding down his cheek, as he spoke all in a rush.

"I don't know! He went off by himself, you know how he does, but he didn't come back."

More tears followed the first. "I waited and waited, but he didn't come back!"

"Didn't come back?" Dash repeated blankly. "Where were you playing?"

"In the hills."

The boy pointed towards the north-east and Dash looked over towards the darkened horizon. He suppressed the instinct to jump on a horse, ride over there and start shouting. The sun had set and the hills were treacherous in the dark. As soon as the sky began to lighten in the morning he would organise a search. He hoped the boy would have the sense to stay wherever he was until they could find him.

"You did the right thing, lad, thank you for bringing back his horse. Don't worry, he's a strong boy, he'll be all right."

He wondered who needed that reassurance most, the boy or himself.

Clearly unconvinced, the tearful youngster nodded. "I've got to get home, I'm late."

"Of course, run along, and ask your parents to come and help search in the morning."

Tish nodded and raced off.

Dash looked up at the lit window of his family's private room. How was he to tell his wife and the other children? He walked heavily inside. He didn't expect any of them would get a lot of sleep

159

that night. He sent a prayer to the Lord of Light to watch over his missing son as he closed the door. He didn't notice the shadow that peered into the courtyard from a point on the terrace above.

Azxet waited impatiently. Lord of the deep dark! Would these lightchasers never sleep? He was one of several Xiantoni assigned to make certain that the day's events were contained. The Xiantona in charge of the fleet had decreed that the lightbrat's existence should be removed from memory as far as possible. Another few days and no lightchaser in the city would be able to be curious about the Xiantu ships, but they had only just begun to lay down the illusions and wards. Thus far only a small portion of the cityfolk had been visited in their dreams, their perceptions and attitudes subtly influenced so that they could look directly at the Xiantu ships and yet fail to notice that they were there. This adjustment required constant monitoring and re-enforcement to remain in place, so they had brought with them many Xiantu gifted in the dreamhold; they would reinforce the spell each night.

Altering the memories of a worried parent of a missing child was another matter. That would take the greater power and skill of a third level Xianton such as himself.

Once just a Jar-Xian, a man of the people of Xian, he had become a first level Xianto at eighteen. As one of the chosen, Azxet had been Gifted with his first power and had learned how to dreamhold - to take control of a sleeping man and bend his actions to serve the Shadowbringer.

After demonstrating his skill and cunning, he had been elevated to second level Xianton, one of the favoured of the great God, Lord Xian. He had been honoured with the Gift of translocation at that time.

More recently, his Lord had elevated him to third level, and he was one of those fortunate few to be given the Gift of shapeshifting. Only one more level remained, and this delightful scheme would give ample opportunity to prove himself again and become a full fourth level Xianton.

Azxet had used the shapeshifting Gift for this mission. Anyone looking at him tonight would see the dark skin, hair, and eyes, of a lightchaser.

He could use his Gifts as he liked and for as long as he needed. Xiantoni did not risk burnout, as did the Guardians, because, unlike the Guardians, they had no Seta to lose. When a Jar-Xian became a Xiantu, Lord Xian replaced his Seta with a supply of his own dark

161

magic. Running short of power was rarely fatal because it could be replaced easily by taking the life energy from some other living creature.

The shapeshifter waited until, at last, the children in the house began to fall asleep, the youngest first.

He crept down into the yard and into the stables, at this late hour he was unlikely to be disturbed but to be safe, he climbed into the hayloft above the animals and hid in a corner. He made himself as comfortable as possible and sent his mind probing into the house. At last! All were asleep. He slid into a light trance state and sent his mind questing out for their dreams. One by one, he slipped into their minds and gently, with great skill, adjusted their memories and attitudes. The adults were the hardest to adjust because he had to battle against the fact that they were not deeply asleep - their worry prevented it. The process became easier as he worked, the more he altered their memories, the less the worry became, and the deeper their sleep.

Eventually, he had finished, and he checked his work carefully but with satisfaction. This was not the total memory removal and replacement that a conversion involved. The memories were deeply buried and the people adjusted to not notice that anything was missing. A Guardian would be able to retrieve the hidden memories, if he knew to look for them, but nothing else would bring them back. These people would never again remember that they had once had another child.

Around the city, other Xiantoni were carefully removing all knowledge of the child's existence from those known to be friends and acquaintances of the family. Soon, no-one would remember that Simet Coe-Jersa had ever lived.

Azxet roused himself, crept out of the stables and, brushing the straw from his clothes, jogged back towards the docks. He wanted to be back in his proper robes before sunrise.

In the morning, Dash rose feeling wonderful. He had slept soundly and felt ready for anything. He walked past the spare family bedroom without a glance and began his usual preparations for the day's work. He had the strangest feeling that he had intended to do something specific, but whatever it was he could not bring it to mind. Never mind, his mother had always said that if you couldn't

162

remember something, it couldn't have been important. He pushed the matter from his mind and got on with his tasks.

One by one, his six children and his wife woke and appeared in the kitchen, looking for breakfast before embarking on their assigned chores. All appeared well rested and cheerful. Dash again had a feeling of having forgotten something. Oh of course! The spare horse! He was going to arrange for its sale, he couldn't imagine what had possessed him to buy an extra one in the first place.

Satisfied that he had remembered the forgotten item he decided to do it immediately before he forgot again, so he went out to the stables and saddled the horse and set off towards the horse market.

Father Arnath gazed across his room at the spacious new travel bag lying empty in the corner, a gift from the Revered Father and smiled in memory of the detailed illusion that had caused the demise of the old one. That dog!!

He had, of course, allowed no trace of his amusement to appear on his face when the two students were disciplined over the incident but, afterwards, he and Revered Father Teiron had roared with laughter. They had agreed that the youngsters in question had certainly mastered their Gifts.

The elderly priest wondered what the lads would have thought had they known of some of his own exploits when at a similar age.

His smile grew broader as he remembered the look on an instructor's face when a much younger Arnath had noticed that the man had neglected his armour wards, and that part of it had reverted to ordinary steel. Arnath had taken full advantage of that to transmute the steel slightly and make it magnetic.

The group had been training with daggers at the time, and these had suddenly all flown at the man and attached themselves to his chest plate. Very funny at the time, although he had been lucky that the man had not suffered injury. Still, it *had* been the instructor's own fault for neglecting his armour.

That had been a *long* time ago!

In his nineties, but still vigorous, Arnath was tall and slim with slightly receding hair and a neatly cut short beard. He had been Bishop of Bein for over ten years, and before that had spent many years in other clerical positions. A Tyrean Sorcerer with five of the gifts, he had entered church service twenty-three years ago, after the death of his Ponfour Melsa.

Feeling that he was now called to a different service, he had chosen to not rebond. He was one of the few clergy who were Sorcerers, but who lived permanently in the Protectorates.

Like all other Tyreans, he still returned yearly to Tyreen to refresh his skills both magical and physical.

This year his visit had been prolonged, firstly by the crisis caused by a Zindon taking control of the young Rykatu's Ponfour, then by several Church matters, and finally by the need to learn a new skill to send seta across a dreamwalk.

A new skill, at his age! He chuckled while settling himself to sleep. Tonight was a test that he had mastered the new skill. His instructor would be waiting for him to dream. He closed his eyes and within seconds was asleep.

The same day that Tam threw Crystu in the lake, Father Arnath, together with several others who were leaving Tyreen, rode out of the Cave of Cleansing to begin his journey home to Bein. He said goodbye to his companions and urged his horse along a side path into a secluded area.

He had been gone too long and intended to translocate home, The wards around Tyreen prevented translocation out of or into the country so he, like everyone else, had to leave the kingdom via the cave first.

The limiting factor for translocation was not just distance, but also weight and size. It was his strongest Gift and he was quite strong enough to send himself, his horse and luggage, and a great deal more if necessary, the long distance to Bein.

Closing his eyes, he brought to mind the view visible from a favourite viewpoint: the city on the plain, the sea to the left, and the rolling hills beyond, all bathed in sunshine. It did not matter if the weather was actually cloudy or rainy, as long as he knew where he wanted to go, he would arrive in the right place. He released the power slowly and allowed the translocation nimbus to develop around him and the horse. He checked to be sure that the misty nimbus enclosed everything and then made the mental flick that sent him to his destination.

Arnath opened his eyes, expecting to see the familiar beautiful landscape, but what he saw made him gasp in horror!

The city and plain were shrouded by a large dark-grey cloud. From his vantage point, the elderly priest could see that the cloud originated from beyond the horizon across the sea. He remembered that the distant volcano had been in one of its periodic active phases when he left, but he had never known it have such an effect as this! He could only just see across to the docks, which seemed to be unusually full of ships.

Most shocking of all was the sense of magical residue that tickled the edge of his mind. Somewhere in the city, magic had been, or was being, used in quantities large enough that he could feel it even at this distance.

For a moment, he considered translocating back to Tyreen to report this but rejected the idea. He had no real understanding of what was happening down there. If he went back now, someone

166

would have to investigate and that someone might as well be him. He was known in the city, expected to return, and no one knew he was Tyrean, except possibly Dash, but *he* was only guessing, and Arnath knew that his friend would have never told anyone of his suspicions.

Arnath would play the unsuspecting bishop, innocently returning to his post after his regular sabbatical. He ignored the small cautionary voice in the back of his mind that was pointing out that any Sorcerer sent to investigate would be accompanied and defended by a Ponfour, whereas he was completely alone.

He directed his horse down the path towards the nearest road into the city. As he came down from the high point and approached the city, he discovered that the cloud, which had been so black and threatening from above, appeared much thinner and less menacing from below but was still unpleasant.

As he breathed, grit made his tongue feel dry, while the faintly sulphurous taint to the air made his nose itch.

Dust lay over the road and was visible on the surfaces of the leaves of the roadside plants. It was a coarse dust, which seemed too heavy to be disturbed by the gusts of wind that caught at Arnath's cloak.

Passing several outlying farms, Arnath noticed that the people he saw seemed lethargic. They moved slowly and seemed not to notice the dust around them. He saw one woman placing washing from the line into a basket, oblivious to the grey dust coating the folds of the clothes. She made no attempt to shake it off.

The priest was a regular patron of The Sailors' Well and usually made it his first stop when returning from a journey, even before going home. He decided that he should not deviate from his usual pattern. In addition, the Well was the best place to learn about recent events.

Riding through the outskirts of the city, he called cheerful greetings to people he knew. Most replied, but did so in an absent-minded fashion, and seemed to forget his presence almost immediately. Here, closer to the centre of the city, Arnath could feel the tell-tale residue of magic use all around him. The quality of the tingling that he could feel suggested that the magic use was widespread and continuous. Dear God! How many magic users were here? Could they be anything other than Zindons?

167

He was careful to bury his own abilities as deeply as he could. So long as he avoided magic use himself, he should be able to pass without any enemy recognising him as a Tyrean.

When he reached the Well, he rode into the stable courtyard and dismounted, He settled his horse into a free stall, then, carrying his bag over one shoulder, he went into the Well.

"Arnath! Welcome back. Come through. What will you have?"

Dash gestured towards the door to the private bar and followed the priest through. He seemed much as usual, Arnath thought as he sat down in his favourite chair.

"I'll have a mug of pengar please, to wash away the dust of travel," he replied, "and some savoury snacks. Whatever you've got."

"DARA!" Dash shouted through the hatch. "PENGAR, AND SNACKS FOR FATHER ARNATH, IF YOU WOULD BE SO GOOD. It will just be a few minutes, Arnath," he continued at a more normal volume. "You arrived at the perfect time: the afternoon rush has yet to begin."

He sighed.

"To be honest with you, though, the *morning's* rush has also yet to start, and I'm still waiting for yesterday evening's rush to appear."

"How unusual," commented Arnath mildly. "Usually the Well is full of people."

"True, usually it is," Dash agreed, "but not at the moment. Everyone you saw in the main bar is a guest here in the Well. Very few Bein residents are coming in. No one wants to go out in the dust if they can avoid it, so they stay in their homes and only leave to buy food supplies to take home. All the businesses are affected, except those selling groceries."

"I noticed the streets seemed a little dusty, why is no one sweeping it away?"

"Because it seems to make no difference if you do," Dash replied gloomily. "I tried at first to keep it off the yard, but as fast as I wipe it off, it comes back. If I leave it alone, though, it doesn't seem to get any worse, so now I just leave it. No one wants to eat outside now anyway because you just end up with grit in your food. So why bother trying to clean something that won't stay clean, for customers I haven't got, who wouldn't want to eat outside anyway?"

"That makes sense." Arnath nodded sympathetically. "Hopefully the wind will change or the volcano settle down again."

"I'll drink to that," said Dash, pouring something into a glass and taking a sip. Arnath was surprised - in ten years he had never known Dash to sample his own wares unless someone was paying for him to do so.

"Let's talk about something less gloomy, my friend," Dash decided, his hearty voice sounding a little forced. "How was your trip to the hidden kingdom?"

"Oh, the same as usual," the priest replied.

"Indeed?" Dash looked astonished. "You've been gone so long I thought you must have walked back for a change."

"Instead of riding my horse you mean? No, I let his legs do the work, not my own."

Arnath knew that Dash had been alluding to translocation, but this game was an old one that they played each year. Dash would try to get him to admit that he was a Tyrean, and Arnath would misunderstand or mishear the questions. The normality of it was slightly reassuring.

The innkeeper nodded but had a glint of disbelief in his eyes.

"Can I ask you something?" he began.

The priest laughed.

"I think you just did. Have you a second question?"

Dash paused for a moment, gave him an artificially patient look and then continued, "I know that all those in service to the Church of Light must spend some time in Tyreen, every few years."

"Of course," Arnath interrupted. "The Revered Father likes to keep in touch with his clerics."

"Exactly," Dash nodded, then continued again. "I've never heard of one who went there quite as often as you do, Arnath. You're away for about a month every year. But you can't spend much time there because, as we all know, it takes..."

"About three weeks to get there from here by horse." Arnath spoke the last words at the same time as Dash and sighed.

"My friend, you asked the same question last year, do you not remember what I answered last time and the time before?"

"As a matter of fact, I do." Dash grinned. "You didn't answer at all!"

"Didn't I? How strange. Oh, here's Dara with my drink and food." Arnath nodded towards the door as it opened to reveal Dara with a tray.

169

"Father Arnath, welcome back. I hope you had a pleasant journey."

She placed the tray on the table beside Arnath's seat.

"And was your sabbatical restful?" she asked.

"Not all of it," he replied, thinking of the attempted Zindon entry, "but it was certainly educational."

Dara smiled and opened her mouth to speak again but someone shouted her name from the corridor.

"I'm sorry, Father, I have to go. I'm glad you're back." Dara bustled back through the door. "I'm coming, Ral, I'm coming!"

As the door closed on her voice, Arnath turned back to his friend.

"How much do I owe you?" he asked, patting the pocket of his cloak where his money was.

"Prices of food have been going up lately, and I've had to put up my prices likewise," Dash replied, sounding embarrassed. "It comes to four suns, one moon, and twenty three stars."

Arnath raised his eyebrows.

"As much as that?" he commented, pulling out his purse.

"Here you are," he said, handing over five suns.

The priest looked at the twenty-seven stars he received in change, before placing them in the purse.

"My purse seems to be darker inside now, losing all those suns," he commented.

"So have our Guardians learned civilised ways yet?" Dash asked.

"Ha, if by that you mean have they started to use coinage?" Arnath paused, delighted to have successfully diverted Dash from his earlier line of thought. "No, my friend, they have not, and they would be amazed and possibly offended at your suggestion that civilisation requires money. They believe quite the reverse: that a monetary system is by far the inferior way to exchange goods. It encourages greed and creates poverty. Their system ensures that all citizens have everything they need and also luxuries too. All work for the society as a whole and none seeks to enrich himself at the expense of another."

"I can't imagine that." Dash shook his head. "People working without pay? No one would put in a full day's work, in fields not their own, without some reward. I certainly wouldn't"

170

"Of course you wouldn't," Arnath agreed gravely. "Changing the subject completely, how are all your children doing?" Dash happily launched into a detailed description of all his children's recent successes and general welfare.

Arnath listened and made the appropriate comments. He forbore to point out that although Dash claimed to have no understanding of doing something for others with no thought of reward, he and his wife, having no children of their own, had taken in seven parentless children over the years.

Those they had adopted were the orphans left by tragic sea accidents. After each disaster, Dash and Dara had simply appeared at the homes of the bereaved youngsters and taken them home to the Well, where they were cared for as members of his family.

The innkeeper had also arranged the sale of the now empty homes and placed the proceeds in trust, held by the Church, for the children's use when they were of age.

Dash finished his lengthy monologue, and the priest frowned.

"And what of Simet?" he asked. "You missed him out. Is he in disgrace for some prank?"

His friend stared at him blankly.

"Who is Simet?" he asked.

Arnath suddenly felt cold. Dash appeared to be serious.

He laughed hoarsely.

"Dash, if it's a joke, it's a bad one. I mean Simet, your second eldest."

Dash laughed and for a moment Arnath felt relieved, but then Dash replied,

"You've been drinking at some cheap bar and were given poor quality. It's addled your brain: I have no son named Simet."

Arnath stared at him in shock. Clearly Dash's memories had been adjusted, but why and by whom?

There was only one way to find out, but if any magic users were nearby they would feel it. He prayed that none were, and then leaned closer to Dash and grasping his shoulder sent a healing probe deep into his mind and body. He was right: Dash's memories had been crudely altered to make him forget that Simet ever lived. The interference had also reduced his curiosity and made him unlikely to even notice anything out of the ordinary.

171

The elderly priest healed the damage and then guided Dash to a chair as his memories returned.

Dash looked around the room as though he might find something that would explain his lapse.

"Simet! I forgot about him? How could that happen? He went to play in the hills and didn't return. I was going to raise the alarm as soon as it was light."

He looked up at Arnath in horror.

"That was two weeks ago. How could I forget? And not just me - Dara has made no mention and neither have the children. What could make us all forget like this?"

"Magic!" Arnath replied grimly. "Your memories were altered."

The innkeeper looked at him in awe. "You healed me, didn't you? You really are a Tyrean as I suspected."

"Yes," Arnath nodded, "I am, and now I need you to tell me everything unusual that occurred here in Bein after I left."

"But Simet, we must look for him."

The man was half out of his chair and looking towards the door. Arnath pushed him back down.

"Dash, since I came within sight of Bein I have sensed the residue of magic. The closer I got to the city, the stronger the sensation. Magic has been used here, and is being used here, in large quantities. Whatever has happened to Simet is part of it: you were altered to forget him. I must know what has caused this, and you are the only person I can ask. Everyone else is affected by it, and I'm sorry, but if Simet has been missing for two weeks..."

He could not bring himself to finish the sentence, but he knew that Simet was almost certainly dead.

Dash sank back into the chair as he understood. He took a deep breath and then nodded resolutely.

"Yes, I understand. I will try to think."

Picking up his glass, he drained his drink. Then he looked up grimly,

"The Shantoo! It must be something to do with them. They were the only unusual thing to happen, and," he gasped, "I also forgot about them. That can't be a coincidence, they must be responsible. Why, whatever is it? You've gone grey! Have you heard of them?"

He stared at Arnath who had stiffened in shock at the name Shantoo.

172

"Tell me about them, these Shantoo," he rasped, being careful to say the word exactly as Dash had and not in the way that he suspected would be the correct pronunciation.

"They arrived just after you left! Enneth told me about them. They said their ships had been blown off course and they would stay until the wind changed."

"Ships? How many?" Arnath asked, thinking of the twenty or so large ships of unusual design he had seen in the harbour.

"Three," Dash told him, "but they wouldn't come ashore. They said their God didn't allow them to mix with others. They come from far in the north where the sun is weaker, so they cover themselves in robes to keep the light from them. And they have pink eyes."

Arnath closed his eyes and made himself breathe slowly and deeply to control the sudden surge of fear. It was not a coincidence. Thankfully, Dash was mispronouncing the name, but not by much.

"Who are they? Who are the Shantoo?" Dash asked.

The priest knew their real name and how it was pronounced, though he had never heard it spoken aloud. A book in a warded room in Tyre gave their true name, and an illusion spell placed the correct pronunciation directly to the reader's mind without sound.

"It's not pronounced quite like that, Dash," Arnath said, relieved to hear his voice sounded as calm as usual. "I won't tell you the correct pronunciation, but you have heard of them."

He opened his eyes, to see Dash staring at him with concern.

"We say their name differently, that's all. They are Zindons, Dash. There are at least twenty of their ships out there. If they all are full..."

"Zindons?" Dash was aghast. "My boy?"

"I'm sorry Dash, he must be dead. He must have seen something, or been in the wrong place, but I can't think that he can still be alive. Zindons would not hesitate to kill a child if he was in their way."

Arnath thought with regret of the cheeky face, the impish grin, now undoubtedly dead.

He came to a decision.

"Call Dara in here now, I must heal her too."

His friend stared at him but didn't move.

"Dash, now! We have little time if we are to save your family."

The innkeeper swallowed, nodded once, and hurried through the door without a word.

Arnath considered his position, alone in a city full of Zindons. He must hope that none had been close enough to sense his healing of Dash, and that his healing of Dara would likewise go un-noticed.

All who had left Tyreen had been warned to look for signs of the Shadowbringer's activity, but he had never imagined he might find such a large-scale incursion. He had never heard of such a thing happening before. He must get word to Lord Jareth.

Dash returned with Dara, and even as she began to speak, Arnath stood, gripped her arm and healed her.

"Father, Dash says you... Lord of Light! Simet! What? How? Dash? We didn't even look! Father, what did you just do?"

She allowed herself to be pushed down into a chair, and Dash poured her a drink.

"We were made to forget, and Father Arnath has healed both of us." He told her grimly.

"Healed?" She looked at Arnath. "Then you're a Sorcerer? A Tyrean? But who made us forget? And why? The Shantoo, was it them?"

"Yes," Arnath replied, "I am a Guardian of Reyth, a Tyrean Sorcerer, and yes it was.." he couldn't bring himself to repeat the name that sounded so close to the true pronunciation, "your visitors." he finished.

"But why?" she asked.

"They're Zindons Dara, we've been invaded, and enspelled by Zindons," Dash told her.

Dara gave a small shriek, then took a deep breath.

"Then Simet's dead," she looked at Arnath, eyes pleading with him to tell her she was wrong. "Isn't he?"

Arnath nodded.

"Almost certainly, I'm sorry."

She put her hands over her face and shook.

"I'm sorry but you do not have time now for grief," Arnath told her urgently, "All of your children are in danger now and you must leave Bein immediately. The other children are all here, aren't they? You must think of them or they will *all* die." He said it bluntly and it was the truth. Their only chance to save their family was if they could put grief aside and remain strong for the remaining children.

Dash grasped Dara's hand.

174

"What do you need us to do?" he asked Arnath. Grief warred with horror and fear for their family in their eyes, but Arnath knew that his friends would not panic or collapse while their other children were in danger.

"I won't heal them, there isn't time, and the damage should eventually correct itself once you are away from here, but you must go - now! Get everyone into the yard and take only what you can carry. I can translocate the carriage and all of you with me. Lord Jareth will want to hear everything from you. Quickly! We have little time!"

Dara jumped to her feet.

"The healing! Could they have sensed you do it and be coming here?"

Arnath nodded confirmation.

"Then we go right this minute, Dash, with what we can carry and nothing else."

She hurried through to the family rooms and began pulling travel bags from a cupboard.

"Pack for me, I'll go and warn our customers to leave," Dash said.

"No!" Arnath stopped him before he took two steps, "Dash, I'm sorry, but I can't heal them and get your family to safety. There just isn't time and without healing, they will not take any notice of your warning. They won't believe you, they can't. We must leave immediately. I'm sorry."

He wished that he had some way to get *everyone* safely away, but he knew that their best chance lay in getting word to Tyreen as quickly as possible.

Dash stared at him aghast. "We can't warn them?" He shook his head. "No, I understand. You're right. If you had told me before you healed me, I would not have believed you." He took a deep breath.

"I'll be out in the yard in five minutes." He ran out of the room.

Arnath hoped that they had five minutes. Every passing second increased the risk. He was not much of a gleaner, but he could feel the danger increasing by the second. He raced outside and saddled his horse.

Dash, Dara, and their children came hurrying into the stables, the children asking questions but doing as they were bid. Arnath had

175

directed the grooms to bring through the large carriage. Arnath could translocate the family without the carriage, but the spell would be easier with them enclosed, and they could drive it from the Cave to Tyre.

"Quickly, get in!"

Arnath ushered Dara into the carriage and lifted a child in after her. The feeling of time running out intensified and he made a fast decision. The more people, the more time it would take the nimbus to form. He would send them first and then follow if he could. He started to make the nimbus, which had to cover the carriage and the horses.

"I'm sending you now, as close to Darrow as I'm able. I'll follow if I can, but if I can't, ride west into the city and tell everyone that there are Zindons here. Go to the cathedral in Darrow and talk to Father Jedia; he's Tyrean. Warn people not to come here," he told Dash as he lifted in the last child to Dara. "Even if they don't believe you, warn them. Start rumours! Tell everyone you meet that there are Zindons in Bein!"

"What about you, Arnath?" said Dash worriedly.

"I'll follow if I can, but…" he stopped; the sensation of danger was over-powering. "Light go with you!"

He translocated the carriage as far as he could towards the west. So many people, plus the things they had carried, and the carriage and horses, were too much for him to send all the way to the Cleansing Cave and if he was unable to follow they wouldn't be able to enter Tyreen. If they reached Darrow, there were several Tyreans in the Cathedral who could send a message to Jareth. Arnath breathed a sigh of relief as the nimbus cleared and immediately started to form one for himself.

He stiffened at the sudden feeling of being muffled that told him that a ward had been activated nearby. His nimbus vanished. He had sent Dash and his family away just in time and he had been right to not take the extra seconds, which he would have needed to enlarge the nimbus further, to translocate himself and his horse with them.

Something moved by the opening. He didn't bother to check who or what it was before creating an air-ram that blasted through with such force that both gates and part of the wall smashed outwards. He was thankful that transmutation was unaffected by the ward. They

176

evidently did not want him to leave but were not worried that he might fight.

He jumped onto his horse and cantered through the settling dust. Fire blazed through the street, around him and around several black-robed figures; he had attacked them at the same time that they had attacked him. He dampened the flames with a wave of his hand as his terrified horse screamed, reared, and then raced uncontrollably up the street with Arnath clinging on. He looked behind. Most of the Zindons had also successfully stopped the fire, and they were racing for tethered mounts. Arnath now had seven Zindons chasing him, no Ponfour, no sword, and he couldn't translocate.

And he had once thought that becoming a priest might be boring!

The noise of the hooves clattering against the cobbles was terrifyingly loud against the unnatural quiet of the city streets and black dust billowed up as he passed.

The translocation ward remained strong. Light! What was its range? Was one of the creatures behind him carrying it, or were there wards scattered around the entire city? Arnath wished that he knew. He looked behind, only five now followed him. Where were the others?

He rode around a corner and made an air barrier behind him. At the same moment, a dragon appeared in the street ahead and spewed green fire. It was an illusion, of course, but, although Arnath could see the reality, his horse could not and reared. Arnath lost precious seconds dispelling the illusion and persuading his terrified horse to go forward. The Zindons came around the corner and their horses ran into the air-barrier just as Arnath reached the next side turn. One animal, at least, broke its neck in the smash.

And still, the translocation ward held him within its grasp. They *must* be carrying it, he decided. They did not need to have the entire city blanketed in this way when no native magic users lived here. If he was going to escape, he had to lose the pursuing Zindons.

Arnath constructed an illusion of his own body, shaping it carefully about himself, and then he set it so that it would remain intact for a good few minutes without further magic.

He rode down a small alley with several side streets and reined in his horse. He slid off, guiltily increased his poor mount's fear with a misused healing spell and smacked his mount firmly on its rump to make it gallop away while he ran down the street and got out of sight

177

behind an abandoned cart. His illusion had remained on the horse and the Zindons, coming around the corner, saw what they assumed was Arnath galloping ahead of them, just as he had for the last few minutes.

Arnath held his breath; if any of them was an illusionist he would know that it was not real.

The Zindons raced past the street without a sideways glance. Breathing again, Arnath ran. He knew that it could only be a matter of minutes before they discovered the deception and came back to search for him. He hoped he could get far enough away from that ward to be able to translocate. He ran along alleys, ducked through shops, dashed past people who might have been sleepwalking for all the notice they took of him. He stopped behind a stall in a dusty market square breathing deeply. He could feel magic residue in the area, but nothing close by. He had run at least a couple of miles but was still warded. He couldn't understand it, but it meant that he must try something else.

He knew the city well, better surely than the invaders, and hoped that this small advantage might gain him some time to find a quiet place where he could eventually hide long enough to attempt a dreamwalk if that gift was not also warded.

He jogged through streets and alleys, easily avoiding the lethargic population. He heard occasional shouts spoken in a slightly odd accent, and once had to duck behind a revoltingly foul heap of rotting rubbish to avoid a group of Zindons who appeared from within a building and ran into the next.

The streets grew narrower and the buildings taller and greyer as he reached a poorer section of the city. Here the streets seemed empty, but every so often, in the corner of his eye, he caught a glimpse of a flickering shadow as if something flew above him. When he looked up, he could see nothing in the sky and tried to persuade himself that he was imagining the movement.

He had travelled at least another three miles and yet the translocation ward was a strong as ever. He wished that he could dismiss the fear that it was following him.

Eventually, Arnath came to a gap between two large warehouses. He dashed along the alley, slipped through a gate, leapt a brick wall, and then dived between a rock and a clump of bushes into a cleft in the rock. At the far end of the cleft, rough-hewn and worn steps led upwards. Arnath ran up them, wishing that his legs were fifty years younger but glad that he had kept up with his training and exercise even after he became a priest. The path led out into a hidden overgrown garden that few people knew existed. Above him, on three sides, the sheer cliffs were topped by the walls of some of the oldest buildings in the city. None of those walls contained windows. The wealthy lord who had once owned this land two hundred years earlier had wanted his garden to be private and had the wealth and influence to ensure it. The fourth side, up which Arnath had just scrambled, looked out across the city and harbour and the view was usually breath-taking.

Arnath stopped and leant against the cliff, breathing deeply. He looked out at the grey and gloomy scene as his breath slowed and prayed that he had eluded the shadow minions even though the ward still cast its blanketing numbness across his ability to translocate.

Around him, wild flowers were blooming in untended abandon. Fruit trees were shedding blossom, and thorned creepers were spreading across one corner, and several types of climbers wound their way across branches and up the jagged cliffs. Something splashed in the small dust coated pond and sank out of sight.

His breathing eased, Arnath pushed his way through the undergrowth to the clump of trees at the back. Here, the grass was long and the leaves above reassuringly concealing, so he sank down with his back against a tree, took a deep breath, slid into sleep, and constructed a dream to attract Lord Jareth's attention.

Arnath was thankful that Jareth had given him an opportunity to refresh his knowledge of his commander's mind aura. Even so, he was not powerful enough to walk fully into the Rykatu's dreams from this distance, but if Jareth heard his call, the more powerful Sorcerer could use his own strength to make the connection.

Arnath hoped Jareth would hear him quickly; he would be asleep and unprotected during the dreamwalk and sooner or later, the Zindons *would* find him. He hoped that it would be later, but he feared that they were already closer than he wished.

Azxet had followed the bishop almost from the moment his horse set foot upon the main road. He had seen this Light Servant in the innkeeper's dreams and knew of Dash's suspicion that the bishop was one of the Guardians of Reyth.

Azxet thought it unlikely. *They* usually went about in pairs and this bishop clearly had no Ponfour. He did not like to take a chance though, so he had stationed several Xiantu around the edges of the city and had received word of the man's arrival. Accompanied by two second level Xiantoi he watched the man ride up the high street, calling banal greetings to the sheep-like lightfollowers. He could sense the disapproval and contempt radiating from his companions as he continued to shadow this bishop. He ignored them, he would rather tell the Xiantona that he had wasted a few hours than face the consequences should he allow a genuine Tyrean to learn about the invasion, and escape with his knowledge, before all the preparations were in place.

They watched as he dismounted and went into the Well.

"This bishop *can't* be a Guardian!" one of Azxet's companions said in disgust. "He would have sensed the magic residue long before he reached the city. He would have gone back to Tyreen immediately to fetch other Sorcerers."

"That would be the sensible thing," Azxet agreed, "but the Guardians rarely do what we would consider the sensible thing. We will continue to watch him until I say otherwise. Should he prove to be a Guardian, however, you will not partake of his Seta. That is your punishment for speaking criticism without permission. Be sure when I want your advice I will ask for it. At all other times, I have no interest in your opinion."

He stared at the Xianton until sure that the man had accepted the rebuke.

Then all three stiffened as they felt the distinctive surge of power within the Well.

"My apologies, Xianton Azxet, you were correct, the punishment is deserved." The erring Xianton bowed his head. "What action should we take?"

Azxet looked at him with contempt. Xiantoi should not apologise, they should turn anger into hatred into strength. Just being

180

on this over-lit area of land seemed to be causing odd behaviour in some of the weaker Xiantu and Xiantoi.

Possibly it was the need to spend time in contact with the minds of these Light followers. The higher levels were watching the effect closely and noting those who were affected. When the time came, these weak ones would join the Jar-Xian in the coming battle. If they survived that, then the final phase of Lord Xian's plan would kill them along with all the Guardians.

"The punishment stands," he said, in case the fool had thought an apology might cause him to change his mind. "Translocate back to the ship and report to the Xiantona. Request two battlegroups and a translocation ward in my name. One group to join us here with the ward, and one group to stand ready, but hidden, at the cathedral, in case he goes there. You will accompany that group and wait for further orders."

The Xianton nodded. When he had disappeared from view, the other Xianton, a woman named Xareht, spoke.

"Xianton Azxet, will you instruct me? Why would this Guardian continue on to the cathedral? Surely by now he has learned of our presence. Will he not simply translocate away?"

Her question was appropriately phrased and her tone showed only respectful curiosity and a wish to learn. Azxet considered for a moment and then decided he would answer.

"He must have sensed our presence in this city before he arrived here, and yet he still entered. The Guardians are prepared to sacrifice themselves to protect those their Light Lord has placed into their guardianship. He has exposed himself to us by using his power, probably to heal the innkeeper so that he can learn what has happened here. Once he has learned all that he can, I have no doubt that he intends to translocate, and I hope that the ward arrives before he does."

"How do you know he is a Translocater?" she asked.

Azxet shrugged. "This far from Tyreen? The innkeeper has noticed that he travels to and from the hidden land too quickly so I think it likely that he is."

They both felt the second tingle that betrayed the use of powerful magic within the Well.

"I would guess that he has healed first the innkeeper and now the wife," Azxet said. Xareht nodded. A few minutes later, they became

181

aware of activity in the stables. Horses were brought out and saddled, and a small carriage was also prepared.

Azxet swore.

"If they don't bring that ward soon he may escape. We are lucky that he seems to want to assist his friends first."

A translocation nimbus appeared and dispersed, leaving the requested battle team of ten Xiantoni. Azxet concealed the feeling of relief and snatched the padded bag from the hand that held it out.

"I do not want our prey to leave before we have a chance to introduce ourselves," he said as he pulled the ward from within the bag.

He looked at the object in his hand. Fist sized, and a perfect sphere, it had clearly started as a simple ball of glass until a skilful transmuter had altered it. The entire sphere was a detailed tangle of interwoven fine multi-coloured glass threads that drew the eye inwards towards its centre. Normally such an object would glow gently with a warm light that caused the strands to sparkle in a way that made the light seem to move around within the sphere. Now, however, the centre held an impenetrable darkness that seemed to pulsate slightly, and the coloured strands were tinged with grey. His companion looked at it again, then met his eyes. He could see her appreciation of the desecration of the object.

"That is a sun globe, isn't it?" she asked. Azxet nodded.

"We found several in the cathedral. The symbolism is pleasing - the darkness has driven out the light that once was inside. As a converted object, its range is limited, but once activated, it will prevent anyone within that range translocating."

A burst of magic use made Azxet swear as he realised that his procrastination had given the priest time to start to translocate.

He concentrated and the sunglobe began to pulse more strongly as he activated the ward within. He knew it was working because he could feel the dampening of his own power.

Too late! The carriage containing the innkeeper and family had already vanished, but the priest remained. Azxet knew that his error had possibly cost them a great deal but he must show no weakness now where his subordinates could see it,

"And now he is trapped and knows it. Come on!"

Azxet ran towards the open gate, Xareht and the ten Xiantoni following. As they reached the opening, a solid air ram blasted through the opening, destroying part of the wall. Three of the battlegroup were knocked unconscious by falling bricks.

A moment later, the bishop emerged, his horse at full gallop. Azxet, Xareht, and two of the Xiantoni transmuted fire around the fleeing Tyrean and at the same moment flames blossomed around all of them.

Azxet swore again as he shielded himself. Two of the group were not transmuters and were rolling on the ground desperately trying to put out the flames.

"Leave them!" he snarled furiously, "After the priest!"

It was their own fault for not having their robes strengthened against fire, he thought as he ran for his horse.

They chased after the Tyrean at breakneck speed. "Xareht!" Azxet shouted, "I'm going to shapeshift. I can follow him more easily and keep him within the ward's reach. Send one of the others back to report to Xiantona Kajzte that we are chasing a Tyrean, and also tell him that the innkeeper has been freed from our spells and has been translocated out of Bein."

Xareht nodded as Azxet changed shape and launched himself into the air as a derstral. Flying above the city he was easily able to keep pace with the Tyrean and watch as the man successfully eluded first the dragon illusion and then, after a long chase, just as it seemed that the Xiantoni had caught him, he turned out to be an illusion! Azxet wheeled back, predator's eyes peeled for any fast movement. He flew low in a tight searching pattern that spiralled outwards from where he thought the man must have eluded his pursuers.

There!

Luckily still close enough for the ward to be effective, Azxet saw the priest dashing through an alley. He flew closer, trusting the derstral's camouflage ability to keep him hidden from his prey's occasional searching look upwards.

The important thing now was to stop the Guardian escaping. Without knowing what other Gifts the man might have, Azxet was unwilling to attack him alone, but the man was old and sooner or later he would tire of running and stop somewhere to rest and that would be Azxet's chance to signal to someone to assist him.

Eventually, the Tyrean scrambled over a wall and began jogging along the rough track into an overgrown garden. The garden had no

183

other exit that Azxet could see and he suddenly realised as the priest lay down that he might be intending to dreamwalk.

Azxet flew higher and, to his relief, spotted Xareht and the remaining battle group searching a few streets away. He flew down, changed back into human form, and beckoned Xareht and the accompanying battlegroup.

Above them, he could feel magic in use and he knew that they had little time.

"We must be quick!" he hissed, "This way!"

They ran quickly up the stairs towards the source of the power that they all could sense. Following the path, they arrived in the overgrown garden. Azxet could see the faint traces of the priest's passage through the undergrowth and they followed that trail to where the old man lay against the tree with his eyes closed, oblivious to their presence. They could feel the power in him as he attempted to establish his dreamwalk.

Azxet gestured to Xareht to join him. They lay down beside the Guardian and quickly entered the semi-conscious state required for dreamholding. The rest of the battlegroup stood ready in case the priest woke enough to fight. They would drink the Seta that was left after he and Xareht were satiated. Together Azxet and Xareht sent their consciousness down into the Priest's body and entered his dream. One alone could not have overcome his defences, but two Xiantoni working together could do it easily.

Even so, he fought hard and it took longer than Azxet had expected, but eventually they had control of his dream and sealed his mind within it. Then they moved to his Seta and they began to feed.

When they had completely replenished their energy from Arnath's Seta they withdrew and allowed the battlegroup to finish what was left. When they all departed, they left the body where it lay beneath the tree.

After returning to the ship, where Azxet invited Xareht to help him celebrate their victory over a Tyrean in privacy. For a short time, he had been afraid that the priest would escape, but everything had gone well in the end. The innkeeper and family had escaped but they were unimportant. Now he felt exhilarated by his success and Xareht was just as exuberant.

184

In Tyre, Lord Jareth became aware that someone was trying to make contact with him. He excused himself as quickly as he could from his conversation with Tarek and found a chair on which he could recline while he slipped into a light trance to allow him to dreamwalk. He searched for the voice of the other but found nothing. He woke troubled. He did not know who had called to him, but his gleaning power stirred for a moment, and he knew that whoever it was, had died.

Part 5: The Kingdom of Perrest

"The Kingdom of Light was named one hundred and sixty two years after the conclusion of the War of Magic, although at the time it was barely a quarter of its present size. The Kingdom of Tirashon was founded seventy five years later. The two kingdoms grew slowly and it was another two hundred and ninety-two years before the third kingdom, Perrest, was founded on the east coast." Book of Light: History of the Protectorates – The Expansion.

A mountain of ice

Commander Iffrey, of the Angate division of the Perrest Royal Guard, looked at the impossible mountain, which loomed whitely above the ridge, and then turned back to the small group of men waiting on the track behind him. He pushed his gloved hands deeper into his coat pockets and wished he was somewhere else. Anywhere else would do if it had a fire.

They were standing at the top of a high chalk ridge. Behind and below them stretched the low fertile plains of the Kingdom of Perrest, the most northern of the Protectorates. Meandering rivers, forests, fields, roads, and several substantial towns and villages were visible in the distance across the well-populated and fertile plains. Closer, starting at the foot of the ridge upon which they stood, lay the large city of Angate which sprawled for several miles to the south and east.

Above them stretched the undulating upland moors, uninhabited except for the herds of sheep that were pastured up here during the summer months, and for the shepherds who looked after them.

Under normal circumstances, the moors stretched for miles as far as the eye could see - a rolling curving landscape covered in tough grasses and shrubs with just the occasional twisted tree. A few sunken hollows marked places where the underlying limestone had been eroded by some underground water source and had collapsed. In other areas, there was a brighter green to the vegetation, suggesting bogs and peat.

These were not normal circumstances.

The land around them was white with frost and snow, and the leafless trees nearby shook as the cold wind blew down from the uplands. The four men with Iffrey were, like him, well wrapped up with furred leather and wool clothing. The four of them had volunteered to climb up onto the newly formed ice mountain and try to find out what had made it. The last group sent to investigate had not returned. Neither had anyone who had walked up onto the upland in the last few weeks.

Two of the volunteers were men dying of incurable disease, and one was a criminal under sentence of death. Duke Rannis had offered pardons for criminals, and a large amount of money, to anyone prepared to risk their lives to find out what was behind or in the impossible mountain. The fourth man was here just for the money – he thought he would come back alive.

Winter was starting to ease, but the air was still bitterly cold and every breath hung as a visible cloud in front of Iffrey's mouth as he spoke.

"This is your last chance to change your minds," he told the group. "I know that you all volunteered, and Duke Rannis is paying a fortune that will keep your families in luxury for life, but you can still turn around and go back."

Casiol snorted without humour. His deepset eyes and gaunt face evidence of his sickness.

"And what then?" he asked. "The Duke still needs to know what made that." He pointed at the mountain. "Someone has to go. I'm dying anyway and if that's what I think, it's a faster way to go, and my wife and children will be provided for."

Ewail nodded agreement and then turned to cough wetly away from the others. Like Casiol, he had only weeks left to live, although only his cough was evidence of whatever was gnawing his lungs.

Garet laughed derisively.

"We know what you think, Casiol: Snow-ants! Why not Zindons while we're telling children's stories?"

Casiol smiled wearily; they'd already had this argument several times.

"Just because they are stories, doesn't make them unreal."

Garet shook his head firmly.

"Magical creatures? Nonsense. We'll go up there and find that men are behind this. We'll find them, find out how they did it, and come back, and tell the Duke, and then go home rich and let someone else deal with it."

188

Iffrey half agreed with him; He didn't believe in magic or snow-ants either, but he also couldn't think of any human act that could build a mountain of ice so quickly, with no-one seeing anything.

Casiol shrugged. "For your sake, I hope that you're right, but men didn't do that." He looked up at the massive feature. "There must be millions of the things in there. We won't get far."

Malson said nothing. The manacled convict just looked from one to the other as they spoke. Iffrey wondered what he thought and then dismissed it as unimportant. Of the entire group, Malson was the one who deserved to be here, and who definitely did not deserve the freedom, money, or pardon, he would get if he lived.

Iffrey looked at Garet and sighed. He had known the young soldier for several months and decided to speak bluntly.

"Garet, whoever is right, the last group who went up there didn't return. We also have a long list of missing people whose last known movements took them onto the uplands. Whatever or whoever built that mountain, your chance of claiming the reward personally is nil. You are going to your death. These others are dying anyway, one way or another, but you aren't. If you don't change your mind, you are a dead man. You're a fool if you think otherwise... a dead fool!"

Garet laughed scornfully. "I'll be rich and calling *you* a fool when I get back."

Iffrey shrugged, ignoring the insult; there was no point reprimanding a man who was about to die.

"We'll see." He turned to Casiol. "You're in command. Try to stay out of hollows. We need to see what happens to you."

Casiol nodded and without another word, he began walking up the track towards the unnatural mountain. Ewail and Garet followed him. Malson cast one despairing glance at Iffrey and then plodded after the others, his manacles making a tinkling sound as he walked.

The commander beckoned to the two soldiers who had been waiting a few yards back. They joined him and together they watched the small group of volunteers moving along the path above. As the men climbed higher, the three watchers raised their distance viewing tubes to their eyes for a closer look.

Iffrey wished that he could afford one of the larger viewers; the military issue device in his hands gave him a better view than could his own eyes, but the men still looked a long way away.

And then, in the space of three fast breaths, the snow around the volunteers shuddered and rose up and engulfed them. Then the hillside stabilised and there was nothing to see except snow.

Lowering his viewer, Commander Iffrey looked at the soldiers beside him. He wondered if he looked as pale and shocked as they did.

"We'd better get back. Duke Rannis will want to know."

"What can we do?" one of the soldiers, a young man no more than twenty five years old.

Shrugging, the commander replied, "For them? Nothing. About that mountain? I don't know. Captain Pendin said something about sending a message to Tyreen."

"Does Tyreen really exist? I thought it was just a story," the soldier asked.

Iffrey looked back up at the snow mountain. "So did I. Right now I hope that I'm as wrong about that as I was about snow-ants."

He shook his head and the three of them started back down the track to the city.

"We have had so many reports of strange occurrences from around the Protectorates, that I am beginning to think it's a deliberate ploy by the enemy," Lord Jareth informed the king and queen at their daily briefing in the palace library. They sat around a low table with reports and books scattered across its surface.

"Deliberate disinformation designed to make us spread our people too widely and weaken our strength?" asked Queen Elish.

"Exactly, my Queen," Jareth replied. "They may also hope to fool us into taking our army to one place when the true strike is elsewhere."

"So what can we do?" King Tarek asked.

"I don't see that we can much differently than we are. I have sent those whose dreamwalking skills are strongest, or those who can translocate, to investigate the reports. I hope that way to be able to receive their reports quickly and know which rumours I can discount."

Tarek nodded. "I agree, we need to receive that information as quickly as possible." He stood up to look at a large map that hovered in the air in the centre of the room.

"The problem," Jareth went on, "is that I am running out of people I can send. The strongest and the best are almost all travelling now with long lists of things to check or are here learning what people are calling 'Tam's technique'. We have this new report about Bein: a family claiming the city is over-run with Zindons. No one else leaving there has reported any problem, but the man is said to sound certain and he is reported as saying that Arnath translocated him and his family to safety but didn't follow them. Unfortunately, I am unable to confirm this; one report that I have mentions that Bein's priest, Arnath, was found dead in the town." He paused, wondering about that dreamwalk a few weeks ago, which had never completed. Could it have been Arnath?

"Who can we send to check it?" asked Elish, breaking into his thoughts. He pulled his concentration back to the immediate, and currently more important, problem of his king's stubbornness.

"That is the problem, ideally I would want to send at least two Sorcerers, preferably more, and if there really are Zindons in Bein it should be the most powerful. However, at the moment, everyone is fully occupied and likely to be for weeks. I have only Seldar with

Trerin, who are already travelling in that direction to investigate several rumours, and…" he hesitated, knowing how the king would react, "Crystu with Tam."

Spinning around, Tarek jabbed his finger towards Jareth.

"No! Crystu stays in Tyreen until Tam passes my tests."

Elish sighed and looked sideways at Jareth with a wry smile.

"My King, if there are indeed several Zindons in Bein, Seldar and Trerin will be over-matched and in considerable danger without aid, and I simply have no one else, of sufficient strength, free to send with them. We still have Sorcerers hunting for Krell worms in Daria but they *can't* leave until they are certain it's safe and there are no more of the creatures left; even just one missed worm or Rainbowfly could be disastrous. Brelai reported finding another three pupae yesterday. We cannot abandon that search and risk more deaths whatever else may occur elsewhere."

"No!" Tarek repeated stubbornly.

"Tarek, you are being unreasonable! Tam is already as skilful as many who have practiced the gift for some years, and Crystu is not likely to let a Zindon slip past her notice again to attack her Ponfour."

"I'm not taking any more risks with my only daughter, Jareth. She stays in this country, behind our wards, until I am certain that Tam is as capable of defending himself from Zindon attack as any other. Don't forget," he continued, "that Zindon had plenty of time to learn a great deal about both Tam and Crystu. How likely do you think it is that the creature failed to pass on its knowledge?"

Jareth nodded, accepting the point.

"Then we will have to send Seldar and Trerin without assistance. If Jathte and Trerisia finish their assignment earlier than projected I will send them across. They can at least both translocate. Seldar can translocate himself but is unable to manage Trerin too, so they are riding. With the places they have to visit first, it will be a few weeks before they reach Bein. Maybe someone else will become free by then to send to join them."

"Jareth," the queen leaned forward, "how likely is it that there are indeed Zindons present in Bein?"

Jareth shook his head.

"My Queen, I have no way to know until someone goes there, looks, and reports back. However, so far most of the other rumours that we have investigated have proved to be unfounded, or less than reported, so we can hope that this will also prove to be nothing. In all of history, there is no record of an invasion by Zindons; they usually come in ones or twos or threes. I'm far more concerned about this report of an unprecedentedly large snow-ant infestation in Perrest. If true, we'll need to send a lot of people there to deal with it and Light knows where I'll find those people. That's where Jath and Trerisia are and I truly hope that it's another false story. It certainly sounds unbelievable – a snow-ant colony the size of a mountain." He shrugged. "I'm sure that I'll hear from them soon."

Confirmation

"It is surprisingly beautiful," said Trerisia as she and Jathte stared at the astonishing view of a mountain of ice where none should be. Normally at this time of year, the area should have been dotted with of ewes and lambs, but not even Trerisia's sharp Ponfour eyes could see any animals. The rampant growth of the vegetation was evidence that nothing had been grazing here for a long time.

Perrest was a long way from Tyreen, and their current location within it would have taken several weeks of travel had they ridden all the way. Instead, the two of them had translocated to the border of the country and ridden in from there. They could have translocated the whole way, but they wanted to be sure that the land was peaceful and unthreatened before they reached the site of the reported oddity.

Trerisia thought that the landscape of Perrest looked somehow unfinished and needed some mountains to complete it, but it had none, or at least, none of rock; much of the country was plains, river valleys, and chalk downs. Here, near the northern border, the downs rose steadily away from a wide fertile plain with a meandering river at its midpoint. There were ice-covered mountains just visible on the north horizon but they were well outside the land claimed by Perrest. There were no mountains closer except for the impossible one that the Tyreans had come to investigate.

In front of them, though its size made it appear closer than it truly was, was something that could best be described as a mountain of snow and ice. It towered into the sky for a good thousand feet, and its icy skirts spread out across the moors for miles in all directions. The closest snowy foot lay just a quarter of a mile or so from their position.

"If this was the middle of winter, I'd appreciate the view and then find a nice hot fire to stare at, but as it's summer..." Jathte let his sentence trail off.

Trerisia nodded agreement.

"Yes, that is quite clearly not a normal phenomenon, and I know of only one creature that could create such a hill, but..." she moved her eyes up towards the summit, "how many snow-ants would it take to build such a mountain?"

"I have no idea," Jathte replied grimly, "but before we request assistance, let's be sure that we are in fact dealing with snow-ants."

194

"We should leave the horses here," Trerisia recommended. "They don't react well to snow-ants, and we know that we can outrun the creatures if necessary. They move quickly over a short distance but have no stamina. So long as we stay off the snow itself they can't surround us."

They dismounted and walked towards the nearest hillock of snow.

"Are you ready?" Jathte asked. Both of them now held in each hand an item that at first glance looked like a frying pan with a long handle. The inside of the pan was criss-crossed with strips of metal, their outer edges sharpened. They held these weapons ready, eyes alert for the slightest movement, as they approached the snow.

They halted a few feet away and Jathte concentrated, focussing on the snow ahead. A small amount of snow suddenly changed into glowing liquid rock and, with a great deal of hissing and spitting, immediately sank deep into the ice, steam boiling out from the hole. That part of the snow hill rapidly collapsed into water and ran downhill until the rock became visible once more, now partially solidified into a strange amorphous shape. The steam rising from it showed that it was still very hot.

"That should get their attention," said Jathte backing away warily while making an air shield around himself. Trerisia also shielded herself and watched the snow alertly, ready to defend the two of them.

For a moment nothing happened, then the surface of the snow on either side began to move as creatures swarmed out of it and threw themselves onto the hot rock, cocooning it beneath their bodies.

They were not, in fact, ants nor insects of any sort, although they did slightly resemble mouse-sized woodlice. A tough featureless shell-like carapace covered top and base, while multiple pairs of armoured legs propelled them along the ground.

Snow-ants were so called because they created anthill-like mounds of snow and ice for their colonies to inhabit. Any source of heat was attacked and the energy siphoned off to be sealed inside their shells. They would then begin to build their snow hill - transmuting rocks, water, soil, into snow and ice in which they made their home. They would also attack living creatures, swarming over them and sucking out their body heat, turning them into frozen husks that they then transmuted into more ice for their hill.

195

Magical creatures, they could appear from nowhere and start a colony so quickly that they could raise a tree-sized mound of ice within a few days. Their ability to collect and store heat was so efficient that, even in the heat of summer, this mountain could exist in full sunshine with no sign of melting.

Once spotted though, they were usually easy to kill because their carapaces were only slightly stronger than eggshell, and when cracked the creatures vanished in tiny explosions of blue flame. In small numbers, even the unGifted were in little danger.

The two Tyreans had encountered snow-ants a year earlier, but neither had ever before heard of such a large ice mountain as the one that they currently faced.

Within seconds of the creatures attaching themselves to the rock, the steam had vanished and the pools of water had not only refrozen, but fresh snow and ice had begun to form. A few minutes later, the hill looked much as it had before Jathte had disturbed it, except for the ants which, having removed the heat from the rock, now became aware of the heat emanating from the two Tyreans. As one, the ants turned and scurried towards Jathte and Trerisia. As they approached, the closest ants leapt upwards, aiming for the Tyreans' upper bodies.

The two Guardians began using their weapons like bats: the sharpened edges of the metal strips cracking the carapaces and destroying the creatures. They were hard pressed as hundreds of the creatures leapt at them, so both also began transmuting the air into solid air-rams which smashed the ants as they jumped to attack.

Trerisia's arms whirled, and small blue explosions peppered the air around her as she fought tirelessly, a fierce grin of enjoyment on her face. She also leapt and jumped, landing unerringly on the scurrying creatures, her magically toughened boots able to withstand the small explosions as their shells cracked under her feet.

"Zia! There are too many, we must flee and return with aid!" Jathte shouted as he fought those that went around his Ponfour to attack him.

"You can't kill them all yourself!" he continued as she ignored him. He transmuted part of the hill into pure flame. Those ants caught in the fire were destroyed and as the hill melted again, the others were distracted from their attack and raced back to rebuild their nest.

Jathte caught hold of his Ponfour's arm and stopped her chasing after them. More ants were now boiling out of the hill to rebuild it.

"Back to the horses, now! That's an order."

He tugged at her until she stopped resisting him and they jogged back to their mounts while the ants concentrated on their damaged hill.

"The usual method of dealing with these creatures is not going to work! There are too many of them to destroy piecemeal, and that mountain is too large to transmute all at once without a lot of aid. I need to speak to my father," Jathte said as they rode down the side of the ridge.

Trerisia looked at him in surprise, "Jath, the distance is too great to dreamwalk clearly, even if I gave you my energy to use with your own."

Her Sorcerer nodded. "Yes. I will have to translocate back and talk to him in person."

"Then why are we riding down?" she asked. "We could just go straight to the Cleansing Cave from here."

The tall yellow-haired Ponfour could sense through the bond that Jathte expected her to object to his next statement. She reined in her horse and stared at him with narrowed eyes.

"I know that you are expecting me to argue about something, so tell me what it is!"

She waited.

Jathte also halted and looked down for a moment and she could feel that he was choosing his words carefully.

"We know that there are other Tyreans in this kingdom and we need to start gathering them together, here, now!" he began. "I want you to stay here in Perrest and begin assembling a group while I go back to Tyreen and ask Da to contact others to join us."

"Absolutely not! We both stay or we both go," Trerisia said firmly. "I will not agree to this, Jath."

Her partner sighed.

"Have you a better suggestion?" he asked. "As you said, even if you give me your Seta to supplement my own, I cannot easily reach my father's dreams from this distance. We need aid! This infestation is larger by far than the largest I have ever heard of and I think we will need a Rykatu's assistance to deal with it."

"Then we will both translocate back to Tyreen," Trerisia argued.

"No, someone must remain here," Jathte replied. "We know the approximate locations of other Sorcerers who are within your dreamwalking reach and you must start contacting them tonight - you know it is less tiring if you dreamwalk from a natural sleep instead of an induced one. This is the first thing we've found that is a genuine threat, and it is huge. Whatever else people are investigating, once they know that it's nothing, they can come straight here. Da gave me the authority to summon them if necessary and I'm using it, but we will need more aid. I hope that I will be gone no more than a day, but it will take considerable time to assemble a large enough group here, especially if we cannot have Crystu's aid. The longer we take organising, the larger that mountain will grow. We need Da to contact those who are beyond our reach, and I'll ask him to send us Warriors and Soldiers too. I think we will need a great many people for this."

He looked her in the eye, and she could feel his determination through the bond.

"I have to insist on this, Zia. If those you contact can arrive before I return, you will organise a watch on the ice mountain. We need to map it and judge how quickly it is growing, and also keep the curious away from it." He smiled. "I know you don't like it, Zia, and neither do I, but it is necessary."

She nodded reluctantly.

"All right; I will agree, but only until there are others here. If you are not back then, I will leave the organisation to them and join you in Tyreen."

He opened his mouth, but she pre-empted his words. "No, Jath. That is the only way I will agree to this. I am your Ponfour and my primary task is your protection. I cannot do that if you are on the other side of the continent from me." Then she smiled and added, "I am also your betrothed, and I dislike the idea of being so far from you, even for just one day."

"I, too," Jathte replied softly, "but *our* primary task is to defend this land against the minions and creatures of the Shadowbringer. Everything else must come second, including our wedding."

Nodding decisively, she answered, "Then you should go immediately, I will take rooms for us in a hotel in Angate," she nodded towards the city, "and begin the task."

He nodded, but she felt him hesitate, something still unsaid.

198

"What else?" Trerisia asked.

Looking at her, Jathte grimaced.

"Try not to get into any fights, Zia, I would prefer not to have the entire town aware of our presence just yet."

She grinned. "I will try, but you know I never start them. I simply seem to attract them."

Jathte waited, and she eventually nodded acquiescence.

"I will make every effort to avoid drawing attention, Jath. Now go! I would like to find a hostel before the sun sets. A hot bath will help me relax for the dreamwalk."

Her betrothed nodded and walked his horse a short distance away. Trerisia felt him concentrate, and then felt the tingling that accompanied magic in use. The misty translocation nimbus gathered around him and then closed upon him. It and he vanished. Immediately her sense of his location told her that he was far away, in the direction of Tyreen and the Cleansing Cave. In the few years since they had bonded, she had never been so far away from him except once. Her sense of him through the bond seemed strangely stretched and muted, like a sound heard through covered ears. She knew when he had stepped into the gateway to Tyreen because the bond seemed to curve and stretch further as he went through the wards that shielded Tyreen. His emotions now seemed almost to echo through the bond as it passed across the border of the hidden realm. Reassured that she could still feel their connection, she continued her journey downhill towards the city.

Angate city was large and populous. It stood on a well-used highway that ran from the busy port of Tarsh, in the east, all the way to the Royal City of Perestin, in the west.

Several roads from the south met the highway in a large fertile plain beside a deep river, and a thriving market town had grown here. Over time it had become a prosperous city in which many markets sold a wide range of goods. As a result, the population displayed a wide variety of clothing styles and skin shade, as traders from all the Protectorates, and even a few from Kandar, could be found selling their wares in its streets.

Despite this, Trerisia drew some curious stares as she rode into the city centre. An unusually tall woman, dressed in good quality, if travel stained, leather clothing, her cropped blonde hair contrasting starkly against her dark skin, riding alone with an extremely large sword strapped to her back, was an unusual sight even in this cosmopolitan city. The sword was in fact slightly smaller than it looked. Trerisia was using illusion to enhance its appearance. She felt that it made a certain statement about how she would react if accosted and that statement might prevent trouble.

The Kingdom of Perrest, although largely peaceful and Light following, did nevertheless have a criminal element, and a city this large contained a fair number of these. Jathte had asked her to avoid fights if possible so Trerisia hoped that an obvious weapon would deter any but the most determined.

In the centre of Angate, the blonde Ponfour found both a hotel and a cathedral. The doors of the cathedral were open and she could see a number of people entering and leaving. Today was not a service day, so no formal activities were taking place within, but Cathedrals of Light were always open for private devotions.

She decided that prayer would be appropriate given the scale of the task ahead, so she tied her horse to the rail and, carrying her saddlebags and with sword still strapped to her back, she entered the building. Just inside the door, as usual, was a supervised side room in which she left her sword, bags, and also the other small weapons that she kept concealed about her clothing.

The attendant's eyes bulged in surprise at the number of bladed weapons Trerisia produced for storage.

200

Several pounds lighter she walked through into the main assembly area. The cathedral followed the usual pattern of one large central gathering room with many side alcoves, each with sliding doors and walls to allow them to be converted into small private rooms for individual or group use. Several of these were closed and she could hear music coming from one. She paused to listen, as the style of music was unfamiliar. The unseen players showed more enthusiasm than skill, she thought, wincing at a sudden discordant squeal of sound from a wind instrument of some kind. Yet the melody was lively and as she walked on she caught herself walking in rhythm with the beat.

Walking quietly to the Focus of Light at the south end, she looked with respect at the large stained-glass leaded window behind it. It depicted stylised representations of seven Tyreans, each one demonstrating one of the seven Gifts. The figures surrounded a central Light symbol identical to the one Trerisia wore on her forehead.

She never failed to be amazed and humbled at the ingenuity of ordinary people. Tyrean cathedrals had similar windows, but they were crafted by transmutation, a skill, yes, but not like this. The window she looked at had been entirely crafted by hand, each piece of coloured glass created by a craftsman without magic, and then the pieces joined together with strips of lead, also by hand. It must have taken hours of work.

Similarly, the carved stone images that adorned the walls had been carved by hand, by dedicated people ready to give their best for their place of worship. She considered herself privileged to be able to serve and defend people who were capable of such incredible achievements.

Finding an empty alcove, she entered and knelt, composing herself for prayer. She asked for strength, wisdom and guidance in the tasks ahead, whatever they might be. Not just for herself, but for all who would find themselves facing servants of shadow in the coming conflict. She also prayed for her brother Trerin. The first year was often a difficult one for Ponfourii, as they adjusted to the bond and learned how it enhanced their abilities. They also had to learn to understand and work with their Sorcerer, but Trerin might also face a major conflict with shadow forces at the same time as he adjusted to his bond with Seldar.

201

He was now a Ponfour, trained and able, but he was also her brother and considerably younger than she was. She worried about him and found it difficult to place his safety in the hands of the Lord of Light in this troubled time.

After an hour or so, she rose, feeling refreshed and ready for her task. She bowed to the Light Focus and then went to collect her belongings.

Outside the Cathedral, two men in the black and tan uniforms of the Perrest Royal Guard waited patiently. When Trerisia emerged, they walked up to her and bowed,

"My Lady," began the one wearing a captain's insignia, "my Lord Rannis, the duke of this city, requests that you would do him the honour of visiting him at his home."

Trerisia looked at the two of them and lifted an interrogatory eyebrow.

"He requests?" she asked, her meaning quite clear to the two soldiers.

"Oh yes, my Lady, you are free to refuse. My Lord wished me to say that he would never offer any disrespect to a Tyrean, but he wishes to speak with you, and hopes that you will agree to come with us to see him."

He seemed earnest, and Jathte had asked her to avoid conflict if possible so, although regretting the delay, she smiled graciously.

"I have a little time free, and so, because he asks so politely, I will be delighted to come with you. Please, lead the way, my Lord...?" She waited for him to supply a name.

Smiling, the soldier replied, "Just Captain, my Lady, Captain Pendin, and this is Septuar Elkam." The junior man bowed

"I am Trerisia," she responded as they mounted their horses. "Is Duke Rannis's home far?"

"No, Lady Trerisia," Captain Pendin replied, "A short ride only."

As they rode, Trerisia noticed that the two men were careful to avoid flanking her. They clearly wanted to be sure that there could be no question of coercion.

Captain Pendin made light conversation, asking about her journey and commenting on the recent changeable weather patterns. He was advancing his theory that the 'little pile of snow', as he called it, might be responsible for the recent severe windstorms, when they arrived at a guarded gate set in a high wall.

202

The guards evidently recognised Pendin because they opened the gate without question and they rode through into a wide paved track, which wound through a carefully tended garden, then led through a small orchard before arriving at the entrance of a large winged palace.

Aides were waiting and as soon as Trerisia and the soldiers had dismounted, their horses were led away, the unnamed soldier leaving also. Trerisia and Pendin entered through the main door, the guards again letting them pass without comment, and then along a passageway.

The captain opened a door and bowed Trerisia through it, following her into the room. The room appeared to be a family gathering room. It was large and the walls were hung with richly embroidered tapestries. The room contained comfortable looking chairs, low tables, bookcases and decorative plants and one occupant.

"My Lady, I present my Lord Rannis, Duke of Angate. My Lord, I present the Lady Ponfour Trerisia."

After bowing to the figure, who had just risen from a chair beside a low table containing several varieties of drink and a selection of foods, Pendin smiled farewell to Trerisia and withdrew from the room.

"Please, be seated my Lady," Duke Rannis bowed and then gestured to the empty chair on the other side of the table, "and let me pour you a drink. You have had a long journey."

He poured from a steaming jug as Trerisia sat down in the indicated seat. He was a short, thin, man in his early forties, with intelligent green eyes and clean-shaven face. He wore a simple woven tunic over soft leather trousers. Both were well made and embroidered in geometric patterns in contrasting colours.

Trerisia accepted the proffered glass and sipped. It was a hot dark-brown infusion with which she was unfamiliar. She thought it bitter and not really to her taste, but she hid her dislike of it out of politeness. Nodding her thanks she looked her host firmly in the eyes.

"Lord Rannis, I cannot spare you much time. Why have you requested this meeting?" she asked.

Rannis gestured at a sheet of paper on the table.

"You and a Sorcerer appeared at the borders of our realm three days ago, out of a cloud of mist according to the report of the herder

203

you startled. You then rode across the country, camping each night. On arrival in this district, you proceeded to the top of the ridge and out of sight. A short time later the two of you reappeared heading back downhill. You stopped partway, had some sort of disagreement, and then the Sorcerer translocated and you came into the city and proceeded to visit the Cathedral."

He looked at her, obviously waiting for her reaction to his detailed knowledge.

She smiled, not at all surprised that he knew about their arrival.

"Your people are most observant, my Lord Rannis," she commented.

Rannis placed the paper on top of a pile on the arm of the chair. "Gathering information is how I serve my king," he replied.

"You are clearly successful in your work, my Lord, but if I may suggest it, some of your people could do with training in a wider variety of professions. The three who followed us the first night would have been more convincing in their role of herders going to market, had they known how to emit the correct whistles to instruct the dogs they were trying to use. The two who took over from them were better trained but still were too obvious in their observation. And the two who followed us partway up the ridge..." she shook her head, "clearly had no knowledge of wall mending, which was their supposed reason for being on the hillside. The wall fell down almost as soon as they turned away from it."

Rannis stared at her for a moment and then threw back his head and roared with laughter.

"I shall certainly take your advice, my Lady, they should not be so easily identified."

He wiped tears of laughter from his eyes before continuing.

"Very well, Lady Trerisia, I will be forthright with you. Several Tyreans have entered the country recently, presumably in response to certain strange happenings and rumours, and this has caused his Majesty some concern. He is most especially concerned at one rumour which claims that a Zindon recently infiltrated Tyreen, killing a Ponfour in the process."

Trerisia stiffened in surprise.

"I would be interested to know where that rumour began," she told him.

"Is it true?" he asked, leaning forward, and then caught himself. "My apologies, I know that I have no right to ask that."

She did not intend to tell him the whole story, yet neither could she lie, so Trerisia chose her words carefully.

"A Zindon did attempt to enter Tyreen. Rykatu Crystu was returning from her first journey out of Tyreen, and the creature thought that her inexperience would enable him to gain entry when she opened the gate. He was wrong! Her Ponfour chopped the creature into three pieces. The Zindon did not get beyond the gateway. However, no-one outside of Tyreen should have *any* knowledge of the attempt, except, of course, any shadow minions with whom the Zindon may have shared its plans."

"I will have any information about the rumour's origin made available to you immediately," Rannis told her.

Her surprise must have been evident on her face for he continued, "My Lady, I asked you here to find out what I can do to assist you. I hope that you intend to deal with our little problem up there on the ridge, but I am becoming aware that there may be more happening in the world than I had realised until now, and that our troubles in Perrest may be minor by comparison. So how can I help you?"

Trerisia could tell that his offer was genuine, and smiled.

"My Lord, we did indeed come here to investigate the recent reports of this ice mountain. It was one of many strange reports that we have received from across the entire continent, but so far, to the best of my knowledge, it is the first to possess substance. Can you tell me when it first appeared?"

"I can't be sure, but I think that the reports of early snow on the ridge last autumn may have been its beginning. At first, we did not recognise the danger. Some citizens disappeared during the winter, including a prominent artist last seen heading up-ridge with her equipment in hand. Even this spring, we did not realise that anything was amiss until the mountain grew large enough to be visible from down here. I sent people onto the ridge to investigate but they did not return. I sent another group, of volunteers who knew the risk, this time with observers behind them, who saw what happened when those they followed stepped onto the snow. They were sensible enough to realise that they could not help, and they returned to report what they had seen. We have lost almost all the sheep from this

205

region, which will cause hardship later, but I am more concerned about the loss of life of my people. I realised that we would need Tyrean help to deal with what had to be an unprecedentedly large infestation of snow-ants, so I asked the Bishop to send a message with the next cleric to travel to Tyreen."

He looked at her. "To be honest, I expected you long before now, my Lady."

The rebuke was mild but clear. Trerisia sighed.

"As I said, my Lord, we have had many reports to investigate. All so far have proved baseless. We could not know that this one amongst so many was real."

Duke Rannis frowned.

"Is it possible that these false reports were intended to delay your arrival and give these snow-ants time to become so well established?"

Trerisia nodded.

"My Lord, not only is it possible, but this too may be just a diversion designed to sap our strength, for it will take a great many of us to deal with it."

Rannis looked at her for a moment, clearly absorbing the implications. If this was also a diversion, then what worse was occurring that the shadow minions wanted to conceal?

"Then I repeat my offer: is there anything I can do to help?" he said at last.

"My Lord," she replied, "the most important thing you can do at the moment, is to continue keeping your people off the ridge and upper moors."

He nodded. "I have already banned people from going up there, but some are always curious. Despite everything, fools still contrive to go up to see the snow mountain." He shrugged. "In many ways we are better off without such idiots, but I would rather not lose any more citizens to creatures of shadow."

"My Lord Jareth has returned to Tyreen to request aid in dealing with this," Trerisia told him. "He will translocate back here tomorrow. Meanwhile, I am to contact other Tyreans here in Perrest and ask them to come to Angate. We must map the mountain so that we can estimate how many will be needed to deal with it. Any information that you have on the exact whereabouts of other Tyreans would assist me greatly."

206

The duke nodded. "You will have it within the hour."

"Thank you, Your Majesty," she replied, deliberately looking him in the eye as she used his real title.

Rannis stared at her for a full second and then nodded.

"Yes, you are correct," he admitted, "but how did you know? There are few here who are aware that Duke Rannis is also King Perdon."

Trerisia smiled.

"We keep track of the rulers of the kingdoms we protect. I was given a complete profile of you before we left Tyreen. It included the fact that Duke of Angate is one of your lesser known titles, Your Majesty."

"I see." He nodded. "I would appreciate it if you could keep that to yourself if possible. The Duke of Angate has freedoms that the King of Perrest is not allowed. I value those freedoms."

"Of course, my Lord Duke. I will abide by your request," she replied.

"Thank you. May I ask what your immediate plans are?" he asked.

"I must go to the hotel and wash," she brushed at the travel stains on her clothing, "and then tonight I must dreamwalk and contact the Sorcerers here in Perrest. We will need to find lodgings for all. Dealing with this will take many of us and many days I suspect."

"There is plenty of room in my home here for you, your lord, and even an army to stay," Rannis told her. "I offer you the use of it for as long as you need. My people will supply anything you require."

"Thank you, your Majesty. I accept your generous offer. It will also help disguise our presence here in Angate, at least for a while."

Rannis nodded, though Trerisia was sure that he would have liked to ask why they wished to conceal their presence, so she quickly changed the subject.

"Have you maps of the upper land?" she asked him. "We will need to get a clear idea of the extent of this infestation. Hopefully at least one of the Sorcerers, who I will contact, is a shapeshifter and can fly safely over the mountain to gauge its extent."

The duke stood and pulled a bell cord on the wall.

"We will begin immediately, my Lady. And please, I ask you to keep to yourself my true position; even most of my household here are unaware that I am also their king."

"Of course, my Lord Duke," she replied. "I will make sure that all my people are so informed. Thank you again for your assistance"

The scale of the problem was daunting, but Trerisia was confident that they would prevail. In fact, she looked forward to the challenge that this mountain would pose. All of the other reports she and Jathte had investigated so far had been misunderstandings and mistakes.

At last! Something real to fight!

Part 6: Grinnet

"Shapeshifters – Some Tyreans have the ability to change their shape into that of any living creature. The ability is supposedly one of the rarer Gifts, but, in truth, we know very little about the prevalence of any of the magic Gifts amongst the normal population of Tyrean. There are a few well known legends and children's tales but we can only guess whether any of those contain any real fact. The idea of changing one's shape is intriguing; one wonders how deep the change goes. Is it just the outer appearance or does everything within alter? Do instincts and thought alter to match those of the creature? Can a man become lost into an animal life? Can a pregnant woman change her baby's form with her own? What about clothes? Do they fall off or change with the Sorcerer? So many questions."
Extract from the journal of King Perdon III of Perrest.

Tarvinstoft

Trerin folded his wings and dived towards the campfire below. At the last moment, he opened them to check his swoop and released the dead rabbit he held in his talons.

Perfect aim!

The carcass landed immediately behind Seldar making him jump. Trerin beat his wings to return to the thermal updraft and, soaring high, began to search for another rabbit. He was in his second favourite shape: a large eagle with unique colouring. Inspired by tales of derstrals, Trerin varied the colour of his feathers to match the colour of the sky so that his form was hard to spot from the ground. Today his under-feathers were a delicate blue with patches of white feathers in places along his sides and in his wings to blur his outline. From above, his colouring was a mottled green and brown, again with the intention of disguising his outline from any higher predator.

Aside from his immediate family, his former classmates, tutors, and Seldar, there were few who knew that Trerin could shapeshift. When he and Seldar had helped to escort Tam back to Tyreen, he had taken great care not to allow Tam to learn of his Gift.

If Tam had learned of it, the Zindon within him would also have known about it, and Trerin wanted the servants of the Shadowbringer to know as little as possible about his abilities. He would rather that they learned at the moment his teeth or talons ripped their lives from them.

His sharp eagle's eyes quickly spotted another rabbit. A few seconds later, his talons held it as he returned once again to the campsite where Seldar was preparing their evening meal. This time he dropped his burden from a lesser height and further away from Seldar. He landed and quickly resumed his usual form.

Seldar glared at him.

"Was it necessary to drop the first just behind me? I nearly dropped the knife into the fire!"

Trerin grinned.

"I'm sorry, the rabbit slipped out of my claws."

It was the truth: as he had opened his talons, the rabbit had indeed slipped from his grasp.

"It's amazing how often that happens to you!" Seldar replied dryly. "Perhaps you should do some grip exercises to strengthen your fingers. Here start with these." He held out an onion and a knife.

Trerin took them and laughed.

"I'll take your advice into consideration, my Lord."

He bowed ostentatiously before sinking to the ground and beginning to chop the vegetable on the flat board the Sorcerer had pushed towards him. Seldar meanwhile resumed working on the two rabbits, expertly skinning them and removing the meat which he placed into a large pan. The onions, and several other foraged vegetables and herbs, joined the meat and the stew was soon beginning to steam over the fire.

They were eight days into their journey to Bein and had camped for the night in a large clearing within a wood. Due to the threatened strike by the Shadowbringer, each would stand guard for half the night. Seldar was starting to feel the drain on strength caused by such short periods of sleep. This was exacerbated by the need to travel quickly, which prevented the possibility of catnapping in the saddle.

Trerin stared into the flames, letting his mind wander, and enjoying the heat against his face.

Seldar spoke suddenly.

"Trerin, there's something I've been wanting to ask you."

Trerin pulled his attention back to his surroundings and looked at Seldar enquiringly.

"What is it?" he asked.

"Does it bother you?"

Seldar looked at him pensively. Trerin could sense through the bond that this was something that Seldar felt almost guilty about.

Bemused by the unexpected seriousness tingeing Seldar's emotions, he replied lightly, "Was there a particular 'it' of which you were thinking, Seldar, or just some sort of general 'it'? It will make it easier to answer your question, you see, if I know which you mean."

Seldar grimaced and looked into the fire. Trerin could feel that he was trying to find the right words, but having trouble doing so.

"I'm talking about the nature of our Ponfour bond, Trerin. Does it bother you that we don't have that deeper quality that some do?"

Trerin took a deep breath in surprise, and then let it out slowly as he considered his answer.

"To be honest Seldar, no, it doesn't bother me. Quite the opposite in fact: I am relieved. If nothing else, you're not exactly my type." He grinned.

Seldar barked a laugh.

"I didn't really think I was, lad. But I take it from your answer that you are aware of the ...err, *significance* of that extra depth?"

It was Trerin's turn to laugh.

"Oh yes! Once I became a Ponfour myself, it didn't take long to work that one out. I suspect that only those afflicted by it have difficulty seeing what it means. Like Lady Crystu and Lord Tam, and Jathte and my sister."

"You really don't mind?"

"Seldar, if I ever marry," Trerin was suddenly serious, "I hope she is a one Gift craftswoman who never ever has to leave the safety of Tyreen. I can't imagine anything worse than facing danger side by side with someone you love that deeply. I would find it too nerve wracking."

"I, too, lad," Seldar nodded. "It was why I deliberately chose, for my second Ponfour, someone with whom I knew I was unlikely to form such a bond."

He looked candidly at Trerin.

"It has bothered me though, that although I knew what I was choosing, you would not until it was too late."

Trerin nodded.

"It's true that I didn't know then, but I'm quite happy not to have that extra burden." He grinned again. "I may be taller than him, but my shoulders are nowhere near as broad as Lord Tam's. Rest your mind, Seldar, I don't envy Lord Tam or my sister their little bit of extra speed and strength."

Seldar sighed.

"I am relieved to hear it, lad - *very* relieved."

He lifted the lid from the pan and sniffed the delicious steam that rose. "That stew looks about done. Shall we eat?"

Trerin grinned. "I thought you'd never get round to that."

He quickly dismissed the unusually intense conversation from his mind and applied himself to his food. Sorcerers sometimes worried about the silliest things and he was glad that it was all settled.

In the morning, they continued their journey almost as soon as the sun had risen.

"We will have to make sure we get some decent rest before we get too close to Bein," Trerin commented, as their horses trotted along the track. "I think I'd prefer to meet Zindons when we are both fully awake."

"I agree," Seldar said. "Although I would prefer not to meet them at all if it can be arranged, I too would rather be awake for the occasion if it arises."

They slowed the horses to a walk because Seldar's, in particular, was starting to sweat. Trerin looked at it sympathetically and thought that he would not like to carry Seldar on his back.

"Do you realise," he began, "that if you lost that stomach, you would probably be able to translocate both of us, and the horses too, all the way to Bein?"

Seldar looked down at his paunch and grinned.

"You exaggerate lad, my gut does not weigh as much as you and both horses."

Then he tipped his head to one side as he looked at Trerin. "Maybe as much as you," he allowed. "However, it is not likely to disappear overnight so we will both just have to ride. Why? Are you in a hurry to face a city full if Zindons?"

Trerin laughed.

"One or many, it's all the same, I'll wave my sword at them and you can jump on them. But I expect we'll just have another wasted journey and there'll be nothing darker than a few visiting strangers with odd clothes."

212

"True," nodded Seldar. "Like the 'Dragon' menacing hunters in Cartrash wood last week, which was no more than a large boar with an extra-large set of tusks. Or the derstral sighting in Kantir which turned out to be a very lost vulture."

Trerin chuckled.

"At least the boar made a pleasant dinner; the vulture tasted revolting."

"Serves you right for changing back to human when you still had a mouthful," Seldar pointed out. "You'll remember next time I'm sure."

Trerin shuddered.

"Oh, I will, I assure you, never again forget that just because it tastes good to an eagle or wolf doesn't mean it will still taste good to a human."

They rode in companionable silence for a while, enjoying the warm sunshine of early summer. The track wandered through forest for some miles, but eventually they reached a more open area where the trees had been felled long ago to create fields and enclosures for a once large settlement.

The majority of the old fields lay untended, but they could see a few miles ahead of them, nestled near the foot of a hill beside a river, an area of small enclosures with crops growing within them. Close by this was a small group of dwellings, obviously the remnant of the once large village.

The foundations of other former buildings were just visible as lines of tumbled stone, disappearing into the undergrowth, which was reclaiming that area. The riverbed was wide and stony but had little water flowing in it. A series of deep ditches extending away from the riverbed, and circling the small, elongated, fields, were clearly intended to convey water from the river to the crops. These ditches, like the river itself, were dry despite recent attempts to deepen and extend them towards the tiny flow in the river's centre.

The crops in the dry fields were beginning to die. Further along the river, a series of dusty meadows contained a small number of emaciated looking cattle.

As they approached the hamlet they could see that, where the river passed closest to the dwellings, a series of holes had been dug within it in an attempt to create some puddles deep enough to allow buckets to be dipped and filled. The inhabitants of the hamlet were

213

taking turns to fill their buckets and were then walking over to the fields to pour water on their crops or taking it to the meadows for the cattle. Trerin counted seventeen adults and about twelve children of assorted ages engaged in this activity as he and Seldar arrived. An air of quiet desperation hovered over the group as they worked. Two other adults were in the process of butchering some animals. They did not yet show any obvious signs of starvation, but Trerin guessed that they were probably still living off the stores put by in the previous harvest. If their crops failed this year, they would then have nothing for the winter and spring, especially if they were slaughtering large numbers of their cattle now rather than watch them starve in the fields.

One of the inhabitants, a middle-aged man, seeing their arrival, put down his bucket and came towards them, a welcoming smile on his tired face.

"Welcome, my Lords, to our village of Tarvinstoft. I am the Head here, my name is Onvarr. May we offer you some refreshment?"

Trerin and Seldar both looked over at the empty river and the dying crops, then back at the man, whose expression became anxious as he awaited their reply.

Seldar glanced at Trerin briefly before answering.

"That is most generous and gracious, Head Onvarr, and we accept your kind offer. I am Seldar, and my young friend here is Trerin."

He dismounted and led his horse over to the post beside an empty trough. The man's face relaxed and he gestured to a woman who quickly went indoors. Another gesture and some boys emptied their buckets into the trough for the horses to drink.

"Come Trerin," Seldar ordered, "get down and tie your horse. We will sit over here and await whatever these good folk may bring us."

He walked to a corner of the courtyard where there were several crude wooden chairs and tables and sat down. Trerin stared at him in astonishment for a moment, before doing as he was bid. He sat down beside Seldar, and whispered, "Seldar! What are you doing? We can't deprive these people of what little they have!"

Seldar deliberately spoke his reply loudly enough that Onvarr could hear it.

214

"Trerin, by the customs of this area, refusing to eat with these good folk would be a sign that we have hostile intent. We will, therefore, share their food, and perhaps after we have eaten, we may find that there is some way that we can assist them in their current predicament."

He smiled and nodded to the woman who placed a beaker of plain water, and a plate of bread, cheese, and some dried fruits, in front of each man.

Trerin nodded his understanding and reluctantly began to eat.

"My Lords, it is most noble of you to wish to assist us, but I am afraid that the dryness of our river is beyond the reach of even a king's commands," Onvarr said, shaking his head as he looked towards the dying fields.

"How long has it been like that?" Trerin asked. "I haven't noticed that the weather has been unusually dry this summer. In fact, there was heavy rain just a few nights ago."

"There was," Onvarr agreed, "and we rejoiced, thinking that the river would swell again after seven weeks of constantly diminishing water, but none of the rain has left the hills."

Seldar frowned. "Have you followed the river up into the hills to see if there has been a landslide to block or divert it?"

Onvarr laughed bitterly.

"Oh yes, my Lord, three times we have tried to follow the course up and each time we turned back, and yet each time when we had returned to the village, we could not remember why we turned back."

"Really?" Seldar sat up and looked suddenly thoughtful. He glanced at the remnants of the older settlement that were visible in the next field.

"Can I ask?" he began, "how long have your people lived here?"

Onvarr was surprised by the apparently unconnected question but answered readily.

"My father found these cleared fields and the fallen remains of these houses and he settled here with his bride, my mother. Over fifty years ago that was, and in all that time the river has never failed."

Trerin looked at Seldar curiously. He could feel Seldar's sudden intense interest.

"What are you thinking," he asked.

Seldar laughed.

"Come now Trerin, remember your lessons. A deserted settlement, a vanishing water supply, and a compulsion that prevents people from investigating upstream. What does that sound like?"

Trerin inhaled sharply as he understood.

"A grinnet? You think we have a grinnet up in those hills!"

"A grinnet!" Seldar confirmed, at the same time that Onvarr guffawed.

"Grinnet indeed! Since when do legends of the dark abyss come to life and attack honest Light dwellers?"

"Just because something is a legend doesn't make it unreal," Seldar told him amiably.

"Well, what do you think, lad? Shall we earn our meal and take care of this little problem for these good folk?"

He stood and, walking over to his horse, opened the bag containing his armour.

Trerin grinned and likewise began to remove his armour from his baggage and put it on.

Onvarr's wife gasped as she saw the gleaming Ponfourii sun symbol on his chest plate, and moved slightly for a clearer look at the circlet on his forehead.

"Legends do indeed walk amongst honest Light dwellers, Onvarr," she said. "Do you not see what these men are?"

Onvarr looked blankly at her for a moment, then back at Trerin and Seldar who were now both armoured and had mounted their horses. Trerin checked his sword blade and then re-sheathed it.

"Guardians?" The word was barely audible. "You are Light Guardians? A Sorcerer and Ponfour?"

"We are," answered Seldar, then he glanced at Trerin.

"You know, lad, that really is very ostentatious. It would be a lot easier to remain anonymous if you Ponfourii didn't insist on displaying that symbol quite so prominently."

Trerin looked up at the sky and screwed his eyes up as if trying to remember something.

"Anonymous," he murmured. "No, I don't remember that being in the vows. There was something about serving and protecting the Congregation of Light, and I vaguely recall something about protecting your life, but I don't recall anything about having to remain anonymous while I was doing it."

He looked over at Seldar and grinned.

216

"So I think I'll keep wearing the symbol for the time being, but I'll be sure to pass on your suggestion to the elders. This symbol is rather important to us though, so I don't think they will be eager to discard it."

Seldar laughed. "As you wish lad, shall we get on with it?" and he walked his horse out of the settlement and along the side of the riverbed. Trerin followed.

As soon as they were out of hearing of the village, Trerin said plaintively, "Seldar, could you please stop calling me lad? Especially in front of villagers? I am twenty three after all, and there is the dignity of the Ponfourii to be considered."

Seldar regarded him gravely. "Very well, lad," he replied, "I will give your request some thought."

"Thank you," Trerin said. "You wouldn't like it if I started calling you ancient one after all."

"That's true," Seldar agreed, "but irrelevant, I am only in my middle years, while you are still struggling to grow a beard."

He smiled as he felt Trerin's instant reaction to that barb.

"I am NOT struggling to grow a beard!" Trerin said with great dignity. "I simply have no wish to even try growing one."

"Of course, lad, of course," Seldar agreed soothingly. "Of course, that would be more convincing if I had ever seen you shave."

"Seldar," Trerin replied in exasperation, "I'm a shapeshifter! I don't *need* to shave hair off! I can make it just not be there! Or I can make it appear."

His face suddenly sprouted a long flowing silky blond beard, which just as quickly disappeared.

"Now can we concentrate on this grinnet?" he asked.

"Very well," Seldar replied. "Suppose you tell me what you remember about them from your training?"

Trerin rolled his eyes but obediently dredged the information from his memory.

"Grinnets, creatures of shadow, water dwellers, carrion-eaters, solitary, gifted with a form of illusion and possible some form of dreamwalk ability. They find an isolated hamlet, dam its river and create a lair within the resulting lake. Any people from the hamlet who attempt to discover the cause of the water shortage are enspelled such that they give up the attempt and return to their homes. The creature also removes any thought of leaving the area so that no

217

matter how little water they have left, they simply continue to try to cope. When the lake is deep enough, the grinnet lays one egg within its lair which hatches within 2 days. The offspring reaches maturity within six weeks, by which time the inhabitants of the hamlet have died of dehydration or if still alive are very weak. Adult and offspring, use the corpses as a food supply before returning to the lake, breaking the dam, and riding the flash flood downstream to the sea where they live for decades before returning to their birthplace or close by, to spawn a new generation.."

He finished his recital and looked at Seldar.

"Well? Did I omit anything important?"

"Ah, like their description, you mean?" Seldar prompted.

"Seldar, you know very well that they come in such a range of shapes that we do not know which, if any, is their true shape. They are not shapeshifters, so far as we can tell, and yet each one seems to be different from the last. They usually choose a form that includes lots of teeth, but apart from that, anything is possible. However, once the form is chosen it is apparently fixed for life."

"Well done, lad, that was a masterful summation. Did your lectures also cover methods of defeating them?"

"Ward against illusion, make sure you have a very sharp sword and know how to use it, and don't stand in one place too long," Trerin replied. "And speaking of the former..."

"Oh yes, of course, just a moment. Now, what shall I use? Oh, this will do," He pulled a steel fork from a pocket of his saddlebag and stared at it for á moment. The fork glowed a deep violet colour for a few seconds and then resumed its former mottled appearance.

"Here you are. Don't lose it."

He tossed it to Trerin who stared at it in disgust.

"A fork? You use an old fork to hold a ward? Seldar, have you no sense of aesthetics?"

"None whatsoever," Seldar replied blithely. "It's metal and it can hold the ward for several days and that's all that matters. My own skills of illusion will protect me from the grinnet's power, and that ward will protect you. I see no reason to waste valuable energy making it pretty."

Trerin shook his head but tucked the fork into a side pocket of his armoured leggings.

218

A short time later, Seldar reined in his horse and moved his head as though scenting the air.

"We are close now," he said. "Something just tried to coerce me into giving up this journey and returning to the village. It seemed most unhappy when I dispersed the illusion it was building around me."

He glanced at Trerin, who shook his head smiling.

"I felt nothing; your ward is effective."

"I'm glad to hear it, lad. Shall we continue?" Seldar urged his horse onwards up the valley.

They followed the riverbed up the valley until, ahead of them, they saw it disappear beneath an enormous wall of rocks, soil, and tree branches, which spanned the entire width of the valley.

"That's a grinnet dam, lad. This one's no innocent creature mistaken for something else. Be ready!"

Trerin nodded and edged his horse ahead of Seldar's. It was quickly apparent that neither horse would be able to reach the top of the dam, so they dismounted, left the horses tethered on the higher ground away from the river bed, and began to climb up.

This close, the dam was not as haphazardly constructed as it had looked from further away. The stones were carefully positioned, with clay pushed firmly between them, to both hold them in place and make the structure waterproof.

The wall was steep and the men were forced to use their hands to assist the climb. At the top, Trerin saw that the wall of the dam was thick, perhaps thirty paces across, and had been at least partly created by landslides down each side of the valley. At the far side of the dam wall, the lake edge lapped the top stones. The lake itself was huge, filling the valley for as far as he could see.

He wondered how the creature had triggered such carefully targeted landslides, and also if such a large lake could form in just a few weeks without some other power being used, but before he had time to fully consider the matter the grinnet attacked.

The Grinnet

As Seldar reached the top of the wall and straightened, Trerin saw a bulge form on the surface of the lake. The water seemed to be being pushed in front of some large creature travelling just below the surface. The bulge quickly grew bigger and was moving rapidly toward them.

"Seldar! Move! That way!"

He grabbed Seldar's arm and pulled him across the top of the wall toward the hillside, they raced to get off the dam wall before that giant wave reached it. They arrived at the safety of the hillside above the lake just as the wave reached the dam wall and crashed over the top of it. Some of the water travelled sideways from that great wave and washed over their feet, while the main part spilled over the dam and tumbled down to the riverbed below.

Trerin and Seldar readied their swords and stared out over the lake in which the water seethed and bubbled from its recent disturbance. They could not see what had become of the creature that had attacked them. The churning of the lake surface caused by the recent disturbance had masked any trace of its movement.

Trerin triggered his gleaning power in readiness for combat. A sudden flashing image caused him to push Seldar sideways an instant before throwing himself in the opposite direction. At the same moment something large, coming from the hillside behind them, leapt through the space that they had occupied a moment before and then vanished into the depths of the lake. Trerin had only a brief impression of teeth and scales before it disappeared beneath the surface.

He jumped to his feet and gave Seldar a hand back upright, and then they backed watchfully away from the lake.

"Thank you, lad." Seldar brushed mud off his armour. "Did you see where it went?"

Trerin opened his mouth to say 'no', but at that moment, the grinnet resurfaced and stalked out of the lake to pause and stare malevolently at the two Tyreans.

It was large and unlike anything that either of them had ever seen before. Its head was long with a lipless mouth from which protruded gleaming glass-like teeth. The teeth projected for several inches above and below the jaws and looked sharp. The neck was short and the chest wide and muscular. The creature had three pairs of legs all ending in paws possessing four long dextrous and webbed toes. The claws on those toes looked as sharp as the teeth, and each was easily as long as one of Trerin's fingers. The creature's tail was long and wide for propelling it at speed through the water. Its skin was

220

completely covered in overlapping scales, each one about the size of a man's palm.

It roared, giving them a good look at its impressive teeth and then, with surprising speed for such a large creature, it charged up the hill towards them.

Trerin ran to meet it and, ducking under its attempt to bite, swung his sword confidently at its unprotected neck. To his surprise, the sword bounced off the overlapping scales without leaving more than a slight scratch on the surface.

At a warning tingle from his gleaning, he leapt sideways, twisting to avoid one of the creature's paws. He ducked under its jaw and again slashed at its throat to no effect. The creature twisted round and aimed its teeth at his legs, but again Trerin's Gift gave him sufficient warning to leap clear. As he rolled on the rocks with a clatter and came back to his feet running, he reflected that rocks, armour, and acrobatics, are not a good mix.

Only his gleaning Gift, his Tyrean armour, and his Ponfour speed kept him alive as he fought the creature. As he leapt to avoid another strike from a clawed foot, he managed to angle his sword so that its tip flicked under the bottom edge of one of the creature's scales. The scale ripped off and the grinnet squealed and twisted at the unexpected pain.

Trerin grinned. So the scales *could* be pierced from the right angle. He jumped onto a rock and then onto the grinnet's back and off the other side, flicking another scale off as he went. The grinnet span round and, despite Trerin's gleaning, he was unable to evade the strike completely.

The creature's teeth fastened on his sword arm and, in a ripping motion, tried to rip his arm from his body. Luckily Tyrean armour is not simply made of metal but is also altered by transmutation to be, not only warded against transmutation by shadow minions, but also extremely strong.

Trerin's sword flew sideways, and he knew that his arm would be slightly bruised, but the creature's teeth suffered more damage and several broke completely out of its mouth. Trerin jumped, rolled, and came up with his sword in his other hand, and glanced at Seldar who was sitting on a rock higher up, watching the fight.

"Any time you want to help, feel free," he shouted up to Seldar before leaping to avoid an attack and taking off another scale as he passed. If he had to do it one scale at a time, then that was what he would do.

"I didn't want to interfere," Seldar shouted back. "There's that Ponfourii dignity you were talking about earlier to be considered. You are doing so well, I didn't think you would want assistance."

"My pride will recover. I won't be offended if you assist."

"Well, if you're sure?"

"I'm sure." Trerin jumped again and removed yet another scale.

"In that case."

Seldar closed his eyes, and Trerin felt the unmistakable surge of magic use. He saw nothing, but the grinnet suddenly span round and howled in anguish while staring at the dam. Trerin did not stop to ask questions, he ran up behind the creature and thrust his sword into one of the wounds on its belly, where he had previously removed a scale. It was a solid thrust that sent the blade deep into the creature's body.

Trerin twisted the blade.

The grinnet screamed and convulsed, knocking Trerin into the lake, then it writhed and, falling on top of him, lay still, pinning him under the water. He held his breath intending to shapeshift, but then felt the whole weight of the grinnet sink onto him fully.

Trerin suddenly realised that shapeshifting was now impossible. The only reason he wasn't crushed was his solid armour, but if he changed his shape, his armour would shift with him; it was designed that way. If he transformed into a furred, feathered or scaled creature his armour would become the fur, feathers or scales, but would retain its shielding properties and could still protect him to some extent.

The problem was that at the moment he began to shapeshift, he and his armour would become immaterial and the grinnet would sink down to lie exactly where Trerin now was.

Shapeshifting could not be paused once begun - the spell would automatically continue to completion, which meant that Trerin would begin to assume his new form in a space that was already occupied.

The consequences of that would be messily fatal for the shapeshifter!

Trerin tried to move the creature off and wriggle free, but it was too heavy. He could hold his breath for a long time, but knowing that he was trapped seemed to make it harder. His lungs began to burn with the need to breathe.

How idiotic, he thought, I kill the thing, and dead, it's more dangerous to me than it was alive.

He knew that Seldar was aware of his predicament and he seemed to be doing something, but what? The creature was dead, surely he could just transmute it into something a little lighter. Then he realised that the creature must still be alive, if only barely, and transmutation cannot be used on a living creature.

Suddenly, the creature writhed again, the pressure forcing the last air from Trerin's lungs, then just as suddenly, the body was gone and Seldar was pulling him to the surface even as his lungs began to suck in water to replace the lost air.

Trerin coughed helplessly as Seldar pulled him to edge of the lake. He felt a surge of healing energy and was once again able to breathe.

"Thanks," he gasped, pulling off his helmet and taking deep breaths.

"Sorry to take so long, lad," Seldar apologised. "I didn't realise at first that you were pinned, and then I had difficulty pushing my sword through the beast's hide to finish killing it, and of course while it was still alive I could not transmute it off you."

"Your timing *was* a little off," Trerin agreed, "but as I seem to still be alive, I'll forgive you."

His breathing had returned to normal and he stood up carefully, water streaming from his clothes and armour.

He looked curiously at Seldar and asked, "What was it that you did, that made it spin round and stare at the lake? It seemed very upset."

Seldar grinned. "Oh, a little illusion, that's all. It saw the dam collapse and the lake begin to pour down the valley, taking its young with it. I thought that might distract it long enough for you to get a good thrust in, and I was correct. An excellent job, although," and now he frowned at Trerin, "next time, jump away more quickly, I don't want to have to fish you out of any more lakes."

Trerin nodded.

"Of course, my Lord! Thank you for the advice, I'll try to remember that next time."

He said it with exaggerated deference and Seldar snorted grimly.

"Speaking of next time," he said, "I'm afraid that we are not yet finished dealing with grinnets."

223

Trerin looked at him and then understood: the wave of water that came close to sending them over the dam could not have been the work of the creature that they had just killed, so there was a second Grinnet.

The offspring of the first was still lurking within the depths of the lake and must now be dealt with. With a groan, he placed the helmet back on his head; its wet padding was now unpleasantly cold and clammy.

As one, they turned to gaze out over the still waters of the lake.

"I don't suppose you saw where my sword went, did you?" Trerin asked. Seldar nodded and pointed to where it lay nearby.

"It's there, but I'm afraid it won't do you much good."

Trerin looked sideways at him and then asked politely, "And why is that, my Lord?"

Seldar shrugged. "Well, I rather think that the young grinnet has not yet developed the ability to breathe air. It's in there somewhere, and the only way to find it is for you to change into something that can breathe in water, and go in after it. I don't know about you, Trerin, but I am not aware of any water breathers with arms."

Trerin began to laugh.

"Seldar, don't you know anything at all about shapeshifting?" he gasped.

He laughed even harder at the sudden air of offended dignity that he could sense through their link.

"That is not a problem," he continued. "As long as I can imagine it in enough detail for it to be functional, I can change into it, whether or not such a creature truly exists. The problem was solved long ago, and I studied appropriate shapes in great detail in class."

He took a deep breath, and then his form shifted very slightly. His armour, clothing, and small weapons disappeared, reforming as shimmering scales across his skin. His hands and feet widened, and his fingers and toes lengthened as webbing appeared between them. His eyes grew a second, transparent, eyelid and gill slits appeared in his abdomen. Picking up his sword, he ran into the lake and dived out of sight.

Trerin quickly realised that Seldar had been partly correct about the sword being of little use under water. He stopped swimming and gave it a few experimental swings; the large broadsword moved very sluggishly through the water. At warning tingle from his gleaning ability, he dropped the sword without hesitation and twisted downwards. In the same movement, he changed shape slightly to free two short knives from within the scales on his thighs, and slashed at the half-seen form that was trying to wrap itself around his legs.

His knife encountered scales, but went through them with ease, Trerin grinned and stabbed both knives into the creature's back. The young grinnet released his legs and with a kick from powerful rear legs disappeared into the surrounding gloom.

From the short glimpse he had had of it, it seemed to have at least as many legs as its parent, but the ones at the front and rear were short and ended in flippers, while the central pair were very long and flexible. The head seemed to project straight from its large barrel shaped body with no obvious neck. The grinnet's skin was covered with a strange mixture of fur and thin, insubstantial, scales; the immature creature had not yet fully entered its final form and was vulnerable.

It attacked again, this time intent on ramming him. Trerin avoided the head and, catching hold of one front flipper, hacked at the shoulder and succeeded in severing the muscles, leaving the limb limp and useless. He felt the central limbs wrap around his waist trapping one arm against his side, and he slashed at the shoulder supporting the nearest tentacle. To his surprise, it detached easily.

Still held by the other tentacle, Trerin pushed his free knife into the creature's belly and cutting a long slash, reached inside as far as he could and twisted and sliced at random. He could see nothing because the water was by now cloudy with silt disturbed by their battle, and also with blood and flesh from the ragged gaping wound that he had created.

He felt the creature attempting to drag him away from its injury, but its strength was failing rapidly. Within seconds the battle was over, and the infant grinnet was dead. Trerin dragged its body to the side of the lake, and then he swam back down into the depths to look for his dropped sword.

He emerged a little while later, sword in hand, and walked out of the lake shapeshifting back to his human form. His wet scales reformed as equally wet clothes and armour, which he quickly removed to allow them to dry in the sun.

Now that the adrenaline surge caused by his combat was ebbing, he began to feel the bruises that he had accumulated, and also the fact that the rocks under his bare feet were uncomfortably jagged. Ponfourii skin was tougher than ordinary, but not invulnerable.

Not for the first time, Trerin wondered why the Lord of Light had Gifted his people with a healing Gift that could only be focused outwards onto another person and not inwards to heal your own injuries.

He looked around for Seldar and saw the Sorcerer climbing higher up the hill above the lake.

"SELDAR!" he bellowed, "WHERE ARE YOU GOING?"

"I NEED TO GET FURTHER AWAY BEFORE I CAN DEAL WITH THAT DAM," Seldar shouted back. "I WAS TOO CLOSE TO IT TO BE ABLE TO FOCUS MY POWER." Seldar took a few more steps, then turned and shouted again.

"WHY HAVE YOU TAKEN OFF YOUR CLOTHES?"

Trerin looked down at his wet clothing that he had just laid on a rock, and shouted back,

"THEY ARE WET! THAT'S WHAT HAPPENS WHEN YOU GO FOR A SWIM IN ARMOUR! EVEN SHAPESHIFTED ARMOUR!"

Trerin felt a surge of power from Seldar and suddenly his clothes steamed for a second and then were dry.

"IT'S GOING TO GET VERY COLD DOWN THERE SHORTLY. GET DRESSED AND COME UP HERE," Seldar shouted and then resumed his climb.

Trerin shrugged and pulled his clothes and boots back on. For a moment he considered carrying the armour because the day was hot, but decided it would be easier to wear it until they got back to the horses and the saddlebags. He climbed up after Seldar and eventually joined him on a spur of rock that gave a good view of the valley, lake, and riverbed.

"Thanks for drying my clothes," he said, and looked down at the lake. "Why are we up here?"

"The least I could do, lad. I would heal your bruises too, but I'm going to need the energy for that." Seldar indicated the dam. "That is why I climbed up here. We can't just leave it so I'll have to do something about it."

"Why can't we just leave it?" Trerin asked. "It felt solid enough to me to be safe."

Seldar shook a finger at him. "Then you didn't look very closely at its structure when we climbed it, Trerin. It feels solid now, yes, but it is largely made of rocks and whole trees held together with mud. Wood rots into powder, lad, and mud washes away. Sooner or later, and most likely sooner, that structure will give way under the weight of water pressing against it and the lake will descend on that village in one huge devastating flash flood."

Trerin knew that he would never have considered that possibility, but Seldar was right, they could not leave the dam as it was. Neither could they just destroy it without releasing all that water.

"What are you going to do? Transmute all the water into steam, so the dam can be safely destroyed?" he asked curiously. That would be an impressive piece of transmutation, though he had no doubt that Seldar could do it.

Seldar laughed.

"Oh no, lad, that would be a shocking waste of something that could be a valuable reserve water supply for those people down there. I intend to save both lake and dam."

Trerin frowned. "How can you? Even if you try to transmute the dam into solid rock, won't the water just break through, while the material is in transition?"

"You're right, Trerin: it would. Which is why I must first change the water."

Trerin could feel Seldar begin to gather his will, and he felt the build-up of power. He looked out over the lake and tried to see what Seldar was doing.

Whatever it was, it was taking a long time. Trerin looked at Seldar whose eyes had closed to better concentrate on his focused power. While he waited for the results of Seldar's intense concentration to become apparent, Trerin wondered again what had persuaded him to accept Seldar's invitation to be his Ponfour.

He had never regretted his choice, but he still didn't fully understand it. He had known that not many had responded to Seldar's request for applicants, and could understand why. Seldar was a good twenty years older than most of the group of warriors who were hoping to become Ponfourii. In addition, he was overweight and did

227

not attempt to conform to some people's notions of how a Tyrean Sorcerer should look, or behave.

Trerin had gone to the interview almost entirely from curiosity. He had hoped to bond with someone nearer his own age, and preferably female. Yet he had found himself quickly warming to the older man. They had a similar sense of humour, and Seldar's refusal to obey many of the unspoken rules of society appealed to Trerin's own egalitarian leanings.

He would not have enjoyed working with someone who insisted on being called my Lord at all times. In addition, Seldar's untidy appearance hid a strong, and disciplined, power and Trerin had realised that he also had a wealth of knowledge about the Protectorates. They had talked for several hours, and then Trerin had left, not expecting to hear from Seldar again because the Sorcerer had made clear that he wanted someone nearer his own age.

To Trerin's immense surprise, Seldar had appeared in his village several days later and asked him to become his Ponfour. To Trerin's even greater surprise, he accepted the offer.

He knew that he had learned a great deal from Seldar in the few months that had passed since they bonded. He stared out over the lake and finally saw what Seldar was doing. Ingenious!

The water in the lake was rising, some of it spilling over the dam as it did so. In the depths of the water, Trerin could see a growing pearlescent mass, which was spreading up from the depths. It touched the surface and then spread out across the lake until all the water had been replaced with the gleaming solid mass. Trerin was astounded - Seldar had changed the entire lake into ice.

Thousands of tonnes of water converted to ice, and he had not finished. Now that there was no danger of the water bursting through the dam, Seldar was free to transmute its structure into something stronger. Slowly, the components of the dam blurred and began to run together as did the sides of the valley where the dam touched ground. The dam hardened again and now, in place of rocks, trees, and mud, there was just rock. Solid rock now extended from deep within the hills and out across the dam. It would erode no more quickly than the mountain itself. The top of the dam was now slightly lower in the centre than it had been and Trerin wondered why. His unspoken question was soon answered as Seldar continued his work.

228

The frozen lake began to melt. By the time that Seldar eventually sat down exhausted, the valley once again contained a large lake. A small waterfall now spilled over the dam wall down into the riverbed, which quickly began to refill and flow.

"There! *Now* we are finished. The crops of Tarvinstoft will soon be growing again," he said and smiled in quiet satisfaction as he gazed at his work. Trerin stared in awe at what Seldar had made and knew without a doubt that his choice had been the correct one.

Back to Tarvinstoft

"Seldar, do you think that was all just a coincidence?"

They were riding slowly back to Tarvinstoft beside the river. Trerin was staring at the flowing water, letting his horse pick its own path. Both men had removed their armour and repacked it in their saddlebags. Trerin had discovered that his sword arm was now a delightful shade of dark purple, and he consequently was holding his reins with his other hand while it healed.

"Was what a coincidence?" Seldar asked, rousing from the half doze into which he had slipped.

Trerin gestured back in the direction of the lake. "The lake, the dam, the river," he replied. "Think about what we spent several days trying to do before we left Tyreen, and what a large number of Ponfourii and Sorcerers are undoubtedly still doing there."

Seeing Seldar's uncomprehending expression, he continued.

"Tam's technique to transfer energy down a Ponfour bond, remember? The visualisation metaphor he used?"

"Oh, I see what you mean." Seldar considered the point.

"No, I don't think it is likely to be a coincidence," he said finally. "We know that our powers can change the world around us, and for several weeks there have been hundreds, possibly thousands, of Ponfourii and Sorcerers all concentrating on that image. It is quite possible that this could be having an effect on the world outside Tyreen. I won't be too surprised if we find later that several others have had experiences involving dams, rivers or lakes."

"So it's probably not important?" Trerin asked.

"Probably not," Seldar agreed, "but I would keep it in mind; we may encounter other problems for which that image is in some way relevant."

Trerin nodded, and they continued in silence, Seldar resuming his half doze for the remainder of the journey back to Tarvinstoft.

They found the hamlet to be a hive of activity, as its inhabitants struggled to backfill the recently deepened irrigation ditches which, now that the river was widening back to its usual size, contained too much water and threatened to flood the fields they had watered. Seldar sighed.

"Tam's technique may be beyond both of us, lad, but it would be useful right now. I'll have to do something about this, but I'm going to have to have a long refreshing sleep to recover. I have already used a lot of magic for one day."

Saying that, he dismounted and walked towards the river. Crouching down, he placed one hand on the ground and concentrated.

The villagers shouted in surprise and jumped away from the ditches they were working on as the ground suddenly began to move in the bottoms of those ditches. A few minutes later the lengths of the ditches, where they joined the river, had narrowed, shortened, and were less deep, so that the amount of water flowing into them was considerably reduced.

"That should be enough," said Seldar as he straightened.

The villagers gathered round, though they remained a respectful distance from the Tyreans. Onvarr stepped forward and bowed.

"My Lords, thank you, you have saved our lives. How may we be of service to you?"

Seldar beamed at him and slapped him on the shoulder.

"An excellent question, Onvarr, easily answered. Beds for the night will be ample repayment, plus some food in the morning of course."

"One bed will be sufficient," Trerin added. "I'll stand watch," he explained at Seldar's questioning glance.

"But lad, you have been working as hard as I, and I know that you're tired too. Surely we can both rest now that the grinnets are disposed of."

"My Lords," Onvarr protested, "we will keep watch while you sleep. We owe you our lives and we would not allow harm to come to either of you."

Trerin, trying hard not to smile at the idea of a small group of farmers offering to protect a Ponfour and Sorcerer, shook his head.

230

"My Lord Seldar," he said formally, "you must rest after your use of intricate and powerful magic. It is my duty, as your Ponfour, to protect you while you rest, and that I will do."

His tone allowed no argument, and Seldar abandoned the protest.

"Of course, you are right," he said, "and I will sleep the deeper knowing that you are guarding my rest."

Trerin turned to Onvarr, who looked slightly offended at the suggestion that Seldar and Trerin might not be safe in his hamlet.

"Head Onvarr, I have no doubt that your people would guard us to the best of their ability against even the Shadowbringer himself, but it is not your job to do this - it is mine. I intend no insult to you, but I must do my duty."

"Of course you must," Onvarr's wife Cherith spoke. "Don't be stubborn, Onvarr! There's no offence. What would we do if another creature of legend attacked? Wave our hoes at it?"

Onvarr reluctantly smiled at the image as she continued, "You know the legends as well as I do: Sorcerers must rest after they have used magic, and Ponfourii protect them, even the youngest child knows that."

She turned to Seldar.

"If you don't mind sitting for just a few minutes, my Lord, I will ready our room for your use."

"That is very kind of you," Seldar said and sat down on the indicated seat as Cherith ran inside.

A few minutes later she beckoned the Tyreans into the house. The ceiling in the timbered building was low and Trerin had to crouch to avoid banging his head on the beams. He could sense that Seldar was struggling to contain his amusement at the sight, and the slight twitch of Cherith's lips showed that she too felt a similar inclination to laugh.

The room offered to Seldar, surprisingly, contained what looked to be a comfortable bed, with fresh clean bedding upon it.

"I will be most comfortable here," Seldar declared and placed his saddlebags on the floor. "Thank you for this, Lady Cherith."

Cherith looked flustered at being called 'lady' by a Sorcerer and made an unpractised curtsy in return. Then Trerin followed her out of the room and he closed the door as they left. He glanced sideways at the low ceiling,

231

"I will have to stand watch outside, I think," he said ruefully as they walked towards the outer door.

Cherith smiled, "Must you stand? I can find you a chair. If you have other bruises like the ones on your arm, you may find it easier to sit."

Trerin grinned back at her.

"A chair would be welcome," he admitted.

"We have a large one that we rarely use - it was built for Onvarr's father who was very tall. I think it would be a better size for you than those already in the yard."

Trerin placed the supplied chair near beside the main entrance to the building in which Seldar was resting. It was indeed a much better size for his length than the other benches were, and well-made. He looked across over the valley and could see the villagers busily making sure that all their cattle now had sufficient water.

His bruises were already beginning to fade so he stood up and began some basic stretching exercises as the aches reduced.

A young woman, perhaps a little younger than him, entered the yard and began moving tables and chairs around in early preparation for the evening meal. She watched Trerin as he stretched, and saw him wince as the movements found some more aches that he had not known about.

"I thought all you magicians could heal yourselves," she said in a curious tone.

"No," Trerin replied, "the magic will only flow outwards, not inwards, so we can heal others but not ourselves."

"I see," she said thoughtfully. "Couldn't Lord Seldar heal it for you?" she asked.

Trerin straightened from his stretch, looked at his bruised arm, and then smiled at her.

"He could, but I would not have allowed it if he had offered. He used a great deal of power today, and it is best that he rests before using more. Beside which, Ponfourii heal very quickly. By morning these will have vanished completely."

She nodded and placed some utensils and cutlery on the table. Several children had now appeared and were assisting her, but it was obvious from their wide eyed stares that they were far more interested in the Tyrean in their midst than in concentrating on their duties,

232

When they had finished their work, the woman sat down nearby and looked at Trerin, with an intent expression. The children all gathered in a group nearby whispering and staring. Trerin found the attention slightly disconcerting.

"Do you know how wonderful it is that you even exist?" the woman asked at last.

Trerin was puzzled.

"I don't understand," he replied.

She smiled a little self-consciously.

"It's silly and childish, I know, but I always loved the stories that Grandmother Annish used to tell about the Guardians and magic, and battles against terrible evils."

She smiled at her memories.

"I used to dream about running away to Tyreen and learning magic and never again having to plough or harvest or clean a pen."

She looked down at her work-roughened hands, missing Trerin's grin at her mistaken idea of Tyrean life.

"Then I grew older and learned that they were just stories and that there is no real magic, just whatever we can make with our own hands. The world was less bright, but it was more real somehow. I met and married a good man and we have helped my father make this a good place, and I tell my children the same stories so that they too can dream of magic for a while."

She looked up at him. "And here you are, real and proof that magic really does exist, and I have seen it for myself when Lord Seldar raised the ditches."

She grinned and tilted her head. "Perhaps I will again dream of running away to Tyreen. It is nice to have my dreams back."

Trerin smiled gently.

"I'm afraid that you would be disappointed three times over if you did try to find my home."

She laughed.

"I can guess the first -Tyreen is hidden so I would not find it. But what are the other two?"

"The second is that we are born with our Gifts: you cannot learn magic unless it is already within you. I can never learn to do what Seldar did today because I was not born with that Gift. Likewise, I have Gifts that he does not and can never acquire."

"And the third?" she asked.

Trerin laughed and gestured at the table that now held several plates of bread and neat piles of spoons forks and knives.

"We must eat, as all mortals must, and crops do not grow by magic. We plough, sow and reap as you do. We also keep cattle that must be fed, watered, and their pens cleaned. We do all these things as you do - with our hands."

He held up his hand for her to see that, like hers, it was calloused from hard work.

"The magic is for protecting the Congregation of Light, not to save us from chores."

The woman laughed a little sadly.

"Ah, and so the dream is changed to reality again. That is good, for it is in reality that we all must live."

She looked up to see his sympathetic expression and smiled again.

"Still, just knowing that the stories *are* real makes that reality seem brighter. I have a good life here and I am content with it, but a little extra brightness is always welcome."

Delicious smells were beginning to emanate from inside the house, and people were starting to gather in the yard. The woman looked around and then jumped up and ran inside. She reappeared a few minutes with a man, each holding one side of a large stew pot. They were followed by two more people similarly encumbered. The pots were placed on tables and the villagers began filling bowls with the stew. Each also took a piece of bread and found a seat, but none yet began to eat. While the villagers were collecting their meal, the woman, with whom Trerin had been talking, appeared in front of him with a bowl, spoon, and bread, and held them out to him.

"You said that you must eat as must we all, so I hope you will join us, my Lord."

"I will, and gladly, the stew smells delicious," he said accepting the bowl.

"Will Lord Seldar require any food?" she asked. Trerin expanded his awareness of Seldar through the bond and could tell that he was deeply asleep.

"Not now. When he awakes he will be hungry, but that will not be for many hours," he told her.

"Of course," she replied, smiling, "I should have known it! The stories say that Sorcerers must sleep after great feats of magic. Will you not also need to rest?"

Trerin laughed. "Not I! I used some magecraft but mostly swordcraft."

"You will stay awake until he rises?" she asked curiously.

"I will," he nodded, at the same moment that Onvarr spoke from behind her.

"Salnia, stop bothering the lord with questions. Fill your bowl and sit, so that we may give thanks. Everyone is waiting for you."

Trerin glanced around and saw that all the folk were now sitting and were looking towards Onvarr, Salnia, and him. Salnia blushed, and with a muttered apology rushed across to a stew pot and filled her bowl. She then sat down beside a man and three small youngsters, presumably her husband and children. Only Onvarr remained standing.

"We give thanks to the Lord of Light for the bounty of his world that fills our bowls. Today we have more than usual for which to be thankful, because this morning we faced the ruin of our crops, the death of our cattle, and though we did not know it, we also faced death by the workings of creatures of shadow. Today we can eat without fear that tomorrow we may starve, and the creature is dead. We must give heartfelt thanks to our God for sending us his Guardians who have saved us. We thank him, and we thank you, my Lord Trerin and also Lord Seldar, for our lives and our renewed hope. "

He bowed to Trerin, and those seated also bowed their heads and a murmur of thank yous ran around the yard. Trerin nodded back solemnly.

With no further delay, the assembled group began to eat. Trerin found the stew to be as tasty as the smell had promised, and the bread was crusty and fresh. Eventually, all the stew had been eaten, and the pots were cleared away and replaced by large plates piled high with small fruit filled pies, the hot fillings oozing out of the sides of the pastries. When these had all been eaten, trays carrying large jugs containing various kinds of drink were brought outside. There were cold fruit juices and hot infusions and also beer in small quantities.

"My Lord Trerin," said Onvarr, "we usually fill these final hours of the day with music, singing, and storytelling. I do not wish to disturb Lord Seldar's rest so I have decided that we will forego the music and singing. May I ask, would you be so kind as to tell us the tale of your battle with the grinnet?"

Startled, Trerin's first instinct was to refuse as graciously as possible. Seldar was the storyteller, not he, but the faces looked at him with such expectancy that, instead, he found himself agreeing. The conversation with Salnia had given him a glimpse of the importance of stories for a people for whom every day was the same as the last.

"Storytelling is not one of my skills," he said, "but I will make the attempt."

He told the tale factually, as it had happened, leaving out only that he had shapeshifted to fight the young grinnet, and that the ward Seldar had made had been created in a fork.

When he finished, his audience was silent for a few seconds and then to his surprise they began to clap and stamp their feet. Quickly he checked his link to Seldar but there was no sign that his sleep was disturbed by the noise.

Onvarr hurriedly hushed his folk and sent them away to whatever chores yet remained undone, then bowed to Trerin.

"I hope our expression of gratitude did not disturb Lord Seldar," he said, "but once we knew the full tale, we would be ungrateful indeed if we made no sign of our appreciation. We would have been killed and eaten if not for you and Lord Seldar. We will not forget this."

He looked at the empty jug of water on the table by Trerin.

"Do you need anything for your nightwatch, my Lord? Anything we have is yours, you need only ask."

Trerin shook his head, "Nothing except perhaps some more water, thank you."

Onvarr nodded.

"I will have Salnia bring some."

He bowed again and entered the house. The darkening yard had quickly been cleared of dishes and food debris, and the tables folded or stacked as appropriate.

Salnia appeared carrying a large jug of water and a clean beaker for Trerin's use. She placed them on the table and then sat down in a chair near his.

"You told us a good story, my Lord, thank you. I will remember it and make certain that my children do likewise. They will one day tell their children about the day that Guardians of Light came to Tarvinstoft," she said.

Trerin laughed.

"Seldar would have told the tale with far more skill than I," he told her truthfully.

She also laughed and then said, mischievously,

"And do you think he would have left out as much about *his* actions, as you did about yours?" she asked.

Trerin pretended not to understand, which made her laugh again.

"You must have held your breath for a long time during the underwater fight," she told him, and she watched him closely when she continued. "My favourite tales are those of Carin the Shapeshifter. It is said that, like you, she had yellow hair."

Her eyes flicked up to his cropped blonde hair.

"Is it a common colour among Tyreans?"

Trerin knew that she had seen his movement when she unexpectedly mentioned his great grandmother's name, but he answered in as non-committal a manner as he could manage.

"No. It is not common."

"I thought not," she replied. She picked up the empty jug and started to walk away, and then she paused and looked back.

"As you eat and drink like we do, it occurs to me that you may also need to know about the small building on the other side of those barns."

Trerin looked were she pointed, and then grinned back at her.

"You're right: that is something I need to know about. Thank you."

He waited until she had gone indoors before jogging around the barns to find that important building.

During the night a persistent rain began to fall, Trerin sighed and went into the stables where he had left his and Seldar's bags, along with their horses.

He had intended to put on his waterproof cloak but discovered to his chagrin that he had forgotten to pack it. He grimaced at this oversight; he had been sure he had everything this time. He was very glad that his sister was not present because she was always telling him to be more organised.

He peered out of the stable door at the rain. There was nothing else to do - he was on watch so he would just have to get wet.

Not for the first time, he wished that he was a transmuter and could make himself a shield. Then he grinned, everyone was asleep! He might have to stand watch, but there was no reason he had to do it in human form. Quickly he donned his armour and then changed into his favourite land form: a very large cat.

The armour, as designed, shifted with him to enhance his fur with its defensive, and more important at the moment, waterproof qualities. He had studied long and hard to create the exact design for his cat. A skilled shapeshifter was not restricted to creatures that actually existed. They had to be functional, but other than that, he could alter the basic pattern as he liked. Trerin's cat had fur that was unusually thick and very slightly curly. The curls meant that the magically tough hairs were essentially interwoven, making it harder for a sword thrust to go through.

His next modification was to the paws - the toes were longer in proportion to the paws than was normal. This gave him room for much longer and slightly straighter claws and also gave his paws almost as much dexterity as a human hand. The inner edges of the claw sheaths were also roughened, so that, as he unsheathed his claws, they automatically sharpened as they rubbed against this rough part.

If necessary, he could also modify the teeth to be much longer and sharper than was natural, so that the canines projected down below his jaw for a good four inches. He only made that adjustment if battle was imminent, because his teeth were also razor sharp, and he had on one occasion accidentally stabbed one foot when he had forgotten that his teeth were long and had tried to rest his head on his paws.

He varied the fur colour depending on his surroundings, so for the moment chose a mottled mixture of greys and black, to be better camouflaged against the shadows in the moonlit yard. One patch of colour remained constant: whatever he chose for the rest of his body, he always had on his forehead a small circular patch of white and yellow fur, as similar to the Ponfour sun symbol as he could make it.

Trerin padded out into the yard, the rain bouncing off his fur leaving him quite dry, and crossed to the tree beside the gate. It was clearly a very old tree - its girth was enormous and the lower branches were also of large size. He jumped up onto the first branch and lay along it. The cat's night vision and keen hearing meant that it was an ideal form for guard duty.

A few hours later, in the early hours of the morning, the increased clarity that he could sense from Seldar's mind through the Ponfour bond told him that the Sorcerer had awoken.

A short time later, the door of the house opened and a fully dressed Seldar appeared. He paused when he saw the rain and then, creating an air shield above him, walked over to stare into the tree.

"Why have you turned into a cat?" he asked curiously.

Trerin stretched a long, thorough, cat stretch, from nose to tail, and jumped down from the branch. Once on the ground, he resumed his normal form.

"Oh, I see," said Seldar, noting the armour. "You forgot your cloak again, didn't you?"

Trerin grimaced.

"Yes, I did," he admitted ruefully.

Seldar laughed and clouted him on the shoulder. "Well, you can take that off and get inside for some sleep. I'm fully awake now so I'll stand watch the rest of the night."

"I saved you some bread and pastries from the evening meal, they are in the stable, I'll get them," Trerin called back as he hurried across the yard to remove his armour.

"Oh, thank you, lad," said Seldar a few minutes later as he accepted a covered plate holding the food. "Now get inside and sleep for a few hours."

Trerin gratefully made his way to the room and was asleep within seconds of getting on the bed.

Trerin woke at sunrise as the inhabitants began to stir, and he and Seldar joined them in a large side room for their firstmeal.

Salnia brought him a plate of food and turned to hand one to Seldar. She suddenly started and looked back at Trerin's face. Trerin had wondered if she would notice the small change he had made to his features.

For a moment he thought she would speak, but she just smiled brilliantly at him and then turned to give Seldar his plate. As she walked back to rejoin her husband, she glanced over her shoulder and threw Trerin another delighted smile.

Trerin could feel Seldar looking at him closely, and knew that he was deciding whether or not to speak. Then the Sorcerer leaned over and whispered,

"Aren't your eyes usually brown?"

Trerin gave him his best innocent look, fully aware that Seldar wasn't even slightly fooled by it and whispered back,

"Oh, I may have made a mistake when I changed last night."

It wasn't a lie because there *was* a possibility that he might have made a mistake when changing back; he hadn't checked that every single hair was the exact same length that it had been previously.

As he spoke, he altered his eyes back to their customary shade.

Seldar nodded and glanced over at Salnia who was now feeding her youngest child, he met her husband's eyes looking over at the two Tyreans, a tolerant look on the man's face.

"Oh, of course, a mistake! I understand!" Seldar said in a patient voice, "You forgot what colour they should be, no doubt."

"Well, la...Trerin, if you have finished eating, it's time we were getting the horses ready. We still have a long journey ahead of us," Seldar announced a few minutes later.

"Come along," Standing up, he made his across the room and out into the yard.

Trerin hurriedly finished his drink and followed.

In the stables, he became aware of the tingling sensation that told him that Seldar was using magic.

"A quiet departure?" he asked.

"I think it would be best," Seldar nodded and released the illusion that he had prepared.

They led their horses out into the yard. Onvarr was waiting outside, as were Salnia and a few of the elder members of the group. None of them noticed Seldar and Trerin pass by, even though all were looking towards the stable block. Eventually, they would investigate and find the stable empty. It would seem to them that the Guardians had simply disappeared.

240

In the lane, Trerin and Seldar mounted and rode away at a brisk canter. Seldar held the illusion until they were completely out of sight over the next hill.

Once he was sure they would not be seen, Seldar released his illusion and they slowed to a trot. They rode in silence for several minutes, then, "Pretty girl," Seldar commented.

"Married," Trerin replied, "with three children," he continued conversationally.

"Unlucky!" Seldar commiserated.

Trerin grinned.

"I think her husband would have become less tolerant if we had stayed much longer though," Seldar continued.

Trerin stared at him, shocked.

"Seldar! You don't think I would actually have become..." he paused as he searched for the right words, "over-friendly? With a married woman?"

As he said it, he felt Seldar's internal laughter reverberate through their bond and realised that the comment had been intended to make him react. He grinned sheepishly, as Seldar reached across and clouted him on the shoulder.

"No, lad, I don't think that, but that's not really the point is it? Her husband might have. We do have a reputation as Guardians of Light to maintain after all. In future save your flirting for the unmarried ones. 'Made a mistake with your eye colour' indeed!" He wagged a finger at Trerin.

Trerin smiled. "Of course, my Lord Seldar, I will do as you command," he replied.

To be continued

Map

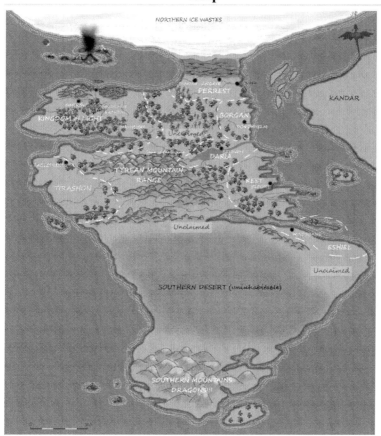

Acknowledgements

There are so many people who contributed to this. First and foremost Tina Newsome, who provided the original inspiration in her medieval challenge, writing contest, in an online writing group, and without whom none of this would ever have been written. (Scenes derived Tina's contest are: the introduction detailing the seven Gifts, the scene in the cavern with the Shadowbringer, and the scene where Crystu tells Tam about the dream.) She encouraged me to keep on going and try to create something worth publishing. Here it is, Tina, I hope that you like it.

Next, Janette Dinse Harrower for encouragement and providing advice on cover art. Also Sarah S. Miles for encouragement.

Helen Stevens for reading and commenting faithfully as I wrote and posted it over several years.

Silvana Kelleher for proof reading and many helpful suggestions and advice. Mike Collins for patiently answering questions about colons and semi-colons.

Chris Broughton for proof reading and making many helpful suggestions, also other proof readers, Judit Sogan, Rob Summerfield, and everyone who I've bored rigid about it over the years.

Thanks are also due the beta readers who read the final edited story to check if I'd left out anything important – Declan Jones, Jamie Fredrickson, and Dave Stohl.

If I have overlooked anyone, I apologise but y'know the old memory is starting to go.

About the author

I'm a fifty-something Christian, archaeologist, martial arts practitioner, and amateur photographer. I was introduced to science fiction and fantasy at a young age by my best friend's dad, who had boxes and boxes of science fiction books dating to the 50s, 60s, and 70s.

In those boxes, I met Isaac Asimov, Frank Herbert, Anne McCaffrey, Zenna Henderson, and many more, and I learned to love the smell of a printed volume.

This story was started as an entry for a contest and continued to find out if I could finish it. I wrote the sort of story I enjoy. I hope that you like it too.

The whole story is written and just awaits editing. This may take a while because it is …rather… long!

Printed in Poland
by Amazon Fulfillment
Poland Sp. z o.o., Wrocław